Skater in a Strange Land

A fantasy novel

David,

D. W. FRAUENFELDER

"Writing books for enjoyment is wicked." Never a

BREAKFAST WITH PANDORA BOOKS

Durham, North Carolina

truer word was said

David

Copyright © 2012 David Frauenfelder

All rights reserved.

ISBN: 0988565609

ISBN-13: 978-0988565609

TO MY WIFE

musa caelestis

CONTENTS

SKATER IN A STRANGE LAND

CHAPTER 1 - KADMUS

There is a saying in Borschland that a hockey puck is akin to the human heart, for as a puck in hockey so the heart in love is fiercely knocked about while seldom reaching its goal.

You will have to forgive us Borschlanders. We are a very romantic and hopeful people, and nearly all of us consider love nobler than a frozen rubber disk. But it is true that Borschlanders are ice hockey mad, and so are prone to sayings that combine love and our favorite sport.

So much is also true of this story, the story of the first North American ever to play ice hockey in the Borschland Hockey League: Sherman Ignatius Reinhardt.

But I, Kadmus Greningen, journalist, eyewitness of this story, must also inform you that what follows is not strictly about love, nor even ice hockey, but about *Te Hart.*

Te Hart can be translated roughly from Borschic as "The Heart," and from this you may conclude that I come to you with a romance. And yes, certainly there is one.

But *Te Hart* means more to us Borschers than the temporary flutterings of passion.

Te Hart is best translated "the deep longing of the heart," and this is in truth that for which all life strives. This is the soul of intrepid adventure, of human beings who bravely step forward onto the slippery ice of their destiny, testing the blades of their grace-given talents, while saints and angels sing in sheltering harmony.

It is, finally, a tale of how one such skater found his talent and changed an entire nation.

Sherm's story unfolded in the year 329 of our reckoning, the year that in North America there was no National Hockey League season. Our hero was a 24-year old of promising ice hockey ability in the lands of North America. But if you look up his statistics in the record books you will be hard-pressed to find them, because though he had very fine promise as a professional, he never quite made it, for reasons known only to the saints and Fate.

In fact, Sherm was so mightily frustrated by the higher-ups and decision-makers of North American hockey that he had become willing to play somewhere else. The tipping point came when the National Hockey League of that year was suspended, for reasons best known only to the principals in the matter. Sherm wrote to put his name in when he saw the Borschland hockey posting on a bulletin board just inside his team locker room.

In due time he received a telegram from Kronus Vujlsbarron, the legendary owner of our most legendary Borschic ice hockey team, Te Staff ("The City," in English), saying he would be glad to have him, based on his written credentials.

No one receives telegrams in the wide world, of course. But our land is different. We live somewhere in the world that isn't quite the world all the time-- more about that presently-- and the only sure way of getting a long-distance communication from Borschland or the peoples of its continent is to send a telegram by our underwater cable to Perth, Australia, where it is then sent by other, more advanced means all around the world.

Sherm received this telegram, so it has been told, on the

very day that he had been on the telephone (another very advanced device only now coming into use here) with someone in Russia, thinking that he might be able to play in that very cold and cruel place.

This telegram said, in good English, because we Borschers are proud of our ability to learn languages, START. HELLO FROM BORSCHLAND. YOUR CONTRACT TO FOLLOW. PLEASE REPORT TO NUMBER 14 WAATERSDRAM, STAFF BORSCH, BORSCHLAND, FOR TRAINING, BY 25 NACHTOBER 12 NOON OF THE CLOCK. END.

Meester Vujlsbarron is famous all about our country for saying only those things that need to be said, and indeed, in our country that is seen as a great virtue (which makes me the greatest chatterbox in Borschland, I am afraid). But Sherm, who is a man of few words himself, understood that his petition to play in the Borschland Hockey League had been granted.

So Sherm collected his equipment, said his goodbyes to his family and friends, and stepped on to an airplane to make the long trek to our nation.

Now to get to our Continent, most foreigners do fly. This might seem normal to you in the wide world.

Flying, however, is a risky business for those of us who call the Continent our home. That is because periodically the Continent is caught in a "phase shift," a phenomenon that takes the entire mass of land upon which we live into a parallel universe whose borders no one has adequately mapped as yet. And when the phase shift comes, anyone caught more than five hundred meters above the earth is liable to be left behind.

That means, one moment you could be flying merrily above Staff Borsch, Borschland's capital city, and the next you could be over a very empty and desolate portion of the South Indian Ocean.

And since most people who live on the Continent are not partial to being left behind (shifts sometimes last years), most of us do not go up in airplanes, and many of us want nothing to do with airships, those floating balloons with gondolas attached, even though they fly perfectly well at altitudes of five hundred meters and below.

Sherm flew first by airplane to the Waterbrownbear International Airport, disembarking on the morning of 23 Nachtober (April 23, 2005) having found that the only way by air into the Continent is by the jetliners of the Upright Bears, our neighbors to the south, who in many ways have embraced the advancements of the wide world that we have not.

From Bearland to Borschland by train takes something like 16 hours, but by airship only 5. So *Meester* Vujlsbarron and his colleagues considered in their wisdom that going by airship would find Sherm in Staff Borsch a day early, and give him time to rest before his first skate on 25 Nachtober.

But when Sherm did not arrive at the airship station of the Borschland Airship Conveyance Concern in Oststaff at the appointed hour, not having been taken on as a passenger on the ship, there was understandable consternation all round, and some suspicion of the Upright Bears, who are not always so upright as all that.

Sherman Ignatius Reinhardt, skater in a strange land, missing person.

CHAPTER 2 - SHERM

I knew I was in deep yogurt the moment I lost my airship ticket.

Let me back up. I knew, before I even got on the plane to go to the Continent, that I was in deep yogurt, but something made me do it, something like a yogurt monster that sucked me into a carton full of very deep yogurt.

See, I have always wanted to play pro hockey. Sherm Reinhardt, professional hockey player. My dream.

I was good enough to play college hockey, at a school called College of the Lakes in central Minnesota, though you can hardly look it up even today, because they are trying to duck the feds for tax fraud.

I'm a pretty good skater, and not small, at 6 feet and 175 pounds. And when I came to Borschland I was still young, 24, but old enough to know what I was doing.

The problem was, I never played on those teams that lead to a good junior team or a good college program.

I always got overlooked.

Some people say when you don't get picked for a sport you ought to try something else. But I didn't want to. I wanted to play hockey.

So when I was coming to the end of my career at College of

the Lakes, where I was a pretty good center, I scored 6 goals my senior year, coach tacked up this message on the bulletin board that was advertising players to travel to this place called Borschland, that no one has ever heard of.

It said that it was a very competitive program but if you were picked you would get a contract to play one season in the Borschland Hockey League for guaranteed money, plus housing, health care, and incidentals. "Possibility for extension of contract exists for the best players selected."

One of my buddies, Cal Campaigner, said that thing was a scam. There is no place called Borschland, he said. It's a scam to get your email address.

But I was finishing my time at College of the Lakes, and after that it was going to be rec hockey for the rest of my life, if that. And I wasn't any nearer to my degree at the College than when I first came four years before, had plenty of student loan debt and no job to go to. I also had almost all my teeth still, and they say you really shouldn't retire from hockey until you need a whole new plate above or below.

So I wrote them, and because they said it was competitive, I told them I was getting ready to be drafted into the NHL, but that since there was going to be a lockout that year, I probably wouldn't get to play, and I needed a one-year job to tide me over. I told them I was in negotiations with the Russian hockey league, but since I was an adventurous young fellow I could stand to go to an exotic place like Borschland and help out whatever team needed me.

That was all at the suggestion of my then girlfriend, Caroline what's-her-face, who was good at words for being a beautician major at College of the Lakes.

Well, they must have bought it, because one day I get a telegram from Borschland that tells me to be somewhere at some time, and that's before the end of the school year, and more details will follow.

And I'm thinking, what's a telegram? What's that supposed to be? Something from 1958? But it so makes sense for Borschland. One hundred per cent.

Pretty soon after that I applied for and got a passport expedited processing, got my plane ticket and some traveling money, and I packed my gear and said goodbye to Cal and Caroline and the coach and everyone at College of the Lakes, which wasn't many, to be honest, and last I said goodbye to my sister Cathy and she said take care and I'll pray for you.

And so I flew, and flew, and flew some more, and I finally found myself in a place called the Maldives, a desert island with an airport, an airstrip, and a taxi between the two. At the airstrip there were twenty palm trees, a shack, and an old 727 parked out back with a logo that said Bear Air and a bear head with wings coming off of it. The driver left me off with my gear, and the first person that greeted me in that shack was a bear.

He was dressed in a navy-blue uniform with a peaked cap and shoulder boards like any other airline employee, except he was furry all over and his voice was rough and growly.

"Good afternoon, Mr. Reinhardt," he said to me, "the plane is right on time." I'll never forget that. It was in an accent that sounded English and maybe Jamaican and something else I couldn't place.

He put my gear on a cart, and we walked out to the plane, which fired up when it saw me coming. And a female bear flight attendant-- I knew she was female because she was wearing a skirt and had a slightly higher voice than the male bear-- greeted me at the bottom of the steps to the plane, and I went up the stairs, and besides one other human I was the only one in the plane, so I sat down next to him.

He was British, and glad of the company. He was also in uniform, an RAF guy, and he said he was on his way to the RAF base in Bearland, and was I the contract man from America who was overseeing the sprinkler installations at the base?

"No," I told him. "I'm a hockey player."

And then I said, "Bearland?" and my face flamed up all hot, because I thought maybe I'd read the flyer wrong, and it was Bearland they were after, not Borschland, and maybe I was going to be playing hockey with a bunch of huge, sharp-fanged animals that could also speak perfect English in a Jamaicanish type of way.

"It's daft, isn't it?" said the RAF guy. "No worries. They're quite civilized, aren't they? More than a lot of places you can go in this world. It's a bit boring, really. Bearland. Daft. But you get used to it."

"But it says I've got to be in Borschland day after tomorrow." And I patted my carry-on bag, a backpack that I used to go hiking with, and began to unzip the pocket where I'd stashed the telegram, airship ticket, passport, and traveling money.

"Borschland?" He blinked, then said, "Oh, yes. Yes, right. Now it all comes clear. You're an *ice* hockey player. Right." He looked out the window, at the sand and the palms and the Indian Ocean, which was as blue as the picture on a jigsaw puzzle, and he said again, "Ice hockey. Right."

And then he checked his seat-back pocket and took out a magazine, and the flight attendant said, "Pardon me, sir" and asked me if I wanted something to drink. So I said, "Coke," and she said, "We don't have that," and she offered me something called Bee Cola, while the RAF guy was ordering a Foster's, which they did have. So I ordered a Foster's too, which came in a big oilcan.

"They are so daft about cola," said the RAF guy. "Anything sweet has to be sweetened with honey. Potty honey guilds."

Then the pilot came on and told us there would be only light turbulence and a small chance of a phase shift.

"Phase?" I said.

"Annoying thing. Bearland's in a bit of a parallel universe, isn't it? Sometimes here, sometimes not. When the place goes into a phase shift, you can't get there from here. Sometimes you wind up exactly where you started. Sometimes you fly right through and you're in Australia before you know it. And it's why the whole daft continent can never be found on a map. But it's bloody well there if you do find it, isn't it?"

Deep yogurt, I'm telling you.

The RAF guy fell asleep with the magazine on his lap, woke up, talked about his vacation condo in Cyprus, about the best topless beaches in the Mediterranean, et cetera. Then we had a meal where all the sauces were honey glazes, and five cans of Foster's, and after about six hours total the pilot came on and said we could see the continent off the right side of the plane, which we could, since it was clear and sunny, and twenty minutes later we touched down at the Waterbrownbear International Airport around 3 PM local time, and the pilot came on and said:

"Welcome to Bearland, the only nation on earth dedicated to the ideal that all sentient creatures are created equal."

The flight doctor examined me for any indication that a phase shift might be coming (how they could tell I'll never know), and then I got my gear and went through customs and took the shuttle to the airship station, where they told me something called the B.A.S. *Goshawk* would take me where I was going.

The airship station was a green grassy field overlooking the ocean. Palm trees waved at the edge of the field. A big silver blimp hovered in the middle of it, hooked down with a dozen ropes. The platform was about six stainless steel pillars with a glass roof over it, nothing walled in.

Everyone was wearing sunglasses because it was sunny and in the seventies; I found out later Waterbrownbear is on a peninsula that sticks down closer to the equator than any other part of Borschland's continent. I felt a million miles away from anywhere they were playing hockey.

I was waiting on that platform, with signs both in English and another language with a lot of backwards B's in it, when this young male bear who's wearing khaki pants and a short-sleeve shirt but no shoes comes up to me and asks am I looking for a guide.

So I reach for my ticket, and he says, "You're taking the *Goshawk*?" And I'm like, "Yes I am," and then I'm reaching for the ticket in the pocket of my sweats and then deeper into that pocket, feeling nothing except an old airplane boarding pass, and then remembering that I transferred the airship ticket from the pocket of my backpack to the pocket of my hoodie that I took off when I got into the sunshine and pulled through the straps of my athletic bag.

And my athletic bag was there, but the hoodie was gone. I'd either dropped it, or it had been stolen.

"No airship ticket," said the bear. "That's serious."

"Really? Don't they have me in their database?"

"No, mate," said the bear. "There's no database. It's not computerized, is it? You're not in the wide world anymore. The ticket says you have a right to get on the airship. No ticket, no airship."

"Oh, my god," I said. "I've got to be in Borschland in, like, less than 24 hours."

"Well," he said. "Do you have a job there in Borschland?"

"Yes, I'm going to play ice hockey for a team up there."

"And you have a guaranteed salary?"

"I don't know, I guess I have to make the team first, but yes."

"Then maybe we can get you an advance."

"What's your name?" I asked.

"Linus," he said. "Linus Black, Jr. But you can call me Junior. That's me, Junior."

"Junior," I said. "Awesome."

"Charrrrmed." He had that same accent as the first bear I'd met, but now I placed that thing I'd missed before. It was like a pirate, but civilized. A genteel pirate.

Junior told me to leave everything to him. I sat down at a café and he went to the ticket office, and when he got back he said, "Change of plan. Airship is chockablock, with standbys. But we can take the train."

The train.

We surveyed the money I had left, and Junior said he'd make it work. We took a taxi to downtown, where I saw more bears in one place than I'd ever seen in my life. Talk about being in a foreign country. I stood out, and how. The ratio was about twenty bears for every human.

The train station was antique, with huge marble pillars and a ceiling that looked like a big glass birdcage. It went about a hundred feet in the air, glass with steel girders like wire. The central ticket area was swarming with bears, families sitting on luggage, bear cubs running around upright and on all fours. Though the bears had their own language, everyone we talked to spoke English to us, and Junior spoke English to them.

There were chimes every time an announcement was made, and after that the PA announcer would grunt and growl in Bear language, and then repeat what he said in English. We walked to our platform, got on the train, and sat in a compartment by ourselves with a luggage rack overhead.

Junior stood up, pulled down the window, stuck his snout outside, then turned back to me and said we would be in for a fine ride.

"How long will it take to get there?"

He looked out again. "If we're on time, about 16 hours." Then he swiveled back and said, "Em. Roger, was it? No, Sherm. Yes, let's find another compartment."

And that's when I knew the yogurt was even deeper than I suspected.

CHAPTER 3 - SHERM

Linus Black Jr.-- Junior-- pulled my gear duffel from the luggage rack like it was a lunch box, and motioned me out. I opened the sliding glass door to the compartment, and he stepped down about three compartments, and to the other side of the train-- the non-platform side. Instead of seeing bears milling around below us, we saw a track, and then another train on the next track.

"That's much better," said Junior.

We sat opposite each other, the only ones in the compartment. I took him in as we waited for the train to pull out. He was not that big for a bear, maybe a few inches taller than me, but with broad shoulders, tan fur, huge black eyes, and a wet dog's nose at the end of his stubby snout. He looked nothing like Yogi Bear, much more like a teddy bear, to tell the truth. But bigger, and with much broader shoulders.

He must have noticed me staring because he finally said, "Nothing, nothing." Then a pause, and, "Except that I do need to get out of the country."

"The country?" I said, like I hadn't heard. He'd whispered, and I just wanted to make sure.

He clapped his paws together, and they made a sound like phump-phump. "Ah," he said. "But you haven't hired me to tell you my story, have you? I'm just going to navigate you through the darkest portions of the Continent, isn't it?"

"Whatever," I said. "But it's going to be a long ride if we don't share."

"Let's get lunch," he said. "I'm going to be nervous until we make the frontier, and a little something on my stomach should calm me down."

The captain in the dining car told us he could seat us during the second service, and in the meantime we could go to the bar car for the "aperitiff." In the bar car it was about seventy-thirty bears and humans, almost everyone male, and almost everyone in black suits and holding round hats. There were bears with mustaches and mutton chops-- that is, fur they let grow that way-- and men with mustaches and mutton chops, and some were drinking beer in tall glasses and others whiskey in short glasses. And every single one of them turned and looked at Junior and me as we came into the car, him in his khakis and short-sleeved shirt, me wearing my College of the Lakes team jacket and ripped jeans.

Just like he'd read my mind, Junior said, "I've spent a lot of time off-continent."

I was going to order a Foster's in an oil can, but Junior put one paw on my shoulder and two claws out to the bar man.

"We'll have some real beer, and that's what it is. Why don't you pay him, there's a lad."

The bar man topped off two glasses with beers that were half head and brown as dirt.

"Here's to your health, and to all your cousins'," he said, and drained half of it.

It was strong beer. No, I mean strong. I can drink beer. I've done it many a time. You don't play hockey and not drink beer. But this was a kick in the head. I took a healthy gulp, and it was like a horseshoe tattoo right between the eyes. I was starting to get woozy, and I thought to myself, this must be the time when the guy passes out and the bear steals all his stuff, and the guy wakes up on a train going to Dogland and he's got no money.

But that didn't happen. One thing I learned about bears in all my days in Borschland, they're loyal. They don't always tell you the truth, but once you have had one of their real beers, they tend to stick with you.

"Oh my God," I said.

"Perfect," said Junior. "You're going to need your rest." It was the last thing I remember him saying.

When I woke up, it was dark in the cabin except for the reading light above Junior's seat. The train was going clickety-click and whooshing past crossings, and the train horn went *beee*-eep, *deee*-eep.

"Better?" he said. He had a newspaper, one in the language with all the backwards B's, that he folded as I sat up. "You were all in."

I rubbed my face. I was going to have a prize-winning beard pretty soon, and wondered if I should shave for Borschland, or whether they required muttonchops.

"Where are we?"

"About an hour from Slausburg," he said, and when I shook my head, he went on. "We've left Bearland, over the frontier into Anvoria."

A little jolt of adrenaline hit me, and I slapped my pants pocket. "What about my passport?"

"No worries," said Junior, like he was completely on top of it. "We'll be checked in Slausburg, then it's on to Celtlands, one more change, and we're over into Borschland and there."

I sighed. "I feel like I've been traveling my entire life," I said, and looked out the window at the dark.

"It's a shock, isn't it?"

I nodded.

"Listen, now that we're over the line, I should tell you," Junior said. "I'm not just a guide."

"I figured."

"I'm part of a political party in Bearland that's, ah, not in favor at the moment," he said. "I'm being watched by the government for, ah, treasonous activity."

"So, you're a terrorist?" I said, without turning my head.

Like, I'm totally not surprised based on all the yogurt I've been diving into lately.

"Of course not," said Junior. "Ridiculous. It's a perfectly legal party. We're for the preservation of democracy. But the party in power now is trying to find ways to stop democracy. Of course they would never say such a thing. They are just trying to pass laws to make it more difficult for them never to be voted out of office. I mean, they never would've been voted in if it weren't for a few bloody foxes making trouble on the borders."

"Bloody foxes?"

"The foxes are our neighbors, and traditional rivals. We had a war with them about a decade back, really a skirmish, since our technology is far superior to theirs. But they're always acting up in one way or another. And we did have an incident of bombs going off in Brownbearking in the past year, which is the biggest city near the Fox lands."

"So there is terrorism, but you're not one of them."

"Certainly not. But there are very few foxes allowed in Bearland, and the government watches them closely, so it was hard for all of us to see how a bomb could go off in Bearland if there weren't any foxes about to set them. It came out that maybe a bear was one that did it. And the other party produced a bear they said did it, and it turned out he was in my party."

"Wow."

"A renegade, obviously," said Junior, cocking his head towards me. "So right now the other party is in power, and they're trying to stay in power, and I've been, shall we say, vocal about it all, and so they're watching me. I gave them the slip this morning, and I would say they are probably still posted at my flat waiting for me to come out to dinner tonight, when in fact I am off to Borschland and other places to speak with, ah, a few people, about our predicament."

"And the next thing you're gonna say is that you're not doing anything illegal that I'm going to be hauled into jail for like, being an accessory to, or aiding and abetting."

"Well, Mr. Reinhardt," said Junior, and he clapped his paws

together, phump-phump, "I am not supposed to travel out of the country, so said a court of our sovereign land. But I have a passport with another name on it, and since this is an Anvorian train going to Anvoria, and it was not a terribly difficult thing to get onto the international platform…"

I rolled my eyes. Never talk to strangers, Mom said.

"…And our first frontier check will be in Slausburg, you could say, technically, very technically, I have indeed broken the law. But I have done nothing that is illegal in a truly democratic country."

"So what are we going to do?"

"We," and he nodded, like he was saying thanks to me for saying we, "We are going to play it cool, as they say in America."

"Chill," I said.

"Yes, precisely. Chill. We should have no trouble with the Anvorian *douaniers*. Their politics are very favorable to mine at the moment. The question will be, will we have any trouble from the consulate bears."

"You mean, the secret agents, or whatever."

"Yes. Because if they have discovered I have left the country, they will have been notified, and they will try to pick me up."

The train horn went *beee*-eep, *deeee*-eep, and a floodlight passed over Junior's face and by it, and I thought, wow. That's about all there was to think.

We got into Slausburg about 10 PM. The train slowed, and I looked out the window at a bunch of twinkling lights and rows and rows of tracks as we crawled into the station.

"So do you have a family, Junior?" I asked as we came under the tall metal skeleton of the station platforms.

"What an odd question," was all he said.

I slung my gear over one shoulder, slung my backpack over the other, and clutched my passport in my hand. There was a big line of people, bears and humans, and we divided into a line of Anvorian citizens and non-. Once we were in that one, I was the only human.

Junior whispered into my ear, "Just do what they tell you. If we get separated, get on the train and good luck to you. I'll catch you up and we can settle affairs then."

"Do they speak English here?" I said, looking up at the signs that were all in languages I didn't know.

"No," said Junior. "But the language is like German. German and French, and a little Dutch. Do you know any German?"

I shook my head, and the image of Mrs. Detweiler came into my head. She was the German teacher at my high school, and we used to call her Debt Piler, because the rumor was she had a shopping addiction.

"I kind of flunked Spanish," I said.

Junior shrugged his big shoulders and leaned on one hip, resting his fake passport on the other.

The Anvorians gawked at my passport. They kept saying *AmeriKANisch*, *AmeriKANisch*, and the lines were held up as a bunch of them came over, all dressed in navy blue with pointy-brimmed hats and leather pencil holders in their shoulder pockets. And Junior came behind me and said something in Anvorian, and they nodded, and took his passport, and gave it back, but they didn't give me mine back.

One of the guards waved me to follow him, and Junior followed behind me, and we left the crowds and went to a small office next to the platform where an officer was sitting behind a desk and smoking a pipe.

"*Glug glug glug glug muh glug ma Amerikanisch, Her Commandant*," said the guard.

"Oh my god, I can't believe it!" said the Commandant, in a pretty good imitation of English.

He stood up, dumped out his pipe, and came from behind his desk. I thought he was going to hit me, but he took my hand, pulled me to him, and did a kind of chest bump.

"You're hockey player! Fantastic. I'm basketball."

I shook my head. Junior spoke to the Commandant, and said, "He's trying to tell you he played basketball in college in the States."

"Man! I'm play, Vestphalia University, Vestphalia Pennsylvania. You know it?"

He must have been a point guard, because he wasn't that big, not even as big as me. And as far as I know, it was a long time ago, because he had a big gut and not a lot of hair. But I said, "Yeah, sure."

"Ha! I think NBA man, but, you know, never happen," he went on. "You play?" he said to Junior.

"*Nay, Her Commandant*," said Junior.

"God, so good to see you. You know, um, I can't say it," and he spoke to Junior and laughed.

"He's says he forgot the name of his girlfriend back there."

I laughed, and he laughed, and we shot the Anvorian breeze for a little while. He had little cups of coffee brought, asked if we were free for a beer, and Junior explained, all in Anvorian, that we needed to catch the 11:10 to Céad Míle Fáilte, the capitol of Celtlands, so we could get another train to Borschland and be there by noon tomorrow. At least that's what he told me he said.

"Of course, of course," he said. "Oh my god. Hockey. Doze bastards, Borschers. You gonna hate dem." And he laughed like it was the funniest joke in the world.

He sent about seven guards to escort us to the Celtlands National Railways train that was going to take us to that country, and he waved us through Celtlands customs, speaking to a buddy of his who was about six foot six and maybe was the center on that Westphalia team, and we stopped at two French fry carts, and he screamed what sounded like "Treat, Treat," and loaded us down with a big wet package of fries and pickle relish.

He paid. But he wasn't screaming, "treat." It was the Anvorian word for French fries, *Friet.*

"Come back to Anvoria sometime," he said as we passed through the barricades. "Play some hoops together. My knee, eh, you know? But I don't care, we play."

And the upshot of it all was that when we saw bears, even bears from the consulate, of which there were definitely a few,

Junior said, they never came near and we never had a half-inch of a problem.

"I bet you're gonna say you planned that," I told Junior as we sat with the fried fat smell of the potatoes and the vinegary sweet relish filling the compartment.

"You did get back your passport, didn't you?" Junior asked.

I patted my pants pocket. It didn't feel like there was a passport there. I stuck my hand in-- all around.

No passport.

"Oh God," I said.

Junior pulled a blue rectangle from his breast pocket and handed it to me. "You do need a guide, Mr. Reinhardt."

CHAPTER 4 - SHERM

It took another seven hours to get to Céad Míle Fáilte, seven hours of raggedy half-sleep, French fry snacks, and French fry farts, which necessitated opening the window several times to let in a blast of cold air that made my fingers numb when I tried to close the window again. We weren't in sunny Bearland anymore.

When the Irish conductor came into the compartment at 5 AM saying tickets please, with his vest and thin tie and black conductor's hat, he put his hand to his nose, punched our tickets, and said under his breath, "*Freet. A thee-ah thee list.*"

"What's he say?" I croaked to Junior.

"You think I know Irish?" said Junior.

At about 6 AM we rolled through one more passport check, platform side, and the Irish train left, and the Borschland train arrived, and I was impressed. The locomotive was black and all shined up, with a black coal car and black passenger cars with a thin silver script across the middle.

"You expecting any friends?" I asked.

"In Borschland, certainly," he said. "This is a backwater, here."

No bears were loitering on the platform, and we saw no bears in our car, and we chose a compartment with a Borschic priest type who was consulting a little red book with gold leaf, and whispering to himself.

I got up, went to the bathroom, washed my face and shaved. I looked like crap and I said to the mirror, "Ready to face the day." I had one small zit over my upper lip, my eyes were bloodshot, and my hair was probably too long for Borschland, all smushed up like a Mohawk on top of my head. I wet it and slicked it back with a comb just so I could call attention to my big, crooked nose. Never got hit with a puck there, it was just naturally that way

When I came back to the compartment, the sun came through the right side of the train, red, then gold, and the cliffs reflected the light where the railway builders had cut into the mountain.

Down below we could see a river in a deep gorge, crowded with rapids, and as we descended down from the summit the river seemed to come up and widen out, and pretty soon we were in a mountain valley with houses on either side of us, and telephone poles, and the houses were made of stone below and stucco above, with wood shingle roofs and shutters on the windows purple, green, red and yellow.

I saw a lot of carts with horses, but no cars, and Junior said we wouldn't see any until we got into the city, because Borschland "does without" cars. And the train really started humming, and everything flashed by in the bright sunshine.

Once we got down on level ground, there were fewer pines, and the trees were all losing their leaves, and many were already bare. It was warm inside the compartment, but the people outside wore long coats and scarves.

"Hockey weather," said Junior.

The clergyperson looked up from his book and nodded at Junior, said a few words. "He wants to bless you," said Junior.

In those days, I never gave religion much thought, though my sister always did, especially after our parents passed. But I said yes, because there is never any harm in being prayed for or blessed.

The clergy opened up a little case next to him, and took out a little bottle of water, and a little bottle of oil, and he dabbed a little of both on to his fingertips. And the guy made a sign over me-- not the sign of the cross, I'm pretty sure, because we are German Catholic, and I know about that type of stuff-- and he touched my forehead with the water and the oil.

"Amen," he said, and I said Amen as well.

So that was that. Around 9 AM it clouded up, and around 10 we pulled into Staff Borsch Central Station, and I got incredible butterflies in the stomach.

"So what's the drill here?" I said, gripping my stuff.

"No worries," said Junior, in his in-charge voice. "You are home free."

He got off the train first, and at the bottom of the stairs there were two bears in black ankle length coats with fur collars. One of them had a mustache and the other had muttonchops, and they were big, about 7 feet tall.

Junior put up his hand, like he was saying *hi*, and then he hit the platform running, pushing past one of the bears, bouncing off him like a pinball. The clergy was behind me and said something like *Highly Outrageous*, but it was in Borschic, so I didn't understand.

Junior ran. He bent over as he sprinted away, one paw almost touching the ground.

He was fast. He was fast for a bear, fast for anyone.

The bears took off running after him, through the crowd that was getting off the train. I had no guide anymore.

The clergy shook his head at me, like he was saying *Bears. What are you going to do?* And he motioned for me to follow him, and we went with the crowd to the front doors of the international platform, and before I knew it I was on the street in Borschland, surrounded by people I didn't know and who didn't know me.

It was cloudy, and cold, but with a kind of brightness to the sky, like the sun was trying to get through, and there was a taxi stand with horse-drawn carts all lined up. Across the street there was a big sign that said SUB with an arrow pointing down. Subway, I thought. Wow, a subway, and horse taxis. I had no idea where 14 Waatersdram was, so I went to the taxi stand and showed them the address on the telegram, and the taxi captain called for a guy.

"*Hahh-keeee?*" said the taxi man. "*Amerikanisch?*"

The universal word. I nodded. He nodded. He looked my gear up and down. Then he said something to the driver that didn't include anything like 14 Waatersdram, and I got into the horse-drawn cart for a short ride to a place that was not on Waatersdram, but this unpronounceable street named Sanktvujtenswej, and he stopped at the bed and breakfast of the taxi captain's brother and sister-in-law.

The driver carried my gear into the place, which was a tall, narrow building with steep steps, flower boxes in the windows, and a peaked roof right next to a bunch of other buildings just like it. He motioned for me to follow him, and we went through the door with a bell over it, and came into a kind of living room/dining room where we were greeted by this huge woman with the biggest, well, let's say the biggest bosom I have ever seen on a woman who is about five feet even.

She came up to me and hugged me full on so that whatever kind of bra or corset she was wearing dug completely into my ribs, and she kept saying *Amerikanisch Amerikanisch*, and she told me to sit down along with the taxi driver, who didn't seem to be in any hurry to leave.

Then she put this big steak in front of us with some fried vegetables that turned out to be shredded leeks (really good, you should try some), and the taxi driver and I ate and sort of gestured to one another like we were playing hockey, and the first word in Borschic I ever learned was the word *gool*, which means "goal," and sounds like the way we say goal, except they say the "o" sound a little longer than we say it. I'm sure he thought he taught me everything there is to know about playing hockey in Borschland, because he set up the salt and pepper shaker as a goal mouth and he used forks and knives to make the boards behind the goal, and he took a little peppermint candy in a bowl on the table to represent the puck. He was an expert, I have to say.

Then the lady ushered me up to a room upstairs, and patted the bed, and put her hands to her head in the universal sign of naptime. I figured, why not, I've got about a half hour before I have to be there, and I was out like a light by the time my head hit the pillow.

The next second-- I swear, it was the next second-- I'm woken up by about ten thousand people singing at the top of their lungs, and in the background, church bells, ringing like it's the king's birthday or whatever. I don't think there's any way to describe how loud it was. I've been at hockey games. I used to go to the crappy NHL team they've got in Minneapolis and I know what a large crowd of people sounds like. But this was over the top.

So I'm up on my feet for two seconds, and they come get me, and pull me downstairs, and the crowd just sort of surfs me over for two blocks to 14 Waatersdram, which turned out to be the headquarters of Te Staff hockey club. The whole street was full of people, mostly men, but at the front door of the B&B there were some women who tried to drape roses over my shoulders. I think some of them were pretty good-looking, but I don't remember.

Then I'm on top of the crowd, and in the middle of the street is this overhead electric tramline with the cars like train cars, and there are more wagons with horses, stopped because the whole street is full, and everybody is singing, everyone's got mustaches and muttonchops, and they're throwing their hats up in the air, and the only thing I can think is, *Is this for me?*

They put me down right in front of the door for 14 Waatersdram, and the door opens and someone kind of pulls me inside.

And it's a guy who puts his hand on my shoulder, looks at me straight in the face-- he's a redhead, about five seven, with freckles, and blue eyes-- and he says, "Welcome to Borschland. I'm Busby."

CHAPTER 5 - RACHAEL

I was not in the crowd that day.

I was not even close to 14 Waatersdram, although I was in the city on the day, and I did hear about the uproar. There is always some kind of uproar in Staff Borsch.

I am not strictly a fan of ice hockey, you see. I am a poetess. My name is Rachael Martujns.

That agglomeration of vowels and consonants must look frightful to a non-Borschic eye. My name is pronounced something like the French name Raquel, and my last name in English would be Martins, really not that unusual, I don't think.

You also may be thinking, what is a poetess, and what kind of career is that for a young Borschic lady who happens to be the daughter of an archdeacon, and one of the most prominent archdeacons in Staff Borsch, indeed.

The fact is that there have been many poetesses in the land of Borschland, almost ever since Borschland began, and the first people landed on the shores and met the Loflins, who are very poetic, as an aside.

I don't think we Borschers are very poetic by nature, but the Loflinlanders are so. They have their epics that go back a long, long way, and their love poems (I do so adore those) and they have their religious poems, and wisdom poems, and almost everything they say is a kind of poem. So it was impossible for the Borschic people not to have some kind of poetry pass into them, despite that we have not always been on the best of terms with the Loflinlanders, to say the least.

Being a poetess is not a lucrative career, I will admit, and I will admit as well that poetesses tend to rely on their fathers for their livelihoods, and then on their husbands once and if they get them, unless they become deaconesses, at which time they cease to be poetesses, although I can't imagine why the two can't mix.

At the time that *Meester* Sherman Ignatius Reinhardt came to Borschland, I had not yet thought on deaconhood or marriage, being just past twenty years old, and newly graduated out of the Borschland Women's University, or as it is called in Borschic, the *Daamensveltinstitut.* I was much encouraged by my professors to be a poetess-- that is, to write sentiments that unite all of Borschland with their beauty and universality and sometimes their subtlety, and to perform this poetry everywhere, for in Borschland it is customary to start things like state dinners and openings of steel mills with a bit of verse.

My professors, in fact, encouraged me to become a kind of celebrity, for a good poetess does engender notoriety amongst the common people, and is invited all over the country, and does sometimes sell enough books to be well off on her own, though, I dare say, that is getting more and more seldom for some reason. Perhaps the murder mystery is cutting in to our market.

But as I say, I was nowhere near the offices of the great ice hockey club when this uproar over Sherm Reinhardt took place, and yet I feel as if I were.

I, being a poetess, must always follow my intuition and inspiration, and that afternoon as my mother set the evening tea before us, and my father the deacon took his leisure to bless it, and there was a newspaper open on the piano bench as I came to the saloon to take our meal, that I spied a picture, a lovely engraving, as our newspaper artists are wont to make, of the face of this young American man.

My father read aloud from the newspaper story, about Sherman Reinhardt, who had missed his airship in Bearland and turned up some eighteen hours later at the bed and breakfast of a lady not two blocks distant from 14 Waatersdram, the legendary digs of Te Staff hockey club.

Those eighteen hours had been a frenzy of extra editions of our newspapers, of which they are seven major dailies, including papers devoted entirely to sport. These extras contained the headline NO NEWS ABOUT NORTH AMERICAN HOCKEY PLAYER several times, which might not sound to you like news. To us, to whom nothing much happens most of the time, it was riveting. We made so much of it, and fancied so many terrible and ghastly outcomes of the story, that when Sherm did turn up there was a citywide paroxysm of joy.

How it was that Sherm was able to arrive in Borschland without attracting notice (except for the lucky hansom cab driver who conveyed Sherm to his sister-in-law's establishment, thereby securing her widespread fame and some fortune) is easy to determine if you understand that we, having never seen a North American hockey player in the flesh, had no idea how one must look.

The engraving in the paper was not like Sherm's face, not as I came to know him, but it did capture something of him. It was of his profile, with roses about his neck, and looking off to the side, to the advertisement about the ladies' foundations on that page, and there was something noble about the angle of his jaw, and the circle of his ear, that touched me. He seemed entirely himself, even though he was not really himself, just a picture. It was as if the artist had received some kind of essence from Sherm and had transferred it to the picture, with that essence intact.

Around the face lay the black and white pattern of the young man's extraordinary story:

The whole street was filled with singing Borschers, some with flags, some with beer steins, some with *topfenz* [flasks] of brandy, some with hats and some with hockey sticks. Besides the singing, there was the pealing of bells from every chapel tower in the city, which made a great noise indeed.

There was even a contingent of women with a very large display of white Borschic roses, with which they would have brought an elephant to its knees if they had draped it over its back, but which Mr. Reinhardt shouldered with a single shrug.

When Mr. Reinhardt looked out the window of his room for the first time, what a great roar came up from the crowd. For his likeness was already in the midmorning editions of our humble sheet, having been relayed to our expert portrait maker by Mrs. van Dijer, the proprietress of the bed and breakfast.

The North American then pointed to his wrist, which is to say, what time is it (as Borschers point to their vests). So Mr. Reinhardt came downstairs, still in his sleeping clothes, or in the very brief pantaloons that exposed his muscular legs for all to see, and he asked in loud and clear American English to the press, that was sitting there in the lobby with Mrs. van Dijer trying to take orders for coffee and tea, "Does anybody know what time it is?"

A young witness, Aadam Strijklen, who said he has spent a year studying Traditional Continental Drama in Bearland, where the language of the university is English, stepped

forward, as a good actor does when he has
been cued, and said, "It is time for hockey!"

What an extraordinary young man, I thought.

"Mother, did you see the papers?" I asked as we sat down, and Father was finally finishing his prayers and blessings.

"Yes, I did," she said. "It's going to be nothing but ice hockey for the rest of the year up until Epiphany, Kandelmaas, and long beyond."

My father grunted, and poured Mother a glass of Anvorian wine.

"Did you see the picture of that man, the American, who's arrived from the wide world?"

"I did," she said. "Imagine. The first American ever to play the game in Borschland. What a feat."

My father sipped at his own glass of wine, grunted in approval, and rubbed his hands over his fish cakes. He loved his fish cakes, especially with the dill cream sauce that my mother directed our cook to make for them.

"I think I may have a poem for that man," I said.

"Saints," said Mother. "Already in love, my dear Rachael? What about that suitable Kejls? He has such good manners."

"I am not in love, Mother," I said. "This is a national poem I am thinking about."

"Then you are smitten and soaked already," said Father, cutting his fish cakes in fours.

"A national poem about a North American?" said Mother. "Come now."

"It is going to be about how we are a welcoming nation," I said, although I didn't really know what the poem was going to be. "And I am going to write it both in Borschic and in English."

"But you don't know English."

"I know English literature. I took a course of it with Professor vaan Flucht. I read *The Great Gatsby*. And we broke our pen nibs doing compositions. It should not be that difficult to do."

"My dear," said Father, buttering bread.

"Well, keep it short," said Mother. "And ask Kejls about it before you submit it anywhere. He has good judgment and he is patient. That is why you would be such a good match."

Kejls Muttik was the last person I was going to ask about this poem. Kejls was not a poetic person or even an academic person, though he did have some pretensions of that. He was a university graduate, of the University of Borschland, and he was on track for a commission in the Borschland Navy to be a naval airship captain, so I expected that I would not be seeing much of him in the very near future.

Mother was hoping that Kejls and I could get married someday. His family knew my family, and his family was a very pious one, contributing much money for the restoration of Father's chapel and the care of the deacons and deaconesses who keep our religious traditions strong. I was grateful to Kejls' father, who owned a lot of factories in the city of Tarlunz, next to Staff Borsch. But Kejls himself, well. I was hoping for quite a bit more, frankly. Yes, he was patient, as impassive as the statue of a saint! And I, alas, have an impatient and even impulsive streak. But is it too much for a woman to want to stand behind a great man, one who is not only great in patience but in something more?

As an aside, a young woman in Borschland is not like a young woman in the wide world. I have done some study of the so-called twentieth century, and I understand how it is that women are emerging from under the broad, many-feathered wings of their men and standing in the bright light of the sun. But that is a long way from coming true in Borschland, I'm afraid, and I don't exactly know if that is what is best for us Borschic women in the long run. I hope I do not disappoint any female readers.

In any case, I thought the very first thing I must do in order to begin work on this poem was to meet the estimable Sherman Reinhart. What an intrepid young man he must be, I thought, to have come from so far away, to have understood the depth of what it means to play ice hockey in Borschland, to know that he would have such a great weight on his shoulders of being the first man ever from America to play the game for us, and for our legendary team, Te Staff.

First I took out pen and paper and composed something I thought would please the editor of *Te Taglik Staff* newspaper, *Meester* Chrujstoff Dookens, with whom I had lately developed something of an understanding. I would write small, topical poems for the women's society pages, for which he paid me a shilling or three. The poems were beginning to find a readership, if any of my friends' talk was worth anything.

This time, I wrote *Meester* Dookens, I would write something of the same character, but I would like to see it published in the sporting pages, where poetry is not so familiar, though not unheard of.

"*Meester* Dookens," I wrote, "I feel as if something great and grand is about to happen in our nation. With the arrival of the American in our land, can we finally be close to a moment where the whole world might be flooding to our doorstep, to follow the people of Borschland into a life that is decent, gentle, restrained, and yet joyful?"

I thought that last perhaps an overreach of the truth, and I started anew, but when I came to that spot again, I realized it might not be, and I left it that way.

"This will be the first of my poems about the estimable Sherman Reinhardt, a series of poems that will culminate in a grand work both in Borschic and English. I give you, sir, rights of first refusal to publish the entire series."

And I finished the letter, put it in an envelope, stamped it, and left it in the box for the evening mail delivery.

Then I went to work on the poem itself, and that took me some time, for I did not finish it till well after soup, and after my mother scolded me for leaving on the electric lights so long, and not switching to candle. But it was worthy, I thought, worthy enough for the moment.

This is what it said, translated, of course, from the Borschic:

Ode to a Face

Hope's an odd thing, you ring
a bell and all a city's looking
to heaven to sing.

Saints among us, someone paints
a picture of a face that newsprint
cannot taint.

Of what is that tracing? Of a long-awaited lacing
of boots and a crunching race as steel
cuts into ice.

Reinhardt, lion of a man
Scion of the Wide World, ion broken
free from the orbit of an atom

That one, not massive enough
to contain his courage.

Ah, the Borschic muse was stingy enough to contain my poem in only those few lines. I could've written more. But I am aware of the journalistic imperative! So much news, so few column inches.

I hoped he would like it, Mr. Sherman Reinhardt, for, I thought, he would certainly be reading the sporting pages in the newspaper, and certainly not about women's society.

But soon after I posted the poem to *Meester* Dookens with my thanks, a terrible sense of regret darkened my insides. How silly to have written a poem based on an engraving! There was nothing for it but to meet the man himself, if I were to write anything significant for the nation.

It was my patriotic duty.

CHAPTER 6 - SHERM

Busby and I walked down the narrow corridor that was the front of 14 Waatersdram, past about a thousand reporters. Busby put up his hand and said something in Borschic, "Not now fellas," I figured, and he took me through another door and down some stairs and we came out into a locker room that was filled with guys getting suited up to play hockey.

They cheered, and Busby introduced me around, and I remembered none of their names, but I saw that most of them were smaller than I was, and lean, and un-buff, similar to the College of the Lakes team I played for. And we went into the manager's office, where I sat down with two fat, bald, guys, and one really tall, skinny guy with black hair and silver sideburns.

They gave me coffee, and Busby interpreted for me.

"How do you feel, Reinhardt?" one of the fat guys asked me.

"Like I could sleep for three days," I said, and Busby said something that I was sure didn't include the number "three."

"Excellent, you must skate with us today," said the second fat guy. "Just a short workout."

"We are counting on you to score goals," said the first fat guy.

"As long as there's no goalie, I'm your man," I said.

They laughed when Busby translated. The second fat guy said, "Excellent. We hear you have many hat tricks to your credit." And he tipped an imaginary hat from his bald head.

The only credit I knew about was the $68.41 I had left on my Visa back in the States, but I didn't say anything about that. They must have read my mind, because the next thing they did was hand me an envelope.

"It's your meal and lodging money for the first week of training camp," said Busby.

I opened the envelope. There were a lot of red and black bills inside.

"Don't go crazy. It's not as much as you think. But you can buy me a beer after practice. You get more than I do, let me tell you."

We left the office, and I asked Busby who was the tall guy with the silver sideburns.

"That's the head coach," said Busby. "Chrojstenkaamps."

"Why didn't he say anything?"

"He never does. Just points. It's good for a guy who doesn't know any Borschic. He makes himself perfectly understood."

I found out quickly. Busby showed me to my locker, where I put on a rig and a uniform with a scary lack of padding, and no helmet.

"Don't worry," said Busby. "It's about skating in this league, not hitting."

Yes, it was. I followed the guys out to the practice rink, which was in this big brick windowless cavern lit by globes hanging from the ceiling. We didn't touch a puck the entire day, just skated in drills clutching our sticks. I don't know, I threw up over the boards about twenty minutes in to the first end-to-end sprints-- threw up that steak and the vegetables the lady at the B&B gave me, threw up the fries and the relish, threw up the coffee I'd drank in the manager's office, everything. But after that, my head was clear and it didn't seem so bad. By the time I got back to my locker and Busby met me to go home, the only pain I was feeling was in my entire body, minus the stomach.

"My God," I said. "How long was that workout?"

"Only two and a half hours," said Busby.

"Only?"

"Yeah. Tomorrow you'll be in it for five or six. And a lunch break."

A guy came over to see me, short, squirrely, maybe five foot five, but a faster skater I've never seen in my life. With a little triangle goatee and eyebrows that seemed to point up at the ends. He patted my knee and smiled, and gave me something wrapped in paper and tied with string.

"That's Chrujstoff Anselm," said Busby. "He's going to be the second line center. After you."

"After me? That kid's a beast. Did you see how fast he was?"

"Open the package."

I did. Chrujstoff leaned on his stick and smiled, and the other guys came around. As I opened it, I smelled none-too-fresh meat.

"What is this?"

I unfolded the last fold, and there in the center of the paper was a greasy, veined pouch, sickly pinkish grey.

Everyone laughed until they were about to fall down.

"It's a pig's stomach. The guys thought you might need a new one after today's practice," Busby said.

Chrujstoff pointed to the stomach. "*Appne, appne,*" he kept saying.

"There's something inside," said Busby. He pulled out a pocketknife and gave it to me.

I shook my head, but cut into the rubbery skin, and I felt something moving. "Oh, great," I said. "What is this, like a bunch of cockroaches or something?"

Chrujstoff and the guys just laughed. I kept cutting, and finally I heard a tweet, and there was a flutter and feathers in my face, and I threw the stomach in the air. A bird flew up and started circling around the locker room.

More laughter, and the guys came around and started

punching me on the shoulder and rubbing my head.

"They said it's an American eagle," said Busby. "Smaller than they thought it would be."

That kind of did it. I'm not that patriotic, and I'm not a fighter, but I snap sometimes, and this was one of those times. I stood up, snatched Anselm by the collar, and shook. He was about 135 pounds, I figured, not the biggest dude on the team, but he was the one who did the joke, so he was going to get punched.

I reached back to give him one straight in the nose, but before I could do it, a couple of bigger guys stepped in. One took my hand from Anselm's collar and the other got me in a headlock. I hunched down, twirled, and the guy with the headlock went flying into the guy that had me by the arm. Both of them crashed to the floor and I landed on top of them.

I tried to pop up, couldn't-- after that skate, I had no legs left, not even a foot, not a toe-- and just lay there on top of the big guys, out of breath again, just like I had been for the last two and a half hours.

Anselm leaned over, put his hands on his knees, and howled with laughter.

Then the whole locker room went quiet, and a face loomed over me. It was Coach, the silver-haired stork, Christen cramps or whatever.

He didn't say anything, just glared. The other guys got up fast, and I rolled on to the floor. Busby pulled me up and said, "He's fining you for fighting."

Coach put out his hand, and Busby gave him my meal envelope. Coach opened the envelope and took out about half the bills. Then he left.

Then something happened I'll never forget. I went over to my locker, sat down, caught my breath, and guys started parading over. Each guy on the team gave me a little handshake and a red or a black bill. The money kept coming, kept getting stuffed in my envelope, up until the very last guy, the reserve goalie, a beefy mug who was shorter than Chrujstoff and yet wider, it seemed, than a car door.

I ended up with a fatter envelope than I started out with.
"Welcome to the team," said Busby.

CHAPTER 7 - KADMUS

That first day, we the members of the third estate, otherwise known as the press, did not have the privilege of speaking face to face with the newest darling of the city, Mr. Sherman Ignatius Reinhardt. It was all business, indeed, a closed skate, as *Meester* Chrojstenkaamps calls it.

I do not think the city was ready yet for any words from Sherm himself. It was all too big an affair for us. We had been asking for someone to come from America for many years, nigh on twenty, and it was a terrible and terrifying thing for us to have done and to have continued to do for those many years when no one replied to our invitation to skate and play our beautiful game-- and then, the one year that there was a yes, it seemed for a time, for a few hours really, that the player promised would not arrive.

Borschland is not open to the wide world, as you must know by now. We have lived by ourselves for most of our history. We have not known whether our mariners would come back to our shores when we sent them out, for the great Creator of the world saw fit to make the Continent a place apart, half in the world where we come from, and half out.

So we began to send fewer and fewer seafarers out-- back to Europe or parts elsewhere, and spent more and more time circling our own continent and becoming familiar with all the other peoples who have been here all the time or have wandered here from somewhere else. And we had become content with our isolation.

But now there is a great movement inside our land that says, maybe the Creator, the god of our Saints, is asking us to bring our light outside, to the wide world, for we see how much that world is burdened with hurt and destruction. Maybe we were incubating our light for the sake of the world.

That is what the deacons and deaconesses told us, in any case. There were-- and are-- skeptics of this particular philosophy. Those opposed (many of them call themselves the *Baandesbegejwing Borschland*-- United Borschland Movement) believe that if we let in others, then others will change us, and for the worse. They do not want anyone to come and change anything about this little egg yolk that is Borschland. They do not want us to hatch into a bird that may join the wide world and someday end up in some greater land's pot.

So here was a great test for us, the Borschers, to see if we could welcome someone from that great country to the north, the United States, that beacon, the place to which all peoples of the world look in hope. If we could welcome that person and he could play our game and team with our players and make something beautiful, why, then, we all might see this as the first beginnings of something greater, then he might go back to his home and tell everyone about us and our challenge to bring the light could begin.

I am a journalist. I tell of what happens, and if people dream, then I tell of that, too.

So Sherm and I did not speak together until a few days into training camp. I believe the honor of the first interview went to my colleague at *Te Taglik Staff*, Mort Voorbelz, not because Mort is more august than I in the world of sports scribbling, but because, apparently, Sherm had read the poem in that day's edition of Mort's paper, and was intrigued to know who the author might be. In typical fashion, the authors of poems use only their initials, and we had an inkling it must be the young

Rachael Martujns by the R.M., but this was the first time we had seen a poem in the sporting pages of the newspaper in quite a long time, so it could have been anyone.

It was a beautiful poem and expressive of that longing and hope of which I have just written. Rachael is such a lovely spirit. She might be the reincarnation of Sankt Rachael herself, friend of the Loflins.

I read the piece that Mort wrote about Sherm, and I must say it did not, in my humble opinion, capture that which we were all wanting to know: who is Sherman Reinhardt, really?

So my interview was set for 28 Nachtober, four days after the arrival of the forward in a strange land.

We met in the dining room of Te Gruis, an establishment known for its large plate glass windows and ornate mirrors. It is a place to see and be seen. They also prepare a beautiful broiled fish known as a *terveelluj* that is stuffed with our local freshwater Borschic lobster, the *Kraackenscheeln.*

Sherm arrived in a carriage wearing American sports clothing-- a brimmed cap, long nylon pants with a stripe down the side, leather exercises shoes, and a padded jacket zipped to the neck. It was a bit blustery out, and he may have forgotten to unzip the jacket once he came into the well-warmed restaurant. But he did remember to shake my hand and take off his cap as we met, exposing a shock of hair taller than many a draft horse's mane.

The team interpreter, the exiled Canadian Kevin Busby, gave me all of Sherm's answers.

At my question about lunch, Busby said Sherm was in training and would not be taking anything with a complex sauce. In fact, he said, a simple *bujfsteek* and mineral water would do.

Sherm looked a bit worse for the wear, I will confess. Though he was a full six feet in height, he hunched over in his seat and appeared much smaller. He was pale, had dark circles under his eyes, and a growth of beard that made him look a bit like a criminal on the run. His thick, wavy hair was molded by the cap and unkempt. But his flint-blue eyes flashed with life, despite his evident fatigue, and he tucked into his rare Bjaward Sudmaas *bujfsteek*, the finest our land has to offer, with obvious relish.

"The training regime," Busby said for Sherm, "has been demanding for me. There is a bit more endurance training here than in the States."

"Clearly," I said. "Our ice rinks are very large. We need to be able to skate back and forth."

Sherm nodded, hunched over, and put a bite of steak in his mouth.

"And how do you find Borschland so far?" I asked.

"I confess I have not seen much of it yet beyond the practice rink, the trainer's steam room, and my bed," said Sherm. "Though I did enjoy seeing the multi-colored shutters on the houses in the valley of the Borschland River."

"We are very proud of those," I said, and paused, a fear coming up in my heart.

"We will be seeing more of Borschland soon," Sherm volunteered. "When training camp is over, I hope to make the social rounds."

"Good!" I said, in more vehement tones than I'd wanted. "We want you to feel welcome. Skating is not the only thing for which we brought you here. There is a ball at the beginning of the season, the Premujr Ball, and that will be a wonderful chance for you to meet some of your admirers. I hope you dance."

"I will learn," Busby reported Sherm said, though he said a good deal more than just that.

"Are you planning to learn Borschic?" I ventured.

"I hope to have the time," Busby was in the process of reporting, and Sherm interrupted with "*Gaadtak*," which means "good morning," and I felt *Te Hart* strongly in him. He had already learned some Borschic. He was of good stock. He was a fine young man.

Sherm hobbled back out of Te Gruis and into a carriage again once he had finished his *steek* and *mineralwaater*, back to the stern discipline of our legendary manager, C.

Chrojstenkaamps.

I was left with the impression that he should drink a measure of brandy-- the kind that comes from Lisandran apples. There is no discipline that cannot be managed with a measure of that homely vintage down one's gullet.

My piece came out in the evening edition, a short one but heartfelt, in which I said that it was upon *Meester* Chrojstenkaamps to ease up on the sprint-skating to let our American find his legs. It is no small thing to travel 6,000 miles, and into a new world. We might find a bit of mercy is in order.

After all, we are a people of *Te Hart.*

CHAPTER 8 - SHERM

That first week was hell.

In fact, I was thinking of quitting all through it.

That's just how out of shape I was.

I don't drink a huge amount of beer. And I kept up pretty well in my last season at College of the Lakes. But that was recreational compared to the pace at Te Staff.

After that first day that was only skating, we started using pucks, passing, skating in between cones, stickhandling. I felt rusty, slow, and stupid. Coach never talked, which was a bonus, but the other two guys, the fat ones, Assistant Coaches numbers 1 and 2, were constantly chattering, and I had no idea what they were saying. Busby didn't skate next to me, whispering in my ear.

I thought, *if I make this team, I will learn Borschic.* It was the first time I'd ever seen any use for learning another language.

But I had to get over the soreness and the little voice that was saying, "quit." I'm not a quitter, and I don't quit over something as easy as hockey, but there was this other little voice that was saying, "You're gonna get cut."

I knew I had a contract, and I knew it had numbers on it, but it didn't say, "guaranteed" anywhere-- at least not in English. So all through that first week I was in fear. Fear of not making the team, fear of failing, but most of all, fear of having to take that hellacious trip all the way back to the U.S.

No one should have to come this far and have to go back so soon.

I got a lot of attention that week. I mean, attention from the press. On the first day they printed a poem in the paper by someone named R.M. The guys brought it up to me and laughed and nudged me, and I turned to Busby, and he said, "We're going to have to find a way to translate that one. I'm not terribly good at that." Busby was a rock and he was from Canada and knew about hockey, but he was no literary genius.

Finally we found out that she was talking about a picture she'd seen of me in the newspaper.

Newspaper dudes interviewed me. There are a lot of newspapers in Staff Borsch. I once told Busby that the newspapers in Staff Borsch were like the Internet because they updated just as often as there were about as many of them as there are websites about one town. They must have killed a thousand trees a day for all that newsprint. Staff Borsch is actually a small city, but it has a bunch of cities right next door, and there's a million people overall in the area.

I trusted Busby to get my answers right, because to tell the truth, I was hurting. I'd never had to do, in a row, fifty end-to-end cone runs with the puck on my stick. Especially on a rink that was about 25 percent bigger than a normal rink. It was like a soccer field on ice. My ankles hurt like they were broken. After my go I knocked over so many cones they were always putting the cones back in place.

On Day 4, Kadmus Greningen interviewed me. Busby said he was one of the most respected hockey columnists in the nation. We went to this fancy restaurant with mirrors hanging everywhere. I had to look at my sorry ass self from three angles.

Somehow we got on to the subject of the training regimen, and Busby told him I was adjusting to all the skating. But I couldn't lie all that well. I didn't need to put on eye black, the circles under my eyes were dark enough.

Chrujstoff and the guys were always goofing on me. Once they pinned a piece of paper that said "REINHARDT" on it to the back of one of the guys, and the others all lined up, and when he skated between them they all tipped over and fell down one by one. They did great imitations of cones. And they never stopped laughing after that one. Comic geniuses.

I had a hard time sleeping. People would parade past my B&B, and serenade me at 3 AM. The trainers handed out a lot of aspirin but they didn't have any anti-inflammatories. I got a mineral bath and a steam bath and a massage every day after practice, but that only helped so much.

Then the worst thing happened.

At the end of the first workout on Day 5, we were going to break for lunch, and Busby told me Coach wanted to see me in his office.

"I'm getting cut," I said to Busby as we took the walk up the stairs from the practice rink to Coach's glassed-in office.

"Somehow I don't think so," said Busby. He was Canadian and nothing fazed him.

"What makes you so sure?"

Busby wouldn't answer. We knocked on the door, Assistant Number One said "*Kam Ujn*," which sounds a lot like someone saying "Come in" with a foreign accent, and we stood there while the Coach looked us over.

Assistant Number One said, "Reinhardt, you've been skating hard. You deserve a break. Take the afternoon off. Get your training and take the afternoon."

"Yes," said Assistant Number Two. "A break's what you need. Get out and see the city if you like." And he handed Busby an envelope.

Coach scowled, but nodded.

Busby looked in the envelope. More black and red bills.

I said, "What about the other guys? Do they get the afternoon off?"

"No, they need the work. You need the rest," said Assistant Number One.

I looked at Busby. He looked at me. We both knew I was

dying. "Okay," I said.

I told Busby I would spend the afternoon off my feet. I would've watched TV or played video games, but they didn't have those. So I said I'd read a book. He could get me one of those Learn Borschic books and I'd study it. I figured, a good afternoon of rest and I'd be back at it the next day. The funny thing was, as bad as I'd been, none of the other guys, with the exception of Anselm, out-athleted me. I could skate fast and I could stickhandle with them. But they were three hundred percent better in their wind than me, and they were at home. They made me look like a beginner.

Busby was for the plan at first, until, while I was unlacing my skates in the locker room, the front office sent him a note saying I was needed for a PR appearance at a local brandy tasting.

"You haven't been seen drinking brandy yet," Busby explained. "It's the national drink of Borschland. They're very proud of it. It's what all the fans drink to stay warm at the games."

"Stay warm?"

"You play all your games outside. It's a tradition."

So instead of spending the afternoon off my feet, we went to a tailor to get fitted for a Borschic suit of clothes, and we picked a pair of trousers and a shirt and a suit coat off the rack for the PR appearance. The black and red bills I'd received from the coach were plenty to pay for it all. Around 4 we went over to the *Brandujwejngarteen Ter Apfeldaam*, and the place was packed. Again, mostly men, but there were some young women and some older women and they all congregated around me and gave me kisses on the cheek as the photographers blazed away with their old-style flash bulbs that sizzled and smelled like burnt oven crumbs.

The brandy was total firewater, stuff you don't drink unless you cut it with something goofy stupid like Gatorade or whatever. We sat at a table and they brought me glass after glass, little shot glasses of the stuff, and I couldn't tell the difference between any of it, but Busby kept saying things like

"This is northern apple. It's subtler. Not as sweet."

I got ripping blitzed just sipping that stuff, and round about 7 when they brought in hors d'oeuvres I was done. But it turned out the party was just beginning.

After the hors d'oeuvres there was a fish course, and then a potato course, and then an apple course, and the photographers flashed away again with me behind this big pile of apples, and there was this older lady, she must have been fifty, who posed holding two apples on either side of her chest, and they took a picture of me and her. Everyone got a bit happier than is good for anyone.

After that they pulled back the tables and a band with a fiddle and a little horn and a standup bass started playing country tunes, and everyone got out and stomped around. The women dragged me out there, and I don't remember much of it. I saw the pictures in the paper the next day-- the guys put them up in the locker room-- and I had to deal with the most massive hangover of my entire life.

But there was one good thing that happened that night.

Pretty much after all the screaming and shouting was over, and Busby was chatting up this young lady in his best Borschic, and I was sitting on a velvet loveseat listening to a song sung by a 55-year old lady in an evening dress with her hair piled on top of her head and a diamond necklace twinkling like stars. One guy accompanied her on a piano, another on a violin, and a third with a little squeezebox accordion.

I couldn't understand a word, but it didn't matter by that time.

Suddenly Busby was by my side, I was sitting up straight, and this face was staring into mine.

She had brown eyes, dark and shiny like black coffee in a white mug. And she was staring at me, so those eyes made quite the impression.

The rest of her was smaller. I mean, the nose wasn't tiny; it was a good strong nose, but not a honker by any means. Her mouth was soft and simple. Her high, sharp cheekbones made her look like a model. And she was wearing a gray hat with a big brim under which she'd pinned her hair away from her face, and on top of the brim was a big, fluffy, black and white feather.

She was the classiest woman I'd ever seen.

"*Wilkaam ind Borschland*" is all I remember her saying. The rest is a complete blur. Busby interpreted some, and she spoke some in English, and I remember thinking her Borschic and her English were both pretty good. But I wished to God that either I'd had less to drink, so I could understand her English, or I'd had more lessons in Borschic.

The next day after practice, when I'd sweated out all the brandy and had taken a junk load of aspirin, I sat with Busby in the locker room and asked him about her.

"Rachael Martujns," he said to my first question. "She writes poems. And she told me she hopes you're going to write a poem on the ice for her."

"She's a fan?"

"Something like that."

"Well, I hope she comes to one of our games."

"I'm sure she will. But you'll see her anyway."

"How so?"

"Because you asked for the pleasure of a dance at the Premujr Ball."

"What?"

"The Premujr Ball is the party they have in the city for the beginning of the hockey season. It's a big affair. Very formal. People dance, the newspapers write about it. Who went, who danced with whom."

"Do I have to go? I mean, do all the players go?"

Busby laughed. "No, most of the players don't go to the Ball. They don't have the class."

"But I don't have the class either."

"You'd better get some, eh? Because the poetess Rachael Martujns has you down on her dance card."

"No way I asked her to dance. I can't even pretend to dance, drunk or not."

"Hey," Busby said. "It wasn't exactly your fault. She roped

you into it, the way Borschic women do."

"Oh."

"Yeah." Busby looked up and said goodbye to some of the other guys, *tah-loo, tah-loo.* "There's no feminism in Borschland. Men run the show, no questions asked. But you'd be surprised how much Borschic women get done around here. So you've got to be on your toes. Or else you'll be married and wearing a stiff high collar every Saturday night at the charity do."

And I thought I probably could handle that if I was married to Rachael Martujns. But maybe that was the firewater talking.

CHAPTER 9 - SHERM

On Day 10, Wednesday, we all got a rest, and I got to spend the entire time in my B&B with that Borschic book. Busby said the coaches would make roster decisions, and we would have our first game on Sunday.

The papers had gotten a hold of the news that I was on Rachael Martujns' dance card for the Premujr Ball, Saturday night after the first week of the season.

I was also on a number of other young ladies' dance cards. The PR department had said yes to a bunch of invitations that came in shiny envelopes. I was given these at my locker every day after practice.

One paper called me Borschland's most eligible bachelor-- after the PR department sent a runner down to the practice rink to ask if I was single. I wonder if Caroline what's-her-face would've objected to me saying yes.

Those last days of practice, we played a lot of situational hockey and scrimmaged, and laid off the skating drills so much. Most of it was passing-- from behind the net, from the flanks, in front, drop passes, headman passes, give-and-goes. There was tons of room on that rink, and still only five skaters, so there wasn't nearly as much hitting and checking as on a North American rink. It felt like you were always playing four-on-four hockey, there was so much room.

And early on, I found out the hard way you can't check in Borschland.

I was skating into a guy on a forecheck and he just disappeared and I went flying into the boards and almost broke my neck.

Assistant Coach Number Two turned into a blazing red skin balloon and screamed murder at me. Busby translated, "Coach says don't do that again."

I have never been a huge hitter in my life, although my coaches at College o' the Lakes kept screaming "forecheck, forecheck" like it was the miracle cure. In Borschland, you are not allowed to wind up on anyone, anywhere. You can't smash someone into the boards. You can't blindside them. Mostly the only thing you can do is shoulder them off a puck if they don't duck first. There is a lot of room on the rink and almost all the time someone can see you coming, and they are small and wiry enough that they just make themselves scarce, like a hummingbird.

If you do connect, even if it is a legal hit by North American standards, you can get thrown out of the game. Penalties, two minutes in the sin bin or whatever, are for things like looking at someone funny.

Forwards are supposed to concentrate on skating around people and putting the puck on net. On defense, you are pretty much waiting for the puck to come out to you. It's not gentlemanly to get in the way of the other side's three forwards if you want to have some offense on their side of the blue line.

I was told that I was mostly to stand at mid-ice during my shift, looking like a lovely lifelike hockey statue. One of the defensemen would stand with me, and we could've shot the breeze while their three forwards went against our two d-men and goalie. It made for a lot of one-on-one races to the net when I finally got the puck, but the goalie always seemed to have the answer when I shot it. I may have scored 1 out of 6 on average on these rushes, which Busby called the Dragonslayer or Don Quixote, depending on how snarky he wanted to be.

The point of the game, I learned, was not to score goals, but to score them beautifully. Coach was dead set on making the extra pass. It was beautiful to be able to send it all the way around the net on four passes and have someone tap it in on at the weak side on the fifth. You weren't commended for vicious slapshots from 50 feet out that were intended to kill and maim before slicing into the net top shelf right.

In fact, it was much more gentlemanly for your stick never to go over your waist level, any time. That meant a half-slap or a wrist shot was the most powerful it ever got, and a lot of scoring was just pushing the puck to somewhere the goalie wasn't. Chrujstoff Anselm was great at that. He would take a pass around the point, skate in between the defenders, stickhandle, then flip the puck through some unseen hole in the goalie's armor.

Gorgeous.

The left and right wingers were expected to stand around the blue line and dip in for loose pucks if necessary, but they didn't do a lot of skating in the defensive zone either. You might think this was a lot of standing around for players, but it takes a lot of energy to battle end to end in Borschland with that huge rink, even if your shift is only a minute or two.

A lot of guys in the NHL couldn't have played in the Borschland Hockey League. Not to be disrespectful, but if you're a guy who's used to skating around a small rink slamming into people for a living, you'd spend a lot of time in Borschland getting treated for a broken neck incurred by missing people and peeling yourself off the boards.

After the last day of practice, we went up to the coaches' office, where there was a piece of paper tacked on the door. The guys pushed me upstairs like they were going to play another joke, and they were laughing all the time. We all stood on the landing below the door, and we all walked up 8 steps from the landing and 8 steps down again after we'd read the list. The old captain, the goalie, Grimm, regulated who went first and when.

Every guy came forward and took a look at the list, and then grunted something like "*Ja, gut*" or "*Klejnzujt*" which meant something like son-of-a-bitch, and when I was going to get in there and look, Grimm stopped me and let someone else go.

"*Altererst*," he kept saying, until finally someone said. "Noo man last."

So I stood there, the "noo" man, until Grimm told me I could go, and as I walked up the stairs I looked down at them grinning at me like pirates, and I got to the door and looked for my name, and it wasn't there.

"*Waass, nijk te hujmer*?" Chrujstoff said, which is like, "What's the matter?" and they all tried to keep straight faces, although some of them were about to fall off that landing, they were shaking so hard.

"This is so lame," I said, and Chrujstoff came up and read the list again, and he threw up his hands and said, "*Nijk Reinhardt, Nijk Reinhardt*!" and then let out a few Borschic curses. He put his arm around me, said he was sorry or whatever, and all the guys said they were sorry and "Bon Voyage, Bon Voyage to America." Everyone said that, Bon Voyage to America.

So I knew they were punking me, but I also knew that there was a chance I hadn't made it, because I wasn't the best guy out there, I had spent the entire ten days just trying to get my wind. The coaches never said anything plus or minus. I was in an English-free zone; I couldn't overhear a coach talking to a coach. It was all Borschic, all the time.

So they took me down to the locker room, and they all stood around and sang me a traditional song and gave me a Te Staff banner and an honorary Te Staff game sweater and they shook my hand, and all the time some of them would be falling down laughing while the others were making speeches or handing me stuff.

Then finally they opened this little brown bottle with a cork and indicated to me I needed to take a swig. One of the guys said, "Trink, olt Borschic goodbye."

And just as I was about to say *forget you, you drink first*, Busby came in holding a piece of paper. "Don't do it," he said, and took the bottle from the guy holding it out to me.

"Where have you been?" I said, as Busby glared at everyone.

That was it. They couldn't take any more. They all bent over double and laughed their tails off.

Busby took the cork out, smelled it. "It's a laxative. You would've been on the toilet all night." He then gave me the paper. "Everyone got one of these in their mailbox today."

This one had the Te Staff logo with the names of the coaches and managers in print. At the bottom there was a wax seal. "This is the official list," he said.

I was first line center.

"They sent me off on a snipe hunt this afternoon," said Busby over the noise. "I knew they were up to something."

When they stopped laughing they started singing, and each one of them hugged me and said *No hard feelings* and *I love you like a brother* and *Welcome to the team*, in Borschic.

First line center.

Then the coaches came down and we went to a swanky restaurant with about a thousand people in it and a hundred five foot tall ladies in evening dresses with big bosoms kissed our cheeks and gave us white roses.

You've never seen anyone drink like those guys.

I don't remember much that happened, except for one exchange that Busby translated for me.

"I thought I'd die," some of the guys were saying.

"I can't believe how much training we did," another said.

And one guy would say to another, "You looked so bad, you looked like death," and he'd punch him on the shoulder.

"But I was worse," said a third.

"What, what?" I kept asking.

Busby said, "The coaches wanted to make sure you understood that the team was serious, just as good as anywhere in North America. So they made everyone train their butts off."

"So it wasn't just me?"

"No, not at all, they were all dying. But they had to make it seem like it was just routine."

"Why didn't you tell me?"

"You didn't ask."

First line center.

"So after this, you're saying, the season is going to be a piece of cake, I guess."

Busby nodded. "Piece of cake."

Then somebody who was listening asked what "piece of cake" meant in Borschic, and Busby told them, and everyone started chanting "piece of cake, piece of cake" and others shouted the Borschic translation "*krustuloff, krustuloff,*" and that was the refrain for the evening and it even made it into the papers that I had felt the first ten days with my new teammates was as sweet as eating pastry, because in Borschic, Busby told me later, you don't say something is easy by saying "piece of cake," you say it's easy, like *en apfelnosch*, biting an apple.

It was a sweet night. But it wasn't a piece of cake season.

CHAPTER 10 - KADMUS

Early in the Borschic hockey season, at the beginning of Eveember, it's not as cold as it's going to be. Sometimes-- rarely-- it has not snowed yet. So the good ice keepers of Te Staff use refrigeration to keep the rink cold.

We in Borschland have been slow to adopt the latest technologies, it is true. We do not have airplanes, only airships, which apparently are called blimps in America. Some say we could not have done so except that we live here in the Continent, insulated from the wide world and the devastating wars of which it is so fond. So be it. But we have found out about making ice cold when the weather is not so cold, because we love ice hockey as much as the wide world loves war. Maybe that is why we have been able to keep war as small as it always has been here. It seems as if the bears and foxes are always at war; perhaps that's why bears have accepted so much from the wide world, to stay above their rivals and defend their land.

But I fear I have become a chatterbox again.

That first Sunday in Eveember is always magical. The first games of the season quicken the whole of Borschland like nothing else. In other countries autumn is a season of melancholy, regret and nostalgia. For us it is a new birth. When it is cold enough to skate on ice, then our blood races. When the day wanes earlier and earlier, light the candles of the deacons and pray with our saints, then we know hope.

In the year of 329, Te Staff began its campaign with its traditional rival, Tarlunz, which is an industrial city a few miles northwest of the government center. It is a place of factories and forges, but of old it is also a place of forests and ponds, a reclaimed marsh, and there are still hundreds of ponds where the young boys skate in the winter, and from these ponds are plucked most of the talent of Tarlunz.

These factory boys have the hearts of oxen and never stop skating, never stop fighting. They are not as well coached as our Staff boys, however, and they have never developed the confidence to beat us regularly. Always there is some shift of the puck that eludes them.

On this night there was much pomp and pageantry at Te Rijngk, our skating place. The river shined with the lights on the far bank, from the longshoreman's city of Natatck and the glittering suburb of Rirlver. The spit of land, Te Saandmaas, that extends between the river and Te Rijngk was full of workingmen, standing, standing, throughout the game, and not seeing very well, for that spit does not rise much above the river level, and they were standing ten and fifteen deep, but cheering none the less as our skaters waved to them under the spot lights and the bands played.

The grandstand proper of Te Rijngk is built into the bluff that borders the river and guides it on, moves it along, saying, you shall not swamp this city. There is room for six thousand here, some of it in seating, some of it in benches, and at the very top in the grand boxes sit the dignitaries of the city, its richest and sometimes its happiest citizens. One level below sit the press, and there is where I am, humble reader, with the river lit up and the spotlights following the players as they skate the oval with grim, determined smiles.

I know not exactly what was transpiring in the mind of Sherman Reinhardt at this time. Surely he had been in bigger rinks, for he had played in North America. And surely he had been cheered louder, for I think in America they have grandstands that seat twenty and thirty thousand fans at a time.

But Sherman Reinhardt never would have been cheered so sincerely. Of that I am humbly confident.

Of the game many thousand words could be written, yet it seemed to pale in significance to the historical nature of the event. To be sure, Te Staff won, by a score of 7 goals to 2, which was an impressive total, though there is no reason for us to have given up any goals at all, but that once we had gotten to 7 it seemed ungentlemanly not to let them score a couple.

But we did not long remember the score. It was our Sherm who shone, our Sherm, our guest, our adopted son.

Sherm lost his first faceoff. The lights off the river must have dazzled him. The venerable center of Tarlunz, Habel Baarda, who has scored a century of goals in his career, slipped the puck back to his defenseman and seemed almost to take a bow, as if to say, *you were not expecting this North American to beat us Borschland boys, were you?*

Sherm went after that lost puck, furiously skating for it, and extended his stick as one defender attempted to pass horizontally to the other. The puck, headed for its intended target, clipped Sherm's stick and spindled high in the air. Sherm plucked it like a ripe Borschic apple, laid it at his feet, and let fly a shot on goal that went so fast it was in the net before any of us had time to pick up our field glasses.

You have never heard such cheering.

Lubert Veeststaff, the Tarlunz net minder of whose age we have now lost track, told us he had never seen a puck struck so hard.

Afterwards, Sherm said through his interpreter Kevin Busby, "I apologize to the nation of Borschland for my selfishness. I was caught in the moment and my blood was up."

It was a proper thing to say. We Borschers tend not to play the game by ourselves. But how can one apologize for a lightning bolt? It is a force of nature, an act of God.

I believe that, by that shot, the will of the Tarlunz team was broken, like dry kindling over one's knee. Through the rest of the game it seemed as if Te Staff danced the Premujr Ball about the slow-footed Tarlunzers. Sherm took his part, but every time he got the puck he seemed to want to pass it, though the crowd begged him to shoot again. Chrujstoff, our young hothead, ended up with 2 goals to take the honor of the flowering crown that night, and Sherm was credited with 3 assists as he skillfully furnished the puck to the blades of his teammates.

He officially took 3 shots on goal, including that first one.

Afterwards there was much talk. Up to that point there had been much talk, but it was of an anticipatory kind. Now there was something we could remember rather than imagine. Most of the men in the press box were impressed, and they wrote in their stories that Te Staff had been blessed to discover a kind of saint from another world.

But one man, a good man is how I think of him, named Henrujk Willbaanz, who writes for *Te Tarlunzer* newspaper, wrote something different that got the entire nation thinking.

"We have only one game to judge," wrote Henrujk,

> but we must all ask ourselves this question: if Sherman Reinhardt is typical of all North American hockey players-- indeed, if there are many players above him, celebrated and decorated in the National Hockey League, as we know Crosby and Malkin are-- then how is it that we can take pride in our game, knowing that the average player from elsewhere can be venerated as the Hero of Borschland for his superior skills?

That sentence stirred something in us. The papers the day after were all sprawling with rebuttals and responses, some of them appearing on the opinion sheets, not just in the sporting pages. Henrujk told me over lunch the next week that he had mainly been interested in selling a few more Tarlunzers that day, that he had not realized what kind of chord it would strike to cast doubt on the skills of our players.

But doubt it cast, and the ink flowed like blood in a battle. Some writers took Henrujk's side, and wrung their hands over the possibility he presented. Others scoffed, saying it was one game, wait and see. Still others said that anything Sherm had done was due to the help of his teammates; even the miraculous first shot was chalked up to the training regimen of the first ten days, or to surprise on the part of the Tarlunz team, or to simple luck. And there was one, a columnist in the feminine pages of Ter *Abendteelegraf*, Noora Oobeest, who wrote what came closest to my hopeful heart:

> We are darkening our hearts over nothing. Maybe we have attracted to our shores a player who, for whatever reason, was not revered in his own country, but who has always had inside him a burning passion for the game, and in his body the talent and skill to excel, but who, for whatever reason, was never properly appreciated in the wide world with its myriads of hockey players smiled on more often and more widely by Lady Fortune.
>
> Maybe, Borschland, we have midwifed from our Sherman the greatness that was always inside him.

But Noora's voice was a small one in those days; most of us were for waiting to see how well Sherm would do in the next games. But there was a small group of influential naysayers who came from, of all places, the steel city of Matexipar, whose hockey team is an archrival of Te Staff's. These naysayers, these spoilsports, called themselves the United Borschland Movement, a political party dedicated to keeping the world out of Borschland and keeping Borschland for Borschers. Most of the time they occupied themselves with trying to uncover spies in the diplomatic corps of the Upright Bears of Bearland, and hoping to pass laws prohibiting bears from selling honey on street corners.

The UBM newspaper, *Te Stumm*, published a front-page editorial calling for Sherman Reinhardt to be expelled from Borschland, and for there never to be any other foreign players. This was impossible, of course, because there were already a number of players from other countries in our land, including several from Vinasola, Zimroth, the Twin Kingdoms of Dann and Kaatsch, as well as Europe, especially Finland. Even a few bears had played, mostly goaltenders, it is true.

But the spell of North America and its legendary hockey league had taken hold in Borschland, and we all knew that this year the league had not been playing because of a labor union dispute. What if, the editorial said, a flood of players from North America came to Borschland and forever changed our national game? Once one player was here, he could report back to his fellows that this was an attractive place and well paid, and there would be no regard for the Borschic traditions or style of play. Following the ice hockey players would be colonists, the editorial read, and after them guns and other governments, and finally Borschland would cease to be Borschland.

Sherm took all of this with monumental good grace. When asked, he downplayed his skills and said that first shot had been a stroke of luck. He said that he was grateful for his teammates' help, and grateful still more for the chance to play in such a storied tradition, in a place where hockey was of the greatest importance.

It was what was expected, what was hoped for, but there have been many players who have not said the things we expected them to say. So I gave full marks to Sherm. And I waited for that game on Wednesday night.

CHAPTER 11 - SHERM

Wednesday morning, Day 15, three days after our first win, I woke up and the sky was bright white.

Most of the time when you get a cloudy sky it is gray, but this was white, and it was white because it was snowing, the first snow of the season.

It didn't stick, just like my boots didn't stick to the pavement when I walked out to the carriage waiting to take me to 14 Waatersdram, and from there to the train station where we'd board a special to take us to our next game against Wrischer, two hours away.

I was on a cloud, swirling around with the snowflakes. I had never been a hero in anything before, not even in midget hockey. I was a good player, don't get me wrong, but there was always someone else better on my team that everybody talked about. I never had a dad who coached and talked me up and brought me to special clinics. I just played, tried to get on good teams, and Dad watched, and he only missed when he was having chemo.

On the way to the train station on the first class tram set aside for us-- second class trams followed, filled with fans-- I replayed over and over that first goal against Tarlunz on Sunday night.

I knew I was going to lose that first draw, because it was my first game in this huge facility under the lights with the crowd and all the pomp and circumstance, and all through warm-ups I couldn't feel my hands. I dropped my stick a couple of times before the game started and I felt like I should take off my gloves if I wanted to have any chance at holding on to the stick in the game.

I knew that guy, Baarda, was going to win the first faceoff. He was a gray-bearded guy with a tooth missing, and he smiled at me the way the guys in the locker room do when they're about to play a prank. Guys like Baarda always win the draws.

So I made up my mind that, after I lost the draw, I would skate my ass off into the Tarlunz zone and see if I could just hustle my way into a good play. There wasn't anything more on it than that. Forecheck, forecheck, I could still hear my American coaches telling me.

And I had adrenaline to burn. No one could've been more hopped up than me without artificial stimulation.

So Baarda sent it back to his d-man, the one on his left, and the dude had already decided to go d-to-d, a horizontal pass to the other defenseman. Borschland hockey players pass the puck; I'd figured it out in practice. So I rushed at the guy like I was going to give him a big hit, and he may have thought, who is this crazy American, I'm going to pass and then duck. I broke off at the last second and extended my stick as far as it would go to cut off the passing lane.

It was a good move on my part, but it was lucky that the puck hit the end of my stick-- a one out of a hundred type of deal. It was even luckier that the puck flew up in the air. And after that I don't know what happened. Instinct took over. The force was with me, or whatever. I know I hit it hard because I'd been itching to take a real heavy shot the entire practice time, and the coaches kept telling me not to. This time, adrenaline took over.

And the puck went in.

It was embarrassing, really, to hear the screams. I was back to not feeling my hands again when my teammates congratulated me. And I lost the second draw to Baarda because to tell the truth, I was shaking, and only 5 seconds had gone off the clock.

Busby sat with me on the tram and the train all the way to Wrischer. He helped. I got asked a thousand questions after the game, and he sat there patiently and not only translated every answer but, I could tell, made it better.

"Did you ever play, Busby?" I asked him as the train tooted its horn and we picked up speed, turning the apartment houses of Te Staff into a blur. "I never asked you before. Did you play?"

Busby shook his head. "I played. Every kid in Canada plays."

Then a reporter came up to us, and Busby didn't say anything more about himself, because he was on the job.

The Wrischer press met us at the train. We had a press conference in the waiting room, which was a beautiful wood and glass barn, gargoyles etched into the glass and carved onto the ends of the benches.

"Sherm, what do you think of the Wrischer team?" The press kept saying, like I was some kind of expert.

"I don't know, I guess we'll find out," I said, and Busby translated in a lot more words than I had said, and everyone smiled and wrote on their notepads.

We skated their rink, which was on a big pond in the middle of the city, with houses on the far side of the pond and a grandstand that was a horseshoe with the open side to the pond. It wasn't nearly as big as Te Staff. The stands went up about 25 rows at the most, and though the game was a sellout, it felt a little like a neighborhood skate.

The other team was small, much smaller than we were, and though they skated pretty fast, we were bigger and faster, and we muscled them off the puck pretty good and played keep away, and after a while the goals started coming. We kept it in their zone most of the time, and at one point I was behind the goal, receiving and passing, and the third time it came behind the goal, I just took the puck, faked a pass, and wrapped it around the goalie, stuffing it into the bottom right of the goalmouth.

The whole stadium kind of gasped, like that had never happened before. To tell the truth, that had never happened to me before. I had seen wraparounds, but I never had the open ice to try one before. And it worked.

We were up 2-0 in the second when I got my second. I actually won a face off at the right point and passed to my wing-- Oovie, everyone called him, what a great player-- and drove to the goal. Oovie passed back to me and I hit the puck into the top right window.

I scored another late and we won 4-0. It was kind of ridiculous, how easy that game was. We could've scored twenty.

Afterwards the Wrischer press acted like I was the second coming. It was weird, because when I say we could've scored twenty, we could've. The guys didn't shoot all that much; they held the puck and tried to make the perfect pass. When I got it I passed a lot, too, but sometimes I couldn't not shoot because I was taught you need to pepper that goalie. And when I shot it tended to go in.

Busby said afterwards, "They don't call it a hat trick when you get three. They call it a trinity."

"Like, religion?" I said.

"Yeah, and that makes you a saint."

I tried to read my book on the Borschic language on the way back from the game, but people kept interrupting me, and I got about 3 dozen telegrams of congratulations from everyone except the prime minister of Borschland. Most of them were just congratulations from random important people whose names meant nothing to me. But a few made an impact.

One was from someone named R. MARTUJNS, and it said, I LISTENED ON THE WIRELESS. CONGRATULATIONS ON THE TRINITY. BLESSINGS.

Busby said, "She has a serious thing for you."

"Hope so," I said.

"No, it's true," he said. "Sending a telegram. You don't just pick up the phone. You have to actually go down to an office, write it up, and pay for it. Or pay a kid to run it for you."

Another was from the United Borschland Movement. It said, LEAVE BORSCHLAND TODAY. NOTHING GOOD CAN COME FROM YOUR PRESENCE HERE.

Busby shook his head. "No death threats yet. But wait till we play Matexipar."

Then there was a third. It was in English, from an LBJ. YOUR LIFE IS IN DANGER. A FRIEND IS AT HAND. WAIT FOR A MESSAGE.

"Who's LB, I wonder?" Busby said. "English telegram's very rare. Prank."

I didn't say that LBJ was probably Linus Black, Jr. "Could be a friend of mine. Last I saw, he was running from the Bearland spy service."

"You have a friend who's a bear? You never told me."

I gestured around at all the uproar in the lounge. "Who had time?"

"Good point," said Busby.

Then somebody put a glass of brandy in my hand, and we had a toast and a song, so Busby never had a chance to follow up on Linus Black, Jr. As to the message, it didn't scare me. It probably should've scared me, but everything seemed so unreal at the time.

Besides, I had the Premujr Ball to look forward to.

CHAPTER 12 - RACHAEL

To be completely honest, my first meeting with our Sherm did not confirm my first impression of him.

It had been silly of me to think of a giant of a man, a gentle hero, mighty yet discerning.

He is tall, much taller than I, although I am tall compared to my peers.

But when I first met him he was sitting down. Almost sitting down that is.

Although it is an understandable custom to celebrate the annual vintage of our venerable products made from the apple, that noble and yet humble fruit, one should never insist on a guest's drinking of it, liberally or not. I have partaken of brandy, though it is a man's drink, and I find it-- ugh!-- what can I say? Disagreeable at best.

I confess that I was a bit hasty in throwing my presence upon our Sherm in his less than his finest hour. When I arrived at the tasting, late because I had spent too much time on a verse that had been vexing me all afternoon, Sherman was bibulated.

Or, if that is not truly a word, he was applepated, *apfelkoffeld*, as we say in Borschland. Brandy has a way of doing this.

Yet, despite that the tousled condition of his hair, which

does go wild at certain times, sticking straight up or straight out depending on how he has leaned his head, and despite the rumpled condition of his ill-fitting Borschic clothes, his inherent nobility still shined through.

"Good afternoon," I said, in my rehearsed English, curtseying and proffering my gloved hand. "I am the poetess, Rachael Martujns. Pleased to make your acquaintance, Mr. Reinhardt."

He staggered up-- so that I could hardly stop from laughing, bless me-- took my hand, and shook it several times.

"Wow," was all he said.

I wished we could have gone on in English. I had done a bit of brushing up with an English phrase book, but I confess it had all gone out of my head when I saw him, standing over me like a heron looking for a fish in a swamp.

He was like the picture in the paper, or rather more vivid than it, I should say. His jaw was as strong as that sweep of newsprint ink indicated, a triangle that ended in a slight, unshaven cleft. His nose was a bit battered, and bent to one side, I thought, though noble enough. And his eyes: blue like the stones on the bottom of a clear stream, and with eyelashes to spare, which is always an attractive component of a man's face, even if it is considered more of a feminine attribute.

But I can say all this later, afterwards, imagining it in my mind. At the time, his applepatedness made me want to laugh, and yet, he was clearly a gentleman.

He invited me to sit, and said something in English, and I said something in Borschic, then he said something in Borschic, and I in English, and we didn't understand each other at all. Then he said, "sorry," which I understood, and cupped his hand as if holding a brandy glass, put it up to his mouth, and then made circles next to his temple.

"Yes, your head must be spinning," I said. "Brandy." And I picked up a real glass.

He pointed to a half-empty bottle, one of those dedicated and rare ones where a paper label has been affixed with an ink scrawl that says from what lot it comes and what region.

"No, no," I said, and smiled, making a circle about my temple as well.

He put it down and we laughed together, and I was suddenly aware that my perfume was very strong, and that I had put on too much. The whole room smelled like a hospital and an apple press at the same time, and here I was adding to it with my *Lavande ter Ellafuus*, which is not really lavender, it is a flower called the *jujnuj*, which is sacred to the Loflinders and sounds like *ee-nee*, despite all those j's. I had thought it so sophisticated when putting it on, but now it seemed very juvenile, somehow-- a part of my past. Sherm put me into a forward-looking frame of my mind, made me think of possibilities, of all the web of future time's connections.

"Borschland," I said. "Does it please you?"

He understood that. He nodded vigorously. "*Borschland's ergut*," he said, balling his fist and pointing up with his thumb. Then he pointed to me, and said, "*Suj*?"

"I?" I put my dainty gloved hand to my neck, not exactly understanding. *Suj* means "you" in the polite form.

"He's trying to say," said someone behind me, "that before he met you, Borschland was not quite so pleasing."

I turned. It was a young man with ginger hair interspersed with gray, a freckled complexion, and soft green-gray eyes. He was fashionably dressed, in a vest and tie, with a tartan scarf about his neck.

"Busby," he said, and bowed. I put out my hand, and he took it. "I am Mr. Reinhardt's interpreter."

"Mr. Busby," I said, "Tell Mr. Reinhardt that is a very chivalrous thing to say."

The interpreter spoke to Sherm, who nodded and pointed to him as he spoke.

"Mr. Reinhardt says I am... quite a useful person to employ."

"You mean he appreciates your turns of phrase."

"Evidently."

This Mr. Busby had something about him that troubled me. One thing may have been that he was clearly cold sober, despite the presence of all the vats of brandy that had been spilled that afternoon. But I would expect a person who is doing a job to keep his wits about him.

No, it wasn't his sobriety. Nor was it his accent. He was almost completely without one, which is difficult for a foreigner, and his diction was very elegant.

It was something in his eyes, or rather, something lacking, that our Sherm had in abundance. There was an emptiness, as if something had been taken from them. But at the time I couldn't put a word to it.

We stood in a triangle, saying nothing, with Mr. Busby at the ready to interpret if he might need to, but I was suddenly tongue-tied and so was the hockey player with the unshaven chin.

Finally, not knowing exactly what to do, I opened my clutch purse and brought out a rectangle of card stock that had a certain number of gentlemen's names on it. It was my dance card for the Premujr Ball. I did not know whether Sherm would be attending, but I thought to myself that if he were, I should be impolite not to give him an invitation to a dance.

Busby nodded, said something to Sherm, took the card, produced a fountain pen, and Sherm signed.

"He would be delighted, Miss Martujns," said Mr. Busby.

As I walked out, I realized that I had never introduced myself to Mr. Busby. Yet he knew who I was.

The Premujr Ball is held every year at the *Waatersdringblomfontijn*, which is a shorter way of saying a great big arboretum with a glass dome at the top, normally a place of wonder and exotic plants, which for a night becomes a ballroom. There are chandeliers with candles in the center of the room, and strings of electric lights hanging in the trees, and it is all very much a festival of lights in the late autumn darkness above the dome.

Of the trees, in particular I love the rubber tree, which is something that grows only in profound southern Bearland, on a peninsula below the border with Anvoria. The leaves of the tree are very broad, like a pair of closed, pouty lips. They are glossy, and waxy, and of the most decided green, with a flower that is like a tiny orange tongue.

I was standing next to one of these trees when I first came to the Ball. I had come with my mother, and she was standing there as well, and a host of her friends fluttered over to compliment me on my dress, fringed at the neckline with black and white *pavijnjeja* feathers-- a bird like a peacock abundant in Vinasola.

My first thought was of the abundance of women at this ball and the underabundance of men, and certainly I noted that there was no Sherm Reinhardt that I could see at this place, the Sherm Reinhardt of the four goals and three assists in two games, which is in itself a kind of magic of numbers.

But there were Upright Bears.

The entire diplomatic delegation of Bearland was at this Ball, and that is because Upright Bears are great dancers. They are very graceful for being so large, very light on their feet, for they are taught from a young age. Dancing is part of the schools curriculum in Bearland, I'm told. And they love to do it. They love to dress in fancy dress and glide about, showing off what they know while at the same time seeming very grave and dignified about it.

And they can remain very grave and dignified, even after they have had quite a bit of sparkling Vinasola wine in them. You know what they say: 3 bears, 24 bottles.

I had recognized and was about to go to greet my first dance of the evening, a young man by the name of Jens vaan ter Wajld, when I felt a tap on my arm, one that was part fur and part claw.

I turned and met a young bear in black tie and tails. His fur was the color of honey and expertly combed. I took him for the son of a diplomat recently stationed here. It is the young Upright Bears who are most keen to talk to humans.

He bowed to me, and I thought he was going to ask me to

dance, but instead he said, "Rachael Martujns, I presume?"

"Why, yes," I rejoined.

"My name is Linus Black, Junior," he said. "I am pleased to make your acquaintance."

"Charmed. You speak Borschic very well."

He nodded. "It is a tremendous bother, but I wonder if you could relay a message for me to one of your dance partners for the evening."

"Saints," I said, my hand going to my neck. "How very forward of you."

"Forgive me. You are under no obligation."

"Which partner?"

"Mr. Reinhardt."

"He should be here," I said, and demonstrated with my other hand. "Why can't you speak to him yourself?"

"Impossible to explain," he said. "But I presume you think of yourself as a patriot of your native land?"

"You presume correctly," I said.

"Then think of this favor as also a favor to Borschland," said Mr. Black. "Again, it is so very bothersome of me to ask."

"Not at all, if you put it that way."

He produced a small, white, envelope sealed with an LBJ in gold wax. It was very fine paper, the kind one might send with an invitation to a ball.

"Thank you in advance, *mamzeell*," he said, and bowing, turned on his heel and disappeared behind the rubber tree.

I felt the fine fabric of the envelope, almost as fine as silk, and the little glob of yellow-gold wax, resisting the urge to pick at it. Instead, I set out to find our Sherm.

Waylaid as I was by several young men who were not Sherm, it was long before I found and rescued him from several young women.

I curtseyed, took out my dance card from my clutch, and pointed to it.

One of the women said, "Foo! We've been trying to get him out on the dance floor for the last quarter-hour! He won't go. Isn't there anyone around here who speaks English?"

He turned about to all of the women, and kissed each one's hand in turn, very impressive. Then I held out my arm and he took it.

We were out on the dance floor and it was a waltz. He had no idea what he was doing, but it didn't matter. We sort of shuffled along together.

"*Nijkt gut tanzen,*" he said, and I laughed, and said he was a fine dancer.

"How are you?" I said.

"*Ergut,*" he said, then pointed in a circle. "*Mamzeell.* Oh. *Meenich,*" by which I guess he meant he wasn't used to the attention of so many young ladies.

I produced the envelope from my clutch and gave it to him. "*Tangs,*" he said, and smiled.

"No," I said. "It's not from me." And I pointed to the seal with the LBJ lettering.

He straightened, gave me a wide-eyed look, then stared at the seal.

"Open it," I said.

We continued to shuffle along with the waltz, until he produced the card, and read it, and stood stock-still.

His eyelids fluttered, and he looked left and right, then at me. I don't know when I have been given such a penetrating stare; I almost dropped to the ground right there. As it was, my knees knocked for a moment, and he pulled me up.

I whispered, "What is it? May I see it?" and I, more forward than I should have been, moved my hand towards the card still in his hand.

He drew away and put the card back in the envelope, and then into his waistcoat pocket. He shook his head, and said, "*Nijkt versteen.*"

"What don't you understand?" I said. "Can I help? Was the card written in Borschic?"

At that time, a bear lady in a high-necked black evening gown with a jeweled necklace appeared at our side. I knew her; she was the wife of the Bearish ambassador to Borschland, and a very important bearess indeed. Her name was Adelaide

Candlebear.

"Good evening, *mamzeell*," she said in perfect Borschic. Then in English, "Good evening, young sir."

We both said good evening.

"I see that you have stopped dancing. This will not do, will it? I am the mistress of ceremonies at this Ball. I must ask you to continue dancing, or to leave the floor."

"He is… unfamiliar," I said.

"Oh, is he?" she smiled, baring her teeth so that I almost started. "Young sir, we have a beginner's room for you to practice in."

She bowed, and motioned for him to follow her with a fan that was in her other hand.

"I will come as well," I said. "I have need of-- "

"*Mamzeell*, I should remind you of your dance card," said Mrs. Candlebear. "If you should wish to give this young sir another dance, it should be politely after the other gentlemen have had their turn. You are in demand, I think."

That was true. I had over twenty names on my card.

"*Tah-loo*, *mamzeell*," said Mrs. Candlebear. "Young sir, please take my arm." And she proffered to Sherm a great bearish arm swathed in black silk.

I do not know how the bears came to be such a prominent presence at the Premujr Ball, but they take it very seriously indeed, and Mrs. Candlebear was a grand, a very grand bear.

So I went along, puzzled and intrigued to the extreme, until about an hour later, Sherm returned, and with a flourish that I could see had been taught him, asked me to dance again.

This time, again a waltz, he confidently took my arm and danced me about the floor so that I could barely keep up.

"You are a fast learner," I said as we twirled about.

"I will learn Borschic," he said to me in my own language, measuring every syllable. "Because I want speak to you."

"You are very welcome," I gasped, nearly out of breath.

We did not speak about the card or about anything else for that matter, as we danced the next four dances together, and then repaired to a buffet table for refreshments, and a pocketful of photographers surrounded us and took enough flash pictures that the entire room began to stink with the chemicals and I forgot indeed my appetite.

Then we spoke a long time together and he was a perfect gentleman and tried to learn as much Borschic as he could from me. We drank quite a bit of Vinasola, and danced again, and then I regretfully told him that I must not see him anymore that evening.

"Who not?" he said, which made me laugh, and I tried to tell him in English the reason.

"Girl… boy… together… Dance." I twirled, and my skirts twirled with me, the Dome and the lights a creamy dazzle. "Everyone… think…" and I put my hand out to him, and slipped an imaginary ring on it.

"Oh," he said, and again, he said, "Wow," which must be a favorite thing for North Americans to say.

"Borschic people," he said. "So…"

"Traditional?" I said. "Well, it is what we have. It is who we are. There is not much to hold on to in this world, is there, my very kind young gentleman?"

He did not understand all this, but he understood the tone of my voice, and he bowed. I held out my hand, and he kissed it, which is not strictly necessary in Borschland; we are not that formal. But it is considered very romantic and a very good sign for a girl who is taking her leave of a man with whom she has enjoyed pleasant company. There are not very many Borschic young men who dare to kiss a young lady's hand, for fear of being misinterpreted. Alas, timid young Borschic men.

I gave Sherm a smile as sincere as Mrs. Candlebear's, but with fewer teeth showing, and I encouraged him to dance with the other young ladies who were standing about waiting, tapping their feet.

He turned away from me, and was surrounded. I wondered if I could compete with all the pulchritude that was on display for him. Some very prominent young heiresses and, so to speak, princesses wanted to dance with the hero of the ice. I had only a little something to offer, for the daughter of a deacon is not rich in money, only in the prayers of the saints. And so, as I myself turned to the young men who stood waiting for me, I asked that venerable, heaven-inhabiting assembly of brave women and men to pray for me and for Sherm and for the note which he had declined to show me.

CHAPTER 13 - SHERM

DO NOT TRUST RACHAEL MARTUJNS.

That was the part of the message I got from LBJ-- Linus Black, Junior, I figured-- that didn't add up.

WAIT FOR A FRIEND TO TAKE YOU AWAY FROM HER, AND FOLLOW THE FRIEND'S INSTRUCTIONS.

The "friend" was Mrs. Adelaide Candlebear, who told me she was the wife of the Bearland's Ambassador to Borschland. We went to the "beginner's" room for dance lessons, and I was paired up with a nice younger lady bear, who called herself Lavinia. There was a band of bears, and in between teaching me to dance-- other guys were in there, too-- she filled me in on the situation.

"The Bearish special police have you under surveillance," she said. "There... your hand on my paw, like this. They know that you traveled to Borschland with Junior. The ambassador and his wife are on our side, but the special police suspects them. They may pay you a visit."

"And why shouldn't I trust Rachael Martujns?"

"We suspect she is part of their spy ring," said Lavinia. "She is a known sympathizer of the Loflins."

"What does that mean?"

"It's a long story," said Lavinia. "That's good. Now you're

waltzing. We don't have time for the entire tale."

"What about that other message? That my life is in danger?"

Lavinia blinked, and made a little sound in her throat, like a bark. "Other message?"

"I got another message that my life was in danger. Was that not from Junior?"

"I know only of this one."

"Okay, what else do I need to know?"

"Once we get you sorted out dancing, you are to return to the Ball and enjoy yourself. Expect a visit from the Bearish special police. You may say whatever you like to them. It's all the same. They don't understand honey from sugar. You haven't seen Junior since you arrived in Borschland, have you?"

"Nope," I said. In fact, I had been kind of missing him. Having Busby as the only English-speaker the past two weeks had gotten a little boring. Now, having met Rachael again, and sober, I really wanted to learn Borschic.

"Right," she said. "You haven't seen him, you don't know where he is. If you wish, you can tell the truth about me. You can say that Mrs. Candlebear is a member of the opposition if you wish. They won't believe you."

"I don't just rat people out," I said. "If it isn't breaking the law."

"And you are under Borschic law here," Lavinia said. "Which means you have no obligation to say anything to bears."

I nodded.

"But here is the other thing. They may recruit you to spy for Bearland. The present government fancies itself an empire. They see a greater Bearland. They want to conquer the foxes once and for all, then move on to Anvoria. They want the Loflins to take over Borschland and be our allies. And so on, until they have beaten the entire continent."

"That seems kind of stupid. Bearland's not that big of a country, is it?"

"No, but we have better weapons," said Lavinia. "We have

jets." She said jets in a way that made them sound at the same time like she knew about them, weren't a big deal, and the best thing ever. "The British are there to make sure we don't go to war with other nations except the foxes. That was a condition of selling us the weapons. But this government thinks we can put off the British, especially if the Continent goes into another lengthy phase, and we can't contact the outside world."

"What are you talking about? I thought phases were temporary things, like weather."

"They can be. But they have lasted years."

"You mean..." I stopped waltzing. "I could be stuck here for years?"

"It's not a small thing to come to the Continent from the outside world. You have been very brave." She spun me a bit to get me started again. Lavinia was a big girl, probably 5'10" and 200, heavier than me. In a beautiful, white silk gown and three rows of pearls around her very thick neck.

"So the special police of Borschland need me to..."

"Spread propaganda about Bearland. And about Loflinland. Positive propaganda. So that eventually, we can bring in the Loflins as a pro-Bearland Borschic government. One that might willingly ally with us if we were at war somewhere else."

"Yeah, I'm not much for politics. Or war."

"Junior thought so," said Lavinia. "He told me that you have quite a generous heart for a human."

"How do you know him? Are you just, like, comrades or whatever?"

"He is my fiancée," she said, her eyes closed.

Lavinia taught me a few other dances, and then let me go back. As I left her, I said, "So I shouldn't trust Rachael Martujns. Can I pretend to trust her?"

"I would advise any good-hearted man against getting mixed up with any Borschic woman," said Lavinia. "Unless you like taking orders."

I cracked a smile. "What about lady bears? Should good-hearted gentlebears like Junior get mixed up with them?"

Lavinia growled, but it sounded like a happy growl.

"Gentlebears...." she said, and put a claw up to her chin. "...Have no choice."

I found Rachael again pretty soon, dancing with another guy, but when I came back, she came straight for me, and we practiced some of the things I'd learned. Four dances in a row, in fact.

She didn't look any different to me, any different, at least pre-note. She didn't ask me about the note. Just did a lot of happy staring and smiling, because we couldn't talk that much.

I didn't want to think, this is a spy. I didn't have any reason to suspect her. These bears could've been totally crazy as far as I knew. But it didn't matter, because the bears had planted a seed. Was Rachael being nice to me just to get on my good side? Just to get on the side of the Empire of the Bears, to help the Loflins?

Rachael's eyes had no answers. She was just a beautiful, young girl, someone who would've been completely out of my league in the States. Caroline what's-her-name had big shoulders and teeth, and blonde hair chopped diagonally, that she dyed with a green streak when she felt like it. She liked to watch "The Bachelorette" and "American Idol" and her highest ambition was to be a groupie for the local rock group at College o' the Lakes that got to play in St. Paul now and then.

Rachael was perfectly classy, and a lot smarter than me. I knew that once I understood Borschic, a lot of what she said would still go over my head. At the same time she wasn't snooty. She seemed really nice. And I think with that type of woman, I could be smart, too. I was a college guy, after all.

Too much thinking. *Don't trust her*, I thought, as we tried to talk together, and she showed me the names of things in Borschic. This is a champagne glass: *fluut*. Champagne is called *fritschelwijn*. We toasted, and she said *gesondhijt*, and I said, you mean, like, *achoo*? And she said, laughing, *nej*, *nej*, *tu-chuu*!

Then all at once, she cut me off. She told me that if we spent any more time together, we'd have to get engaged. Or at least the press would think we were. They took enough pictures of us.

After what Lavinia said, I knew it wouldn't be a good idea to press the issue. And I thought, if Rachael is trying to get on my good side, wouldn't she try to play up our relationship as much as possible? If she were a spy, wouldn't she want to seduce me or something? Isn't that what lady spies do? On the other hand, maybe she wasn't a spy at all, and didn't like me that much. But that smile, and the laughter. That's hard to fake.

I used my newfound dance abilities on all the other good-looking young ladies at the dance. And they gave me big compliments, especially the ones who had learned English in school. It was a great party. I was a celebrity and everyone liked me. I almost forgot that we had a game the next day.

I wasn't hung over, so I didn't suck against Meechen on Sunday afternoon for that reason. I sucked because I sucked. My legs felt like sludge, and I couldn't hold on to my stick. It didn't help that Meechen had the best defense I'd ever seen, and one of them gave me a pretty big hit that probably looked like I just got my skates crossed over. They were sneaky that way. They liked to trip and hook and mostly got away with it.

Still, we won 1-0 because our defense just decided not to crack, and Captain Norbert the car door goalie stood on his head, and Chrujstoff saved us by taking the puck through two of their guys, jumping over the top of both their sticks and putting the puck through the goal's 5 hole-- in hockey talk, that's between his skates.

We shipped out on Tuesday after practice for a road trip to Lojren, a city on the coast. I was tying my tie in the mirror in the locker room, like a bow tie but bigger and droopier.

Busby appeared in the mirror with an envelope in one hand, and a newspaper tucked under his arm.

"Your travel money," he said.

The red and black bills were piling up. I hardly had to buy a meal wherever I went, and my regular salary was paying for the B&B and the clothes. I tipped people so well at first management gave me a cheat sheet on amounts.

"I can't have a lot of games like the Meechen one," I said to Busby's reflection as I pulled the tie tight. He'd shown me how, and I was getting better. Sometimes the guys would stand next to me in the mirror, acting like it was tough to do. Funny guys. "They're going to demote me lines, and then kick me off the team."

"Then," said Busby, "play better."

I took a comb to my wet hair, one sweep, left it at that.

Busby said, "Meechen is beastly. We got lucky."

"So what's more average? The 12-year olds from Wrischer, or those Meechen goons?"

"Only a couple or three teams can skate with us in this league," said Busby. "Watch out for Matexipar. We've got them soon. You think those defenders were tough? Wait till you try to push it past these guys. They will level you, rules or not."

He showed me the newspaper. There we were at the top of the standings, with Matexipar tied with us, and having given up only 1 goal in 3 games.

We walked upstairs to the offices and towards the tram that would take us to the station. Big crowds were still sending us off. "Do you think I'm a good player?" I asked him. "Come on. You know hockey."

"You were the one who was locked out of the NHL. You tell me."

"I may have padded the old resume a tad on that."

"So, what, you played minor league or juniors or something? Were you drafted?"

"I played college."

"That's good enough."

"You don't think they're letting up on me? Like, they want me to succeed or something?"

"Of course they want you to succeed. Don't you see? You're the golden boy, the first."

"What?"

"You're the first North American hockey player to play in this league."

"I thought..."

"You thought."

"I thought at least you..."

"You thought wrong."

Busby opened his traveling satchel, threw the newspaper in, snapped the satchel closed. We headed out to the tram.

.

CHAPTER 14 - KADMUS

Our Sherm had a difficult time versus Meechen. It was like the Borschic regulars attempting to smoke out the Loflins from their swamp hideaways in the early days of our nation. Sherm was used to playing beautiful hockey, the way he'd learned from our coaches during training. He wasn't used to the guerilla tactics of the Meechenders-- the jostling, the hooking, the tripping. Things that the referees are trained to see, but too often don't.

I attributed none of Sherm's difficulties to the events of the Premujr Ball. By all accounts he had a right to be tired the day after. After spending time in the practice room with the dance-mad Upright Bears who have organized this ball for the last 7 years, he danced with a passel of the most betrothable young Borschic maidens, including, our photographers made no mistake in reporting, the poetess Rachael Martujns.

But he drank very little, and the dancing was much less strenuous than a typical ice hockey game.

And he was home, so our sources report, by an hour after midnight.

It did not surprise me, then, that Sherm was back to his old self versus Lojren, also known as Te Lughoos ("The Lighthouse"). Lojren is not the most ept of teams. Their young men tend to grow up tall and slender, and have made the understandable mistake, borne out of love for one's own offspring, the mistake of thinking that size is the great panacea in hockey, forgetting that a lower center of gravity makes for a better skater.

Sherm scored two goals and assisted on two others, and the final score, 6 to 1, was perfectly fair to what happened on the ice.

We all looked forward to the first great test of the season-- Matexipar, the following week, in Matexipar, after an easy game at Te Rijngk versus Sichebach, the worst team in the league.

Matexipar is tucked into a rise-- a line of short hills-- in the north-central area of Borschland. A small river flows in the valley next to the hills, southeastward to the great Borschland River, and a canal has been cut to the north that ends at the marine city of Bevinlunz, and past the smaller cities of Wrischer and Gottwrischer. On the other side of the rise, the great Borschic swamp extends, and the borders of the Loflin homeland.

Matexipar is the central hearth of the Borschic steel industry. It is a city of smelters, big smokestacks, and hulking men carrying lunch pails. And it is a city that takes it hockey seriously.

On the valley side of Matexipar, on the other side of the river, Matexipar's managers and magnates live. This is a kind land, of blossoms in the spring, and rows of apple trees up and down wide boulevards. The smoke from the factories does not settle here, at least not when the wind is blowing.

On the hillside, the houses are built ramshackle up steep inclines. Steel factories sit on the flat ground available or are tucked into gullies. The city's colors are the orange and red of molten metal, and the gray-black of the smoke and ash that billow night and day from the brick stacks whose tops are only a little lower than the highest hill, the no longer aptly named Grijngkoop, Green Hill.

Matexipar's history influences its hockey team. Of old, it

was the headquarters of the military effort to drive the Loflinders from greater Borschland. The Loflins were there when the Dutch captain Abel Janszoon Tasman landed in 1642, and at first they welcomed us because their lore remembered and held in religious respect the arrival of new peoples. At that time Borschland was quite swampy everywhere, and our founders set about draining those swamps and putting rivers in their proper courses. As such we prospered, and the coastal cities of Sajbell, Lojren, and Bevinlunz waxed.

At a certain point the Loflins became jealous and began attacking our cities to carry off what they could. It became clear, as our population increased and we used more of the land, that we had to do something once and for all about our unruly neighbors.

Matexipar is a Loflin name, and it was a Loflin holy place before settlers came. It means Valley of Peace, and it was the place where the good Loflins would hold their councils and argue against attacking Borschland. These Loflins even invited Borschic people to stay here and live in harmony. But there was a massacre in the year 131, of Borschic peace settlers, and from then on the army set up in Matexipar to attack the Loflins who lived in the swamps beyond the hills.

It took many decades, but finally, with the treaty of Bijfhaaf in 205, the Loflins accepted to restrict their borders to their own nation on the coast, and to leave the swamps of the Borschland River by themselves, until such time as the Borschic people wished, as well, to drain those.

There are still people of mixed Loflin and Borschic ancestry in Matexipar, as well as a small, pure Loflin community. But the great majority of Matexiparitans are descendants of the soldiers who fought the Loflins. They are the fiercest people in Borschland, the most isolated, and the most nationalistic.

This people regard the hockey team as the representation of the spirit of their city. They must always fight to the death, never give up, hold on like a wolf to its prey. That is why the team is sometimes called the *Marajsvolfen*, or Swamp Wolves, although most in the city prefer the name Iron Sticks.

This history has also given rise to a political movement that is small in Borschland elsewhere, but nearly ascendant in Matexipar: the United Borschland Movement. It started in the labor organizing times, and it is now the main power behind the local Labor Party.

The UBM wants to keep Borschland isolated. They see nothing but trouble if we open the Continent more to the outside. And they cannot stand foreigners from other continental countries. They cannot abide the Upright Bears. The most extreme are for the eradication of the Bearish nation. It is one of the reasons why the Bears armed themselves and were under the protection of the British for a time about a hundred years ago.

We came into Matexipar on a Tuesday evening, and were met by a crowd of fans, most of them chanting and singing for their team, and waving banners. We deliberately stopped in a suburban station rather than downtown, and took a chartered tram to our hotel on the west side of the river, so that we wouldn't have to go into the roughest neighborhoods of the city that surrounded the rink, a river-fed man-made pond.

But show up the fans did, and were restrained by the finest of the Matexipar police, who are good at crowd restraint. Unfortunately, they were not able to restrain a small group of UBMers from hurling insults at Sherm and advising him to leave the city.

It was an unfortunate incident, not reflective of the vast majority of inhabitants of Matexipar who are good-hearted and law-abiding.

If any of that rattled our Sherm, he showed nothing to the press who met him at the hotel, nor did he say anything to me when I questioned him about it before the game the next day. Through his interpreter, Mr. Busby, his exact words were, "I have seen much worse in North America."

The game, then, became the thing.

It was a cold night, starry, if the smoke of the city had allowed us to see it, and the great grandstands of the

Ovaalrijngk rose up gray-black. The electric lights made the ice brilliant white, and the black and white of Te Staff's uniforms contrasted with the blood red of the Iron Sticks. The colors mirrored the colors of our flag.

At the beginning it did not go well. Matexipar seemed to have an extra fillip of energy, and they skated faster than we. That is a disaster because they are more muscular and most of the time we must be like hummingbirds to their eagles. It was no surprise that they scored first; it was almost a birthright, it seemed to them. If we were to win, we must give up that first goal and work twice as hard to get two of our own.

Our Sherm had the admirable but misguided idea sometimes that the centerman had to go back into the defensive zone and help the defensemen. This is quite dishonorable to the name "defenseman," but it also leads to confusion. Sherm saw that were having trouble with their forwards and he must have taken it personally to have our goaltender, our Norbert, peppered like a Zimrothian peasant fowl.

So Sherm ventured back to harass their forwards, who naturally took it ill. One of them, Hiltuj Goosenzujns, led Sherm a merry chase and skated him right into one of our defenders, blindside. Both Sherm and the defender went spinning away, and Goosenzujns proceeded to skate up to Norbert's doorstep. Our remaining defender, Chrujstoff Wills, made a valiant attempt to dispossess Goosenzujns of the puck, but he was not to be dissuaded from sending it cross mouth to the center, Jesper Joordan, who neatly tapped in under Norbert's left pad.

You should have heard the crowd, as if it were Borschland Day and the fireworks were booming.

As Sherm took his seat on the bench to wait for his next shift, *Meester* Chrojstenkaamps was seen to lean in to Sherm's ear and speak more than a dozen words. It was the most anyone had seen him say in years.

Sherm learned his lesson. He spent the next several shifts watching as Matexipar continued to work our defense hard and allow very little activity in their own end. But they could not break through the curtain wall of our goaltender, and our wings pinched back in to help the defenders more than they are accustomed.

In the second period, we found our legs and pressed them mercilessly, and finally, after fifteen minutes of siege warfare on their goalmouth, Hauke Sybranduj, our third-line center, came through with a shot from the point that lodged in the upper right corner of the net.

The third period thus became all that mattered, but the players had used their energies and were spent, and the game ended at one to one. So there was no resolution to the question of who was the better side on this night, though it might be said that Te Staff's earning of one point in a very hostile environment was a victory of its own.

There were those of us with the impression that Sherm should have played better, that he should have scored, or somehow shown the superiority of Te Staff through some superhuman effort. But for the first time in Matexipar he did well.

I, at least, had no doubts.

CHAPTER 15 - SHERM

The less said about the first Matexipar game, the better.

It was a rough time. I'd gotten a note saying, "Don't trust Rachael Martujns," but unfortunately I was beginning to fall really hard for her. She was in my brain like a movie, playing over and over.

I'd also gotten a note that said, "Your life is in danger. A friend is at hand." The wax seal implied it was from Junior. I'd talked with his fiancée, Lavinia. But he hadn't yet made contact with me.

So I had all those things to think about, besides having to go into a hostile environment in Matexipar with people yelling things at me that I didn't understand and Busby wouldn't translate.

We got lucky in the game, to tell the truth. I made a bonehead play trying to be a hero and back check when I wasn't supposed to. Norbert the goalie stood on his head that first period and kept it 1-0. Then Oovie made an unbelievable pass to Hauke Sybranduj when it was their goalie's turn to stop everything coming at him, and in the third, to tell you the truth, no one had anything left. It was like a boxing match where you're just grabbing and holding for the last 5 rounds. But it wasn't exactly that no one had any legs left. We just used all our adrenaline. It was like I hadn't eaten in ten years. I was kind of hallucinating at the end. They gave us hot tea and brandy to sip while we were waiting for our shifts. There's nothing like caffeine and alcohol to destroy whatever will to skate you have left.

But it was also the first game where I focused for more than a couple of minutes at a time. I had begun to understand a little more of the language. I was reading, Busby was teaching me, and so were the guys. I understood here, there, left and right, up and down, forward, back, over, under, shoot, pass, I'm open, other technical stuff. I got telegrams every day and used a dictionary to read them; that is, when Busby didn't persuade me to give them to him. Most were from fans. Occasionally one of the governing board of Te Staff would tell me I was doing a good job. I always got one or two from the United Borschland Movement encouraging me to leave the country.

Oos Borschland Te Ooslaandern. Foreigners out of Borschland. That was their motto. They always signed it that way. Sometimes they would try to reason with me. I got one that said, in English, *You don't like it here, don't you?* They did better when they stuck to non-*ooslaander* talk.

And I always looked for one from Rachael. It only occurred to me after that tough game against Mat X, while I was pouring sweat, answering questions from the press, with a fistful of telegrams in one hand, that I could send something to her.

What to write? I obviously couldn't bring Busby along to translate. That would be way too awkward. But I didn't know nearly enough Borschic to send a telegram or a letter in that language. I could do it in English, but who knows if she would understand it?

We slept in our hotel that night after the game and I spent the night composing telegrams that I never sent.

You are incredibly beautiful + can I see you please + thanks + telegrams are a lot like texting + except it isn't instantaneous + Regards + Sherm

We took the train home early the next morning, where Busby had set up a number of real estate agents ready to move me into an apartment and out of the B&B where I'd been staying.

"You need to go someplace a little less central," said Busby. "It's crazy around here."

I agreed. Though it was convenient to be able to walk to practice, I was always surrounded by fans wanting autographs and singing at all hours of the night.

We took a horse cab across the bridge to a suburb called Rirlver. The streets were wider and lined with big, leafless trees. Main avenues had center dividers with patches of grass-- now covered in snow-- and hockey ponds for little kids. A tramline came out here that stopped on Waatersdram. From some streets you could see the river, and all of the apartments I looked at had were on the top floor and had a view of the river.

We stood in front of big windows that opened to let in fresh air in the summer, and I looked down at the two or three photographers that were always where I was, smoking pipes, hoping to get a picture of me for the next print edition of the Borschland Internet.

"Can I afford this one?" I asked Busby.

"Of course," he said. "Your lodging is paid for by the team. You can choose what you want."

I looked back at the place, with its big, furnished sitting room. It continued to a dining area with a table and six chairs, and a big mirror on the wall behind. A bedroom and bathroom came next, behind French doors with paneled windows.

The real estate agent, a put-together, fiftyish, five-foot tall woman with a big, foofy hat and necktie with a diamond pin, fired away in Borschic, and Busby said, "You have maid service, and you can eat in the restaurant on the ground floor, or have your meals brought up. That's also included in the price. They don't turn the elevator off. You never have to walk up."

"*Vij Fijl?*" I said to the agent. She had gray eyes and a lot of makeup.

Busby cut in. "Price isn't important. This is pretty standard for single guys on the team, eh."

My bank account said I had 11,000 Borschic shillings. Every Friday I took my unused per diem and deposited it, and the teller, a thin man with a thin mustache, updated my bankbook in fountain pen. I had no idea whether I could ever exchange that money for actual dollars. Or how much a shilling was to a dollar. It cost 4 shillings, 20 centimes for a huge steak, fried leeks, and a pitcher of beer. If you gave them a 5 and said keep the change they acted like you were some high roller.

"How long by tram to the rink?"

"Twenty minutes. But you'll take a cab. The maitre d' at the restaurant can hail you one."

"I can hail my own cab."

Busby pivoted to the real estate agent, who smiled from under her foofy hat, then back to me.

"*Ten Suj lijk*?" said the agent-- do you like it?

"*Ja, maam*," I said. "Let's take it."

"Right."

Later, we were in a bar that was a player favorite. We were drinking brandies with beers back, and Busby said, "Just between you and me, sport. If you were trying to figure out if that flat was good enough to host Rachael Martujns, it doesn't work that way."

"What are you talking about?"

"You can't take women up to your place. There's a way to get a woman if you want one. But there's no dating, okay?"

"Don't you think I know that?" I raised my voice, louder than I'd wanted to. Busby liked to think he was a mind reader. Sometimes he was, which just made him that much more confident.

"Okay. It's just, you haven't discussed the need yet."

"The need?"

"For a woman."

"Yeah, well, that's for me to figure out."

"I was just thinking, if you're sweet on Rachael, maybe you think you need to be faithful to her or something." He tipped his brandy glass to his lips, though there was nothing in it. He had been drinking, which was not his habit. Normally, he was a pretty button-down type of guy.

"Get off it, okay?"

"I'm just saying."

"What is your problem? Just shut up, Buzz. Shut up and get out of my face."

"Zimrothian courtesans are pretty good. You should check them out. Don't--"

I punched him, low on his jaw. He fell off his bar stool and skidded along the floor on his butt. I felt my hand. It stung. But the follow-through felt good.

Everyone in the bar stopped talking and turned. A flash bulb went off.

"Sorry," I said to the room, suddenly as clear-headed as I'd ever been.

Busby sat up and rubbed his jaw. Two players helped him to his feet.

Oovie came over and put his arm over my shoulder while another guy helped Busby to his feet. He said something like, "Busby, you do a great imitation of a hockey puck." It was the first time I completely understood a joke in the language.

The guys laughed. Another flash bulb went off. Someone said, "Forget the camera."

Busby came over to me, and we shook hands. "We have to be shown making up," he said. "For the papers. It's going to be in there tomorrow afternoon."

"Just shut up about Rachael, okay, man?"

"Okay. Ow." He rubbed his face. "I was out of line."

The papers made some hay out of the fight, we tamped it down, and we kicked tail on Sunday afternoon. It was a team called Domaatische, and they tried, but they couldn't keep up. We won 3-0 and I scored all three goals, and on the third goal all these roses, white roses, started raining down on the ice. Women were throwing them, young, old, in-between. Dressed in furs and wearing fancy hats. Ten-year old girls skated out and picked them all up, and PR guys made them into a bouquet for me, and they took a thousand pictures. The guys said now it was my turn to choose a woman to kiss if I wanted, someone who'd thrown me a rose.

The women all stood up next to the boards and waited, and I skated around and waved. But I didn't see Rachael.

"He's a river eel," said Norbert the goalie. "No fisher catches him with this simple bait."

When we got into the locker room after the game there was no telegram from Rachael congratulating me on my trinity. After I looked through them all in the locker room, I turned to Busby and said, "All right. You win. Is there another ball coming up?"

"You want to see Rachael again?" He handed me a newspaper. "Look at this, champ."

It was a newspaper article with three photos, one each of a man, woman, and Rachael Martujns.

Archdeacon Conraad Martujns is scheduled to travel with his family to the Twin Kingdoms for a ski vacation to start off the Epiphany to Kandelmaas holidays, Busby translated. The vacation will last three weeks and the family will be home in time for the Kandelmaas celebration.

"This is Rachael's dad?"

"He's a big guy in the Borschic religion," said Busby. "They're not rich, but they do fine. And he's part of society. He's like, in the top two hundred and fifty people in the city."

"Let's go get something to eat," I said.

We took a cab to a nice place in my neighborhood, a quiet place that didn't allow paparazzi inside. No one bothered us there, and we could have a couple of lobsters and a glass of wine and catch our breath. It was the kind of place that makes up for the lack of pizza and pitchers in Borschland.

"So you like Rachael," said Busby.

"Yeah," I said.

"Enough to marry?"

"How should I know? I've seen her, like, twice."

"There isn't an option here. You don't just have a relationship with a single woman like that. Especially not a classy one like Rachael. There isn't a test drive. You either have to declare your intentions or stay away."

"Declare my intentions."

"It's called courting. In Borschic, *gaaglfujt.* A mating dance. You need to meet the parents, show your bona fides, whatnot."

"Would I stand a chance? I mean, it's not like I'm some kind of prince."

"A hockey player, a star hockey player, can do it. But you have to build up your reputation, and you have to build up your bank account."

"By how much?"

"You'd need five hundred thousand in the bank," Busby said. "Conservatively."

"My contract said I'd make thirty K in dollars this year. How much is that in shillings?"

"That isn't..." Busby considered explaining, reconsidered. "Listen, if you play well, negotiate carefully, invest wisely, you could approach that figure for a ten-year career."

"Wow," I said. "Ten years."

"That's the thing, too," Busby said. He cracked a claw with a metal cracker, pinched out a shiny piece of meat, and dipped it in butter. "You can't even think" – he pointed with his finger, and the butter made a line on the tablecloth-- "about going to America with her. You would stay here. As long as you were married to her. For the rest of your life, eh? Or whichever."

I looked down at my lobster, which I had pretty much smashed to bits with my hammer. A piece of bread, oval, like a skating rink, leaned against my sauce bowl. I picked up my glass of Borschic white wine. Really good with the lobster. There was a little crumb of bread between my plate and my desert spoon, brown against the white of the tablecloth. I picked it up on my fingernail, flicked it away.

Our waiter, mustache, thin tie, big stomach, appeared. "Will you take your coffee and dessert now?"

Busby said, "Coffee." Then in English, "And some cold water for you?"

"Coffee," I said to the waiter. "*Tangs Suj.*"

"Your accent is improving."

"I need to talk to my sister," I said. "Is there a phone on this continent?"

"Not one that makes calls to the States. You'd be better off with a telegram. Letters can take a long time."

I nodded. "Is there an office open right now?"

"Sure. Let's go find one."

"No," I said, and got out my billfold. "I'm going to do this on my own."

"Okay."

"Buzz," I said, "not to pry or anything, but are you ever going to get married yourself? You seem to like it here."

"I like to keep my options open," he said.

"Zimrothian courtesans?" I asked.

"Yeah," said Busby. "Whenever I get my pennies all saved up."

CHAPTER 16 - SHERM

At 10 PM in Staff Borsch, the city pretty much rolls up the sidewalk. Downtown there's a neighborhood called Krejsberg, there's nightlife, bars, music (not pop-- more like accordion and fiddle), and if you go over to the university in Tujrspaark, students are up late, but everywhere else people go to bed so they can get up and go to work the next day. Plus, in winter, you don't really want to be out at night. It's too cold.

Tonight, even the paparazzi had packed it in.

Busby and I walked a couple of blocks, and he caught a tram back to his place, and I buttoned my topcoat, pulled my hat down low, and kept walking. Telegraph offices are pretty frequent in Borschland, but many only do local cables. A few do continental, but only a few, I figured out, do international.

"*Telegram oosde ter Nordamerika*?" I'd ask when I came to an office.

"Zentraalstaff," the clerks would always say, and point towards the middle of the city. Then they'd say, "Reinhardt?"

And I'd smile and wave goodbye.

"*Tah-loo*," they'd say. "*Fvorwart Te Staff*." Goodbye. Cheers. Go team.

After about an hour of walking and asking, I was in Natatck, the town next to Rirlver, and I caught a tram to the subway, which took me into the center of the city.

The subway cars were almost empty, so when I got out at the central station, Ovaalzentrum, it wasn't difficult to notice the two bears getting off three compartments over from me. They were wearing fedoras and black trench coats, and they followed me out of the station.

"Really, guys?" I thought. "Hats and trench coats?" Like the fur wasn't a giveaway already.

We took the escalator, and at the top I asked a ticket taker where to find a telegraph office. It felt good to hear *reecht*, *linx*, and know that meant the same thing, right and left, that my teammates would say when we were on the ice.

Finally I found it, a big, brightly lit building across the street from a plaza with fountains and statues. The ceilings were twenty feet tall, the windows arched, the floors marble. And even at this late hour, there were still a fair number of people lined up to send telegrams, and half a dozen clerks, though there were windows for a bunch more.

"*Telegraam oosde ter Nordamerika*?" I asked the man.

He barely flinched. "*Eenglisch*?"

"*Ja, tangs*."

He tore off a piece of paper from a pad, pushed it towards me, and pointed to a cup of pencils.

I'd spent a lot of time thinking about what I was going to say. I'd practically written a book in my head by the time I came to the office. But faced with the paper and the pencil, I went blank.

Finally, I wrote this:

Dear Cathy + No problems here in Borschland + Having fun + Getting lots of PT + We're winning +Met a nice girl + I think I may stay a while +Sorry I didn't write sooner + Love + Sherm

The man calculated the cost, over 20 shillings, which is a lot of money to spend on one thing in Borschland. He asked me something I didn't understand. When I didn't answer, he said, "insurance?" and he pushed a card over to me, and explained as best he could. It would cost 50 more shillings to make sure the message got to America, got an acknowledgment from

Cathy, and a complimentary return message.

"*Jas, ergut,*" I said. What was Borschic play money to me? I might as well go deluxe. And I did want to hear she was okay. I wrote down my name, return address for Cathy's reply.

The clerk said, "Reinhardt, *ja,*" and smiled at me. "Good hockey man."

I had been in Borschland a month. I didn't know whether I wanted to stay my entire life. Scoring goals was fun, being a celebrity was fun-- some of the time, anyway. Having money was fun, though I didn't have anything to spend it on. How did people spend before home theater systems and Porsches were available?

I didn't know whether I wanted to marry Rachael Martujns, or any other Borschic woman. But I knew I wanted to get to know Rachael better. I knew it would take time to figure out what I really wanted.

But Cathy was my family.

As I came out of the telegraph office, the wind hit me, and I figured I should take a cab if I could find one. It was going on midnight.

A car-- a real car, a black sedan-- turned on its lights and cruised up to the curb. The door opened, and a growly voice said, "Get in, Reinhardt."

I figured they'd probably maul me if I didn't get in, so I did. It was warm in the back seat and smelled like new car and bear breath-- fruit, meat, and coffee.

"Drive, Bearstens," said a trench-coat wearing bear in the back seat next to me.

"Give you a lift home, Reinhardt?" said a trench-coat wearing bear in the front seat.

"Thanks, guys," I said. "It might be murder finding a cab home at this hour."

"Oh, you can find one," said the one in the back. "But a car is faster."

He said "car" the same way Lavinia had said "jet."

The driver, Bearstens, took it easy. There weren't any traffic lights in Borschland.

I said, "So whose side are you guys on?"

"My name is Honeyhide, this is Grizzlyfaith. We represent the legitimate government of Bearland."

"There's another kind?"

"You know this bear?" Honeyhide clicked on the dome lights and showed me a photo of Junior.

"Maybe," I said. "You guys tend to look alike to a newbie like me."

"Don't let him fool you," said Grizzlyfaith. "He is a known subversive. He's dangerous. He is after the violent overthrow of the Bearish government. And he is here in this country fomenting war against us."

Honeyhide said, "Has Mr. Black asked you to do anything for him? Carry packages or messages?"

"I haven't talked to a bear since I got here," I said, remembering too late about Lavinia and Mrs. Candlebear.

"You mean, not apart from the Premujr Ball?"

These guys didn't miss a beat. "Sorry, I did see some women bears there."

"She-bears," said Grizzlyfaith.

"Yeah. They taught me to dance. Say, can I ask you something?"

"Evidently. If you have a mouth and a brain."

Big, clawed, and witty: what a combination. "Listen, do you guys have Rachael Martujns on the payroll?"

"What?"

"Rachael Martujns. Is she spying for you?"

The two bears gave me the eye, then turned to each other, then back to me.

"What do you mean, Rachael Martujns?"

"The poetess. Daughter of the high mucky-muck of the Borschic church."

Honeyhide gave me a blank stare.

"Well," said Grizzlyfaith, "even if she were, we wouldn't be at liberty to tell you that."

"So she isn't, then?"

Honeyhide growled at Grizzlyfaith. "Any other questions?"

"No, it's more of a statement. I guess you know where I live, then, if you're giving me a lift home."

"We do," said Honeyhide. "But that's not a matter of intelligence. We read the papers, too."

They stopped in front of my apartment house.

"Don't trust Junior Black," said Honeyhide. "Or anyone that associates with him."

"Thanks for the tip," I said, and got out of the car.

We went on the road for two games, one against a team called Rjaward, and the other Bjaward. They were twin cities in the south, cattle towns, and you could see the mountains from your hotel window. They had good teams, and we beat Bjaward, 4-3, and beat Rjaward, 2-1. So after 10 games our record was 9 wins and 1 tie. Matexipar was second with 8 wins and 2 ties.

A telegram from Cathy came while we were in Rjaward.

"Shermy, a girl? Really? Bring her back here," she wrote. "Miss you."

I hadn't expected anything different. Just wanted to hear it out of her mouth.

The winter solstice came and went, but not much mention of Christmas. The big holiday season in Borschland was Epiphany to Kandelmaas, the equivalent of January 6 to February 2. Borschlanders weren't big on the baby Jesus, but they loved to celebrate light. Busby told me that Mr. Martujns, Archdeacon Martujns, would be back to conduct services.

"Could I see Rachael in church?" I asked.

"You don't want to give her that impression," said Busby. "Church-going isn't a plus here for romance. It means you're a little bit nuts."

"So, when?"

"You might run into her at a festival. Holding a candle. That happens quite a bit."

On the night of that dinner, we were five games from mid-season. We played each team in the league twice, home and away, for a total of thirty games. We beat Bevinlunz, Sajbell, and Onatten in the next two weeks, then Atterische tied us on a fluky late goal, and we killed Meenesanne, the worst team in the league. We ended the first half with 13 wins and 2 ties. Mat X lost to Bjaward and were second, 12 wins, 1 loss, 2 ties. We scored 65 goals and gave up 16; I scored 22 of those.

All this meant our road to the championship was laid out for us: outside of Mat X and Bjaward, no one had a legitimate chance to beat us, and both those teams had to come see us in the second half.

I had to speculate why Junior and his political party had told me not to trust Rachael when it was clear the bear secret agents had no idea.

I actually went to jewelry stores and looked at rings. Borschland was famous for its jewelry, imported from the mines of the Outer Territories, over the mountains and to the west of Borschland. That got written up in the newspapers. I told them I was looking for a birthday gift for my sister back in the States. They were impressed I would look for an authentic Borschic gift. Although they weren't at all surprised I liked the diamond and gemstone rings. All without talking to Rachael for three whole weeks. It was maddening.

And then Rachael came home from her vacation.

CHAPTER 17 - KADMUS

We have now come to the part of the story that gave us in Borschland the greatest anxiety and confusion.

The first half of the ice hockey campaign of the year 329 had been nothing short of celestial. The star of Sherm Reinhardt was ascending, along with the fortunes of Te Staff. Only in 6 campaigns previously in 75 years of modern Borschland Hockey League play had Te Staff finished the first half of the season undefeated. The year before, slowed by injuries and bad luck, nearly the same group of players had managed only 6 wins, 4 losses, and 5 draws. With our Sherm, however, we could not be bested.

Sherm himself was easily the best player in the league, scoring 22 goals and assisting on 12 others. Almost half the time he participated in a scoring play for Te Staff, and the number of goals scored by the team went up dramatically.

Sherm could hardly go anywhere without being followed by photographers, although after ten o'clock in the evening, if he was home, they might take the rest of the night off. Some waited on some nights perhaps to catch Sherm going to some forbidden part of the city, but they waited in vain. Our Sherm turned out to be a person who valued his solitude, living on the top floor of a newer building in Rirlver.

Some in the press circulated rumors that Sherm was spending his time learning Borschic, for every day he would say a bit more in our language, and rely a bit less on his translator, Mr. Kevin Busby. By the midseason festival of lights, on Kandelmaas Eve, Sherm was able to say to the press, "*Tangs Suj, alle, fvoor ter groos n ergutwill in Borschland fvoor mujn.*" Or, as it came out in the papers, "I'm extremely grateful to the Borschic people for your gracious support for me."

Nothing in Sherm's behavior prepared us for what was to come on Kandelmaas Eve, in the year 329.

The Kandelmaas Eve festival is perhaps the most beloved of all in Borschland. It is the most attended religious ceremony in the nation, for as a nation we generally do not find ourselves in church, leaving the duty of prayers to those most capable of doing it, our deacons and deaconesses. Kandelmaas Eve is held outside, in squares and parks. In the center of Staff Borsch, thousands gather, while in the neighborhoods, groups as small as a few dozen might make a tight circle around a local deacon or subdeacon. All carry special candles in metal, glass, or porcelain holders that are among the most prized possessions of a family. The holders often have a guard about them to shield the flame of the candle from wind and snow, and some are as closed as lanterns, to be used on the windiest nights.

In the center of the open area, men of the community build a fire and a small wooden platform called a *sternaltaar*. At the proper time, usually an hour after sunset, but up until midnight, a deacon takes a very tall candle made of pure beeswax and climbs the *sternaltaar*, invoking the prayers of the saints and angels, to "catch" the fire of the stars. It is said that in the early days of Borschland, the candle of the sainted deacon Noos flared with fire on its own when raised to the sky, on a moonless night when the stars were blazing their brightest. Ever afterwards the people of Borschland hope for a clear and moonless night for Kandelmaas Eve.

A small child is then chosen to take a burning brand from the fire and light the great candle. When all have seen the great candle raised and lit, the deacon lights the candle of the oldest woman present, or to a selected, respected elderly woman, who then turns to her neighbor and lights his or her candle.

Neighbor lights neighbor's candle, until all present have a lit candle.

A procession forms that is led by the deacon or his acolyte carrying the great candle about the square, park or neighborhood, and followers sing traditional songs for prosperity, health, and peace. Thanks are given for light, both literal and that which lights and warms our hearts.

At the end of the ceremony, the people repair to halls and houses for refreshments and celebrations, as often in a Borschic winter a walk at night will be among the chilliest things one does in a year. Brandy is served; there is music and dancing. The grandest families give midnight dinner parties aflame with candles. Children are given presents ranging from sweets to bicycles, and are allowed to stay up until they fall asleep.

This is often a night when men propose marriage to their favorites, or when women pronounce their favor upon men who are hesitating in asking. In such a case it is often seen that there are children born some ten months after Kandelmaas, as this is an exuberant time and a time of great optimism. And so Kandelmaas is also sometimes called *Brejdsnakt*, or Wedding Night, for Borschic gentlemen who find that they have fathered their first child on Kandelmaas almost invariably marry their love of that night. (Wags calls this night *Brejdnaakt*, which means "naked bride.")

Kandelmaas is a lucky time for betrothal, especially on nights that are moonless and clear, but children who are conceived on this night are said to be fiery and passionate, and it is often a child whose birthday falls 10 months after Kandelmaas who is chosen to light the tall candle.

On Kandelmaas Eve in the year 329 of our reckoning, Sherman Reinhardt and his teammates found themselves in the afternoon in St. Noos Oval, a plaza located two subway stops from Te Rijngk, and one subway stop from Krejsberg, the great quarter devoted to music, art, and nightlife. St. Noos Oval has a skating pond at its center that is refrigerated (when necessary) from the 1st of Detzember to the 31st of Fefvruar, and it is lit up every night with skaters from all over the city.

This afternoon, sunny and cloudless, many of the Te Staff team took to the ice, with an orchestra playing in the winter gazebo, and pair skated with the dozens of young women who had turned out. As many thousands of people as could stood ten and twenty deep watching the young men and women twirl about the pond, the girls with the broadest of smiles on their faces, the men as grave and as neutral-faced as possible, in order not to give the impression of having a favorite.

The young women all screamed, "I give you my favor" to whichever one or dozen of the players they loved best, taking care not to give favor to any of the married players, although these men had nearly as many willing partners on the ice as the unmarried.

Sherm participated in all this with good will. He took a large number of them skating about in a circle, then a quick return. He accommodated the many, but disappointed those interested in holding the great hockey man's mittened hand for a long time. Roses cascaded down on the pond, and girls gathered them to take to the sick in hospital.

It was said to be an excellent winter for rose importers.

Of course, there were many photographers there, and they did not mistake to record each and every one of the women whom Sherm chose, hoping to make hay of some particular choice.

But their fondest wishes were fulfilled when, at one point, Sherm stopped in front of a particularly thick group of women and flowers, and the crowd parted to allow Rachael Martujns to step on to the ice.

She had no skates, but was quickly leant a pair, and off they went, Rachael gentle and graceful and slight next to the tall, broad shouldered stranger and skater who was all our joy.

They were out on the ice for much longer than is decorous, and at one point Sherm was seen to catch Rachael in his arms and kiss her on the neck, but others claimed that Rachael only slipped and Sherm nimbly kept her on her feet, and as she held tight to him he leaned his head over towards hers.

When he deposited her on the side of the ice, she thanked the young lady who had leant her the skates, who then, as a reward, was the next to skate with Sherm. But if that lass or the others had thought that Sherm would stay at St. Noos Oval for the Kandelmaas ceremony-- and celebrate, as many of the younger players did, in Krejsberg that night-- they were disappointed.

Three skaters after Rachael, Sherm unlaced his skates and was lost in the crowd. Some claimed to have seen him coming out of a restaurant later that evening, others getting into a horse cab on the periphery of the Oval. Whatever happened, he was next seen in the great crowd in Cathedral Square in the center of the city, where he was a special guest of Archdeacon Conraad Martujns for the National Kandelmaas Lighting of Borschland, and was seated next to the Archdeacon's daughter, Rachael.

One might have thought the young man would accompany a lady so obviously his favorite to the official banquet attended by the Prime Minister, his cabinet, the greatest of the diaconate, and assorted dignitaries of all types, but the last anyone saw of Sherm that night was at the convivial and highly attended consular celebration of Bearland, where, it is said, Sherm danced with Upright Bears until the very wee hours, and received a ride home in one of the consular automobiles.

The next day, Rachael Martujns was reported missing.

The Martujns family are very prominent in Staff Borsch. The father, Archdeacon of St. Ellafuus Cathedral, is not the highest-ranking official of the Church of Borschland, but then there is not a single highest-ranked deacon, only a Council of Archdeacons and a rotating ministership. Let us say that Archdeacon Martujns is the sixth most senior member of that Council.

Rachael was known as a dutiful daughter, and the only child of Conraad and Lynneet Martujns. She was not given to disappearing and reappearing. Having finished her degree at the Women's University, she was living at home and making her way as a poetess, with no prominent suitors and no scandal about her.

The early morning papers made no mention of Rachael, because they were printed even before photographers returned to their pressrooms to inspect their cache of Sherm-Rachael skating films. The next editions, appearing mid-morning, showed prominently the Kandelmaas festivities, along with the best of the skating couple. Then an extra of Te *Staffische Tag* appeared about half past three, with the headline, "Archdeacon's Daughter Abducted."

Now, abduction is a strong way of putting it, but Te *Staffische Tag*, unlike its near-named competitor, *Te Taglik Staff*, is a paper known for its exaggerations if not outright fabrications.

Soon, other extra editions appeared, correcting the first story, which said that some had seen Rachael whisked away from the Kandelmaas ceremony in a horse cab, never to be seen again.

By the next morning, a truer story emerged, narrated by Rachael's mother, which said that Rachael had told Mrs. Martujns that she felt ill and to give her apologies to all at the official banquet. That explained the horse cab she was seen getting into that evening.

When Archdeacon and Mrs. Martujns returned from the banquet that night, somewhere about one in the morning, Rachael was nowhere to be found. Her passport and purse were gone. Some articles of clothing had been taken; her favorite scarf, a winter coat. But no jewelry was taken or books. Also, the pantry had been disturbed, and a chunk of pork roast taken from the larder. The only thing of value that was missing was two place settings of heirloom silver, a carving knife and fork, and a thermos.

The family asked for her at any number of friends' houses before alerting the police, who sent officers to the central train station with pictures asking about her. By this time it was about 8 AM.

No one had seen her, even when they roused the overnight ticket sellers who had gone off shift at 7 AM and would have seen her buying a ticket.

Telegraphs crackled messages to all the border crossings, to alert officials if anyone with the name Rachael Martujns attempted to leave the country. She, of course, being of age, was free to do as she wished-- if she was, indeed, free.

No one could fathom any reason for a kidnapping, for she had no enemies, and was a friend of the Loflinders, a small splinter group of whom had some time ago been financing their anti-government activities by kidnapping, though this was a decade past, now.

Neither parent had noticed much of a change in Rachael's behavior, for she had been much delighted in being able to persuade Sherm to attend the candle-lighting ceremony with her. After Sherm took his leave, however, she reported feeling ill. No one had heard anything between the two that would have raised suspicion.

Afternoon grew into evening, and there was no news of Rachael, and at the various chapels and cathedrals of the city, deacons and deaconesses began imploring the saints to pray for Rachael.

But morning next brought nothing, not a ransom note, nothing, and that evening was the first game of the second half of Te Staff's season. The team played miserably, losing to an undeserving Bevinlunz team by a score of 2-1.

But that was understandable. For at the beginning of the game, Te Staff's management announced the unthinkable-- Sherm was gone too.

CHAPTER 18 - RACHAEL

The holiday with my parents to the Twin Kingdoms has always been a great and cherished joy for me, but this year, for the first time in my life, it was not.

The Twin Kingdoms of Dann and Kaatsch are located south of Borschland and east of the Celtlands, and they are sparsely populated, mountainous, and very rustic. The central city of Dejndeech is charming, nestled in a valley where two stony rivers rush together. The people of the Twin Kingdoms believe they are descended from a lost tribe of Israel, and their coming to our Continent was very ancient. They are calm and quiet and devout, and have been through much. They are satisfied to live in their lands in peace.

From Dejndeech, one may travel to the east, north or south to stay in lodges and chalets where the countryside, blanketed in snow, is a paradise for skiers, skaters, and sledders.

I am partial to cross-country skiing, for in the long draughts of solitude taken while skiing it is so much easier to think, to work out the words of a poem, and to be inspired for new ones. It is a small thing in Dann and Kaatsch to be greeted by an Upright Bear in the morning (there are quite a few who holiday and live in the Twin Kingdoms), and then to see a beastly bear in the afternoon while skiing. It is good to have a guide with a rifle skiing behind one, for bears have been known to attack a skier in the Kingdom mountains, which is why Upright Bears have always worn clothes when holidaying there, even though their fur gives them warmth enough, and there are many who are sun-worshippers and worshippers of their beastly heritage.

The Martujns family has always retreated to the village of Ujbur for our winter holidays, a twinkling little town on the banks of the Skujbu River that tumbles down into the valley of Plesulder. A sledge pulled by a stout draft horse takes us up to our chalet, a lovely, cozy place with a staff of three-- a guide, hunter and woodchopper; a housekeeper; and a cook and nanny. When I was a child this woman would play with me the day long, and we would bake sweets for ourselves and for the children in town, who, when not in school or working with their families in their various endeavors, would frolic with me like cousins.

In those days, the three weeks of our holiday flew by, with skiing and sledding and skating-- the boys of the town were great hockey enthusiasts-- and roaring fires, roast meat, storytelling and puppetry, music and being carried to bed late at night after insisting I was not tired.

That changed gradually as I grew older. The children grew and became distant towards me, for they are simpler folk than we, and are not given to university study. The girls married in their teens and began their own families, and the boys, of course, must work, or go to military service, and attend to the matters of being a person of a certain lower station than their adopted Borschic cousin, nor a candidate for marriage.

I took this change with grace and even a little gratitude, for at that time I was discerning my vocation as a poetess, and I had much to read, and much to study while in school and then university. I began to prize solitude, as my father did, and the past few years of our time in Dann became as cherished as it had been in former times, but for different reasons.

The long train ride from Borschland had always been the worst part for me as a restless young girl. Dann and Kaatsch are truly not that far from my homeland as the crow flies, but directly between Borschland and Dejndeech are some of the highest and most forbidding mountains on the continent, and so far the engineers of neither country have wished to build a railway through them, for there are few travelers and little need for goods to flow so quickly to the center of the Kingdoms. In an airship one could be there in a few hours, but there are few airships for commercial travel, and because of the phase shift they can be dangerous. Therefore one must take a train southwest out of Borschland, then south into the Celtlands, then due east to the Twin Kingdoms.

Once we stepped off the Express in Céad Míle Fáilte and on to the National Railways of Dann and Kaatsch, time seemed to slow to a crawl, as did the engine and its cars, and it seemed forever before we arrived in the city and to the comfort of the first night in my father's friend's house, the Great Teacher of the Twin Kingdoms.

At these times I wondered why we could not stay in a Borschic ski station, such as those above the wonderful towns of Eerichels and Daafna, or about the city of Alma. There are beautiful towns just over the border in Dann. I could not understand until I became a full-grown woman, and a person of deep thoughts, how important it was for my father to get so completely away from his life as Archdeacon in Borschland.

"We do not see the God of our world so clearly," he once said to me, "as we do in the place so unpeopled that we hear not one voice of a suffering soul."

This year, of course, was utterly different from any of those before. I had never left the city thinking about anyone as much as I had our-- or as I had begun to tell myself, my-- Sherm. Although so few words had passed between us, and I had been as decorous a Borschic woman as there is on the face of the earth, I felt deeply a knot of consternation and confusion as we stepped onto the train on Epiphany Day. We were going to a place so unpeopled that we would hear not one voice of a suffering soul, but neither would we hear the voice of Sherm.

This troubled me, and it was troubling that it troubled me.

A North American, of all people. Sherman, such a name.

I knew there would be but little possibility of our spending time with each other without rumors arising that he was courting me. Although I wanted nothing more than simply to sit in his presence and learn of his life, learn of North America, and what it is like to be a man of such skill in his sport, in Borschland we must take all contact between man and woman to be something related to marriage and children. I suppose this is because much contact between man and woman does lead to such things. We are a very practical people.

So that day, as the train sped south through the mountains into the Celtlands, that high and barren place of wind-bent grass and clear streams, I turned over in my heart and head what it might mean for Sherm and me to open ourselves to the possibility of marriage. At first I thought it would be a convenient thing to tell others that there was courtship, and it was leading somewhere, and then, later, when our curiosity was sated, to tell everyone that no, it were best for us to remain apart.

This possibility remained with me for the better part of three days, through the entire train ride, the first night in the house of the son of the Great Teacher (for the Great Teacher had passed away) until the first few strides on my cross-country skis, under a sky so full of goose feather snow I felt as if I were inside a mattress.

I distinctly heard a voice inside say, "This will not do," and I listened to that phrase over and over again as my skis slid back and forth over the fresh snow and my legs stretched out and uncrooked after sitting so long on trains. "This…" *swish* "will…" *swish* "not…" *swish* "do."

Why would it not do? I suppose my heart was telling me that the longer I spent in Sherm's presence, the less I would ever wish not to be in his presence. And I thought, if he were not to feel the same way, that would be rather a disaster.

But why? My life could go on like this forever, or nearly so, without Sherm. And it would be a good life, and someday I would meet a sensible Borschic gentleman and we would have a sensible life with sensible children.

So for the next several days I tried to convince myself that it would be better not to have any more contact with Sherm. In between, I thought about all the things Sherm and I could do together, including spending our honeymoon alone in this winter place, if, indeed, we were to wed in the winter.

On the last of those several days, my Borschic practicality won the day, and I thought, "What kind of bird on a post am I! There is nothing for it but to ask his intentions! For if he has no intention to marry, there is no reason to be stewing over this like a proper *schuunmoute* (cabbage and mutton stew)."

By that time, less than a week had passed, and the only contact we had with the outside world was a telegram posted to Dejndeech and carried up to us that Te Staff had vanquished Bevinlunz by a score of 3 to 2, and that Sherm had scored one of the goals. How my mother and father endlessly discussed that game, though they had not a scrap of newsprint to bolster their arguments, for like everyone else they had become fans of Te Staff after hearing about our Sherm. And when they finally noticed me (for I had said nothing during their entire festival of words), they asked if anything was amiss.

"Everything and nothing," I said, and burst into tears.

It was the most difficult of things to keep from my parents my true feelings about Sherm, for I had never kept secrets from them, having no reason. They must have understood, however, and exchanging glances, let me be. I did not ask to cut the holiday short, though I desperately wanted to, and every hour of dead silence in the white wasteland of the alpine meadows of Dann became like a lifetime of purgatory. I understood what it meant to be a soul in the bondage of purification. Ten thousand years without hearing a bird sing--that was what the utter silence of our winter retreat became to me.

I wrote and rewrote many telegrams to Sherm, and hiked down-- in snowshoes, twice-- to the little village where the telegraph master would always give me a peppermint, and sit blinking behind his thick glasses as I composed and recomposed, tapping his little gnarled pencil against my lips as I considered.

Once I got even so far as to give the scrap to the master, who was turning to his apparatus to tap out the address to the central station in Dejndeech, where it would wing its way on to Staff Borsch, and a messenger would deliver it to Sherm, perhaps at the end of a training session.

But I cried out, and the master turned sharply, and his glasses flew off, and a crack was made in them from hitting the stone floor. I was heartbroken and told him my father would wire an advance to be paid out to him for his glasses and his inconvenience. After much imploring he agreed, for they were his only pair, and he must needs travel down the hill to a larger village in order to have the lenses grinded.

I told my father and quoted what I considered was a reasonable sum for the telegraph master's trouble. He, because he is a frugal Borschic man, gasped at the amount and took off his own glasses.

"Rachael," he said, as if I had blasphemed, "You have been taught economics."

But being a compassionate man, Papa agreed to the sum and went with me to wire it to the telegraph master, who went to the bank in the village down the hill and collected it. He came back with a smile, new glasses and money left over, for he had skied down to the village and back rather than hire a horse and sledge, a sum for which we had allowed in the advance.

I went to pay a call to the telegraph master every day after that, and we received a handful of telegrams, all of them having to do with hockey or church business, and none from Sherm, whose performance on the ice, it appeared, was not affected by my absence. Te Staff won all its games while I was away, completing a nearly perfect first half of its campaign.

Finally the day came for our departure from Ujbur. We were to be carried in a sledge at the unkind hour of 7 in the morning down to the cable car line, and thence to Dejndeech, where we would transfer to our train to the Celtlands and home. I was up and sitting on my luggage at the door at 6, according to my parents.

It took 5 hours to get to Dejndeech, then another 7 to get to Céad Míle Fáilte, and finally, on the Express again, 4 hours to Borschland, two days before Kandelmaas services. We got in near midnight, and, exhausted, I slept late the next day. After waking and breakfasting, I spent the afternoon reading all the newspapers we had missed.

Every photo of Sherm seemed to beckon me. And even the story of Sherm's tiff with Mr. Busby made me long to see him, for I knew, somehow, that there was something of me in that dispute.

On the day of Kandelmaas I read that the players of Te Staff would be skating at the oval of St. Noos, and that endless roses would be thrown and many girls would have the thrill of their lives, skating with the brave young men of the stick and the puck. That very morning, my father said it might be something if Mr. Reinhardt were a guest of honor at the Kandelmaas service at the central cathedral, and that he would send an invitation by personal messenger to that effect.

"Oh, no, Papa," I said, suddenly hitting on a great inspiration. "The invitation should come personally, from someone in the family."

"And that would be you, I expect, my dear?" said my mother.

"You both will be so busy with preparations. And I? The poem for the steel plant in Tarlunz can wait for a day, can it not?"

They both smiled. "It is highly irregular," said my father. "What would people think?"

"I wish we would stop deflecting ourselves so thoroughly when it comes to others' opinions," I said, with my mouth set a little too firmly for proper respect of one's elders.

"Very well, then, child," said my mother. "Bring the invitation to Mr. Reinhardt yourself. Where shall you deliver it?"

"They are skating at the St. Noos oval this afternoon," I

said.

"Will you be taking your skates?" My mother said, with a little upward crook forming on the edges of her mouth.

"By no means," I said. "I am not a silly little teenager with stars in my eyes."

And at this both of my parents laughed.

Truth be told, they were anxious to meet our-- my-- Sherm, not only as a prospective son-in-law, but as a star of the ice-- as if, like the more common people of our city, they had been partisans of Te Staff from their wee britches.

I arrived at what I considered to be a decorously early hour to meet Sherm, but even then it was near impossible to see the ice oval, much less the people skating on it. I stood five deep in starry-eyed teenagers for more than a half-hour as the players chose and skated and posed for pictures, and finally, as the crowd seemed not to be getting any smaller, and I not any nearer to the front, I cried out:

"Way for the Archdeacon Martujns! A message for Sherm Reinhardt. Way for the Archdeacon Martujns." And I held out the snow-white envelope in which my father had penned his invitation.

No one, of course, paid any attention to me at first, but there was a gracious police officer and an official of the St. Noos Park grounds crew who finally spied me and heard me out. They then pushed me through the crowd, which was not at all pleased to see me until they realized who I was, and there was whispering that the daughter of the Archdeacon Martujns had come personally to see Sherm Reinhardt.

Sherm, my Sherm, skated up with the most perplexed look on his face. It was as if he had never seen me before. I was wearing a purple beret that was more like a snood, with my hair pinned underneath, so that might have deceived his eyes a bit, if the last time you have seen a certain woman she was in an evening dress, bejeweled, barenecked, and bareheaded.

He read the invitation, but of course did not understand it completely, so I supplemented, making clear that he would be our guest and that he would be sitting next to me during the ceremonies. There was much pointing back and forth, much to and fro of the first and second person singular pronouns and altogether too many instances of the word "with," a word which thrills women and with his beautiful face so close to mine thrilled me even more.

Then he asked me to skate with him, distinctly, in Borschic. He had already had much practice with it that day.

"But I have no skates," I said, for it was proper to demur. Secretly, I was mad to do it.

"What size are you?" said a strapping young girl with the pinkest cheeks I'd ever seen. "You don't say no to our Sherm, deacon's girl."

I told them, and in a moment skates appeared, and I laced them, and he took my hand, and we were off.

It was the beginning of my downfall.

CHAPTER 19 - SHERM

Up until Rachael appeared I'd been having a good time at the St. Noos skating rink.

After she came I had a fantastic time.

I had just finished skating with my third or fourth girl. They were all sweet, they all asked the same questions and I could answer a couple of them at first, then when I heard them twice I could answer another. I was thinking, this is going to be a piece of cake, when I cruised in and there was a commotion at the side of the rink.

Two guys in uniform were holding back the crowd for a woman with a purple headscarf and a fur-lined jacket. It took me a second to realize it was Rachael, but her smile gave her away finally. It was her "you big goof" smile.

She gave me an envelope, an invitation to church, basically, and after I accepted I asked her to skate with me.

It was the gentlemanly thing to do.

Three weeks can do a lot for language learning. Almost everything we said to each other this time was in Borschic.

"How are you?" I said.

"Very well," she said. "Your accent is improving."

"Thank you."

"Good time skiing?"

She smiled. "You must visit Dann and Kaatsch sometime. It is so beautiful."

"We are doing good in hockey."

"Yes, I read in the papers. You make the city very proud of you."

"And you?" I pointed at her, and then jabbed my chest. "Proud of me?"

We looked into each other's eyes, and she slipped. She lost an edge, or her knees buckled, or she went over a rough spot in the ice. I wasn't really ready, because all the other girls had been great skaters and a couple of them were totally into being twirled.

But Rachael slipped, and as she did, with her back to the ice, I did what came naturally, caught her at the waist, brought her around, caught her wrist with my other hand, and bent at the knees. She was really light. We did a 360 and as we did, she put her arms around my neck and held on, and there was this incredible perfume that my nose injected into my brain. The next thing I knew I was kissing her neck where the perfume was most concentrated.

"Saints!" she cried as we came out of the clinch still on our feet.

I was about to say sorry, because it sounded like she was mad, but she took my hand and stared at me, her mouth open, and then she broke out laughing.

"I'm so clumsy!" she said over and over, while the crowd cheered. Her face was bright red, but it was cold, so she might not have been blushing.

"You okay?" I kept saying. *Alles ergut?* It was something my teammates would say when anyone got hit in the face with a puck.

"All is well," she said. "I am embarrassing you, I think."

"I can hold on to you," I said, and passed my arm around her waist, lightly.

"Thank you," she said, then went into a long, poetic burst of Borschic that I didn't understand.

We took our sweet time with the skate, and the flash bulbs

went like mad. I had never known such a perfect feeling having my arm around her waist, her perfume dancing in my nose, her breath coming out in steam and her eyes like moons.

The guys would skate up with their girls on their arms and give me a pat on the back or say something like, "Your partner is very beautiful."

And I would look at their girl and say, "Your partner is very beautiful."

"We are making quite a scene," Rachael said finally, and we skated back, where many girls were both cheering and yelling at us to be finished.

As we came to the edge of the rink, she said, "I had better see you tonight. If you are going to kiss me without my permission, I think you must keep your appointments with my father." And she smiled a very mysterious feminine smile that usually women only smile in the movies, the kind of smile that Caroline what's-her-face couldn't have even faked.

"Don't worry," I said, somehow not surprised that I understood everything she said.

"I do not," she said.

Rachael curtseyed to me. I didn't know exactly what to do, so I bowed.

All the women went crazy.

The guys-- the single ones, anyway-- had made plans to have dinner at a restaurant in Krejsberg and dance the night away, but something inside me changed for good after Rachael left. I got bored. I wanted to see Rachael. The ceremony began at 8 PM, and it was only 5:30.

I decided to take some time to myself to think. I skated a few more times, then begged off, and tried to get through the crowd on my own. Everyone had to shake my hand or pat me on the back. A lot of folks invited me to dinner. But no one really caught my eye until I saw, standing across the street and leaning against a lamppost, an Upright Bear dressed in a full-length overcoat, bow tie, bowler hat, and no shoes.

Junior, full name Linus Black, Jr.

Once he saw I saw him, he motioned towards his left with a

tricky turn of his head, towards an alleyway that at the moment had no shady types in it.

I crossed the street and went down the alley, and he followed me. Before we got to the other end, he tapped me on my shoulder, and motioned for me to go inside a door.

We found ourselves in a narrow hallway lit by a single bulb. I smelled fish and hot grease.

"Keep walking," said Junior, light and cheerful.

"Nice to see you again," I said.

The hall opened up to a large, bright kitchen with copper pots hanging up, bears in white aprons and with white hats bustling about, all to the sound of oil sizzling and popping in frying pans as big as canoes.

"Fancy some supper?" he asked. "The salmon is very good."

We made our way through the kitchen, where a tuxedoed bear maitre d' met us and walked us into the main dining room, which was nearly empty-- only two massive bears sitting near the front, smoking pipes. The maitre d' led us to a room with French doors, the windows of which were frosted. There were about a dozen tables here, but no one eating. He seated us, and closed the doors.

"Private banquet later tonight," Junior explained as we were seated. "The whole place has been hired."

"Bear or Borschic?" I asked.

"Bear, of course," said Junior. "Diplomatic function. You don't hire a Bearish restaurant for Kandelmaas if you're a good Borschlander. Bad form."

A waiter in an apron and black bow tie came and set the table for us, and another came and brought us little glasses of a gold liquid for the *aperitiff.*

"What is it?"

"Mead. Honey liqueur."

"What are you going to do? Drug me up and dump me in the Celtlands?"

"Don't be ridiculous," said Junior. "It's Kandelmaas. Drink."

I did. It was good. Sweet, with a kick. Junior said, "The consular bears had a little talk with you, didn't they?"

"Yes."

"Well, that makes sense. Did you tell them anything?"

"No, I didn't even tell them I knew you."

"There's a good fellow. But here's the thing."

The waiter came, and brought us filets of salmon topped with berries, deep-fried potato cakes, and a mound of greens. Another guy came with quart bottles of beer, which he left with the corks dangling from a string.

"You can help us," Junior said when the waiters had left.

"Yeah, they told me you were going to ask."

"You don't understand. They think we want you for some kind of messenger boy or a go-between. That's not what we want."

I tried the salmon. It was really, really good. Perfectly done, with some kind of butter and herb sauce melted in.

"We've been watching you. You've done well for yourself so far. Congratulations."

"Thanks." I cut into the potato cake. A puff of steam came up. The potato was tender inside and the crust crispy and salty. I thought to myself, this is good and I didn't realize how hungry I was.

"So, we've been thinking, when you marry Rachael-- "

I just about spit out the potato, and caught myself just in time with my napkin.

"I mean to say, when you're even better known than now."

"Hmmmf."

"We want you to come to Bearland."

I wiped my face and took a swig of beer. Very strong, like the kind we'd had in the bar car. I almost choked.

"Let me put it to you. We have a game that is like ice hockey. It's field hockey with a ball. It's our national game. We'd like to bring you in to play in our league, just as the Borschlanders have brought you."

"Why do you need me?"

"You see how popular you are. Your opinion is going to

carry more and more weight. You are adaptable. And when you become a star in our game, you can advocate for democracy. You can become the spokesperson for a change in Bearish politics."

"What makes you so sure I would be good at this field hockey thing?"

"You are good on ice. Why not on grass as well?"

"What about all these bears mauling me?"

"It is a gentlebear's game. Besides, the players would be for you. They would make sure you weren't hurt."

"Why would the players be for me? Won't most of them be trying to beat the crap out of me?"

"No, we would tell them not to. The players in the field hockey game are for us. Or can be paid to be for us."

"What are you talking about? Are you saying they'd throw games for me?"

"Throw?"

"Cheat. Not try hard. Let me win."

Well," said Junior. "Is that not what your Borschic friends are doing now?"

He looked down at his food, cut the potato cake in half, cut the salmon in half, piled a piece of potato on a piece of salmon, stabbed it with a fork, and tossed the whole thing into his mouth.

I waited till he looked up, and he cocked his head as he chewed, like he was saying *Is it not?* in his genteel pirate way.

"How can you…" I began.

"Everyone knows," said Junior, and lifting the beer to his lips, threw down a healthy belt. "They are just deceiving themselves. They are playing a game of make-believe."

"Why?"

"Because there is a political party that wishes to open up the Continent to the wide world. They are very idealistic. They are very religious, really. They believe that it is time for Borschland to bring its light to the world. They think that they have been chosen by God to be like… an incubator for goodness in the human spirit. And that it is time to give themselves to the world, to convert the world. So, if they bring in a wonderful hockey player to Borschland from North America, the people of Borschland will want to see more of you, and be drawn to you, and soon they will be traveling out to the world in addition to you coming in."

"And I guess that that would mean the end of Borschland as a land that time forgot. It would mean new technology, maybe new war technology."

"That's possible, too." Junior shoveled in a heavy forkful of steaming greens. "Try these," he said, chewing. "Winter greens. A bit like dandelions, but boiled in a lobster broth. Very savory."

"And if they got the new technology, you wouldn't be superior anymore."

Junior nodded. "Did you read politics at university? That is a theory that has occurred to us as well."

"I work pretty hard in those hockey games. Have you noticed? Have you ever been to one?"

"I'm sure you do." Junior wiped his mouth with this napkin. "But face facts. You are not the second coming of Saint Noos."

He was right. I sat there, and let it sink in, and a big pit opened in my stomach. I knew all along I wasn't that good. I'd had a suspicion. Busby was so sure I'd make the team. I'd even asked him if I was that good, and he tiptoed around it. You don't just come in to a place where they've been playing pro hockey for 75 years and set it on fire with your 6 goals in your senior year at the College o' the Lakes, Flippinfinger, Minnesota.

I must have looked like I'd gotten my teddy bear taken away from me, because Junior tapped me on the shoulder and said, "Hello? Buck up. It's not the end of the world. Far from it."

"What about Rachael?" I said. "Since you know everything. Is she just playing nice with me-- to get married to me-- so I'll stay in Borschland?"

Junior took another swig of beer. "I wouldn't put it past

them."

"You jerk. You complete jerk."

"What is worse? To find out the truth now, before you are well and truly entangled, or to have me, a friend, open your eyes? I'm giving you a chance to do good for a country and a party of bears who want to do good. This is worthwhile. This is something on which to build a life."

"Rachael wouldn't come to Bearland with me if we were married."

"Yes, she would. Because a wife must obey her husband. Of course, you would want to return to Borschland for holidays. That would be reasonable."

"I don't believe this," I said, and pushed back my plate.

"You have come to a different world, my friend," said Junior. "Many things are not to be believed. And yet they are real."

I stood up. "Well, I'm not going to play your game in your world by your messed up rules." I jammed a finger on the table. "I'm my own man. I'm my own man."

"Who saved your passport in Anvoria?" Junior said. "I'm not a thief or a bamboozler. I'm a friend, just as I said in my note. I only want your good."

"Another thing I don't believe," I said, and took a couple of steps towards the door.

"You can ask anyone," said Junior, who was still piling food on his fork. "They will tell you."

"Tell me what?"

"That you are not your own man. That the goals you scored were not goals you made on your own, by your own skill."

"Kiss my ass," I said, and left.

CHAPTER 20 - SHERM

The two bears startled when they saw me, and as I walked towards them, they put down their pipes and stood up shoulder to shoulder, blocking the way out.

"Step aside," I said. I was mad enough to punch one of them, but I knew they would've made hamburger out of me.

The goons folded their arms over their chests.

"Get out of my way," I said, "or I'll tell Honeyside and Grizzly Bear, those guys at the embassy, that you're in with Junior."

They eyed each other, then stood apart. "So long, suckers," I said, and left.

So much for the grand exit. It was dark outside, and cold. I walked for a bit until I saw a clock. Little hand 7, big hand 9. It was quarter of seven. I had more than an hour to get downtown to the cathedral and services with Rachael.

I hailed a cab, and told the driver to go around the central loop boulevard several times. He was foreign, from Vinasola I think, and may have been the only guy in Staff Borsch who didn't know me. At least he didn't ask any questions when I hit him with 4 5-shilling notes.

"*Jas, ergut, mejn Sijr,*" he said, in an accent a little better than mine.

We circled the sights, and I considered my options. I could take the next train out, hightail it to Bearland, fly home. That is, if I had enough money in the bank for a plane ticket. Who knows how much it cost?

I could continue on just like nothing had happened. Junior didn't have to be right. I could have done this all on my own.

That one was gone almost as soon as it was out there. There was doubt. Big time. I had to know how much they let me succeed, and how much, if anything, was me. I had to ask someone.

Rachael? How would I ask? What could I say? Are you buttering me up so I'll stay and have all of Borschland fall in love with America, and then Borschland will all go out and convert America to the Borschic way of life?

What about Busby? Was he in on it? Would he level with me? A cell phone would've done wonders for me right then. I didn't know where he was tonight. He had the night off.

As we made our third turn around the city center, I realized I had no choice for that night but to show up for services with Rachael, and keep my options open.

The cabbie took me to the edge of Cathedral Square, crowded with partiers. I stuck my head out of the cab window, showed my invitation to a Staff Borsch policeman. He waved us through, and we pulled up to the cathedral, the doors of which were closed, with police standing nearby. About a million people were filling the square itself, and a reviewing stand had been built to the left of the cathedral building.

Up above, several blimps with lights hanging from their gondolas were slowly circling about.

When I got out, two policemen led me along a sidewalk that was cordoned off. We went up a wooden staircase and up onto the platform, where upholstered chairs had been set up. A chamberlain in a robe with a golden sash led me over to the Martujns' area, and as they recognized me the whole group of people on the platform stood and applauded, and the crowd below looked up and saw me and applauded and started chanting Reinhardt Reinhardt Reinhardt and then Borschland

Borschland Borschland so that I couldn't hear what Archdeacon Martujns said to me when we met.

I took Mrs. Martujn's hand and bowed, and I took Rachael's hand and kissed it, hoping that was the right thing to do for the guy that was courting the poetess Rachael Martujns.

They seated me on the right side of Rachael with her mother on the left, and for the first twenty minutes or so Rachael pointed out to me all the religious stuff that was set up in the center of the square, the candles, the *sternaltaar*, the deacons who'd been chosen to do the ceremony, what would happen before and after.

Rachael was gorgeous. Bundled up in hat, scarf and topcoat, cheeks red with the cold. As long as she was talking, nothing that Junior said mattered to me. I was listening and understanding, feeling really good that I could. She had that same smile, the same happiness at being with me and talking to me that she had always had. Part of me was saying, "Who cares if they're punking you through all this? It feels good. You're doing better than you ever have. Just shut up, get over it, and enjoy it."

But when Rachael stopped talking and I looked up and saw the moon setting behind wispy clouds, and the airships with their strings of lights like Christmas, I felt that big pit open again in my stomach. I heard someone saying, "Reinhardt, the biggest sucker in the history of the world." And for probably the first time in my life I knew if I didn't do something, something to help myself, make my mark, then others would do it for me.

Unfortunately, my first try at doing something didn't come out too well.

I started off okay, by complimenting Rachael on how she looked. She was all done up, her hair pinned under a hat with purple and white feathers and a short brim with a purple mesh in front that made his eyes a sexy mystery. Her scarf was black with a silver stripe and a fur fringe.

"You are very beautiful tonight," I said-- whispered, really, though everyone was talking and there was so much crowd noise her mother could not hear us.

"Tonight, yes. What about tomorrow?" she said, and laughed.

"Sorry, I don't mean that," I began, but she put her hand on mine and said not to worry.

"You make a joke," I said.

"A bad one," she said. "I'm sorry. It's a terrible habit."

"Well, you are beautiful. Today and tomorrow."

"Thank you."

"May I see you tomorrow?" I asked. I'd practiced that particular phrase for a while.

"Perhaps. Are you courting me?"

I thought for a second too long. I wanted to say I was. But I didn't say it.

"Ah. I understand," she said, and turned away. She still had a smile on her face, but some of the life had gone out of her eyes.

"Rachael-- "

"Maybe you misunderstood. I'm sorry, your Borschic is very good, it's getting better every minute."

"I understand courting," I said. "But... in America... it's not the same."

"Not the same? How is it different?"

"I don't have the words."

"Perhaps because the words are a bit shameful," said Rachael. She looked down, and I ate up, drank up her eyelashes.

"We take time..." I said, searching, searching for words. "We don't decide right away."

"How must it take time to decide to be a gentleman?" she asked, slowly. I could hear every word from beginning to end.

Then I said something that I probably wouldn't have said in the same way in English, and that sucked in Borschic. "I don't give you bad hope," I said. "For the future."

Her nostrils flared and her eyes widened. "Bad hope? Bad hope? What do you mean, bad hope? You think I am some..." and she said something I would've loved to understand, then said, "who is hoping only for you? I have many suitors. Bad hope? I am only trying to think of what is proper for us both."

Then I thought, *do you really want this*? My God, this has gone south really fast. I shook my head, and we didn't say anything for a couple of minutes.

I hated not being able to talk the way I wanted, though, really, it wouldn't have mattered if it was all in English. I thought hard about my next sentence, and was about three words in when she put her hand on top of mine, squeezed it and said, "They are starting."

Suddenly the whole place was quiet. Somewhere, a drum banged out three big booms. In the cathedral tower, a bell rang once. The guards with the spears opened the cathedral doors, and a very long procession of men and women in white robes with gold sashes and triangular hats filed out of the cathedral. Next to them young children carried lit candles in long, brass candleholders. In the dark they looked like the headlights of cars on the freeway.

All of them gathered in a circle around the *sternaltaar*, and several children with candleholders climbed the staircase, where they lit torches standing upright at the ends of the altar. The torches flared up and brilliantly illuminated the platform, where there was a thick, tall candle set up and a pile of wood in a metal, four-legged fire pit.

The drum boomed again, and the bell sounded, and the deacons and deaconesses began chanting prayers. Every time they finished a prayer, there would be a drum and a bell.

After about 27 prayers, booms, and chimes, the cathedral doors opened again, and a child walked out. "It is the *fojrkint*," whispered Rachael, close enough that her perfume took the Continental Express to my brain, and I thought, "You jerk, of course you are courting her."

The *fojrkint*-- fire child-- was a little boy dressed in a long robe buttoned at the shoulder; he held a long branch with the bark sanded off of it. He walked all the way by himself from the cathedral to the platform. The deacon took his branch, blessed it with prayers, and gave it back to the boy, who dipped it next to one of the torches. It lit up immediately, licking all along the branch almost down to where he was touching it. The boy then touched the branch to the pile of wood, and it went up like it was doused with gasoline.

As everybody cheered, the deacon took the main candle out of its holder, held it up to the sky, and chanted for a long time. Then he lowered it, till it was almost horizontal to the platform, and the boy took out of the fire a long, skinny piece of wood that was like a three-foot long match. It was burning at the end, and he lit the main candle with it.

The deacon set up the candle again and you never heard such cheering and so many bells.

I turned to Rachael. Her face was glowing, brighter than that fire.

You have to marry her, one voice said.

You have to get out of here, said another.

After the cheering died down, I almost didn't even notice that people were lighting each other's candles. It started around the altar, and radiated out, until thousands of little lights were blazing in a big circle.

A child came up the platform and gave someone light, and everyone looked under their chairs and picked up their own candleholders.

"This is from my family," said Rachael of the holder I picked up. "It was my grandfather's."

I nodded. It was metal, punched with a hundred holes in a swirled pattern, battered, vintage, and covered like a lantern, with a little door. Someone lit my candle, and I lit Rachael's.

She said, "We say this to each other: *lug n frujde*. Light and peace."

"Light and peace," I said.

"Light and peace," everyone said to each other.

Up to then there'd been no singing or music beyond the drum and bell. But now everyone began to sing, Rachael and everyone. It sounded like a national anthem.

I stood there, stupidly silent, waiting. At the end, everyone cheered again, and that was it, and I was shaking hands with everyone, and all the women were giving me kisses on the cheek.

"I want to see you," I said to Rachael as she stood there, not kissing me on the cheek.

"What are your intentions?" she said.

"I have to ask you a question." We took the staircase down from the platform, still holding the lanterns.

"What is it?"

"I have to ask you tomorrow. I have to look and study. I want to have the right words in Borschic."

We stood there with the crowd mixing and milling, and Rachael said, "I will give you the words: When I kissed you this afternoon, Rachael Martujns, it meant that I, Sherman Reinhardt, was determined to have you as my wife. And if I please you, and your father is in accord, I will. That is how we say it. And then I am to say if you please me now, or if you should see me again."

She had never looked more beautiful. Plus, if I had only listened to what she was actually saying, there would have been room for us to get to know each other a bit better before figuring it all out. But I was stung. Of course I'd kissed her, because I couldn't get that perfume out of my head. And of course she took it-- I mean, she didn't take it wrong, but she took it a long, long way.

So I cracked under the pressure. The negative voice in my head won. It said *She is forcing you to propose because they told her to.*

"I have to go," I said. I held out her grandfather's lantern for her to take.

"It's not over. There is a banquet," she said. "My father-- "

"I have to go. I can't stay. I have to go."

She dropped her grandfather's lantern, and caught at my coat. "But you must."

I pulled away. "I must? I must? I don't think so."

And I turned and got lost in the crowd. There were plenty of people. I didn't look back at Rachael. As I was crossing the street I heard a car horn honk.

It was Honeyside and Grizzlybeak.

"You have a place to celebrate?" Grizzlybeak asked.
"I have to get out of this place."
"Yes, you should. Because your life is in danger."
"What?"
"Get in. We'll explain as we drive."
I got in.

CHAPTER 21- RACHAEL

I must apologize. I didn't start the evening by determining myself to disappear. I didn't even have the idea of it when I stepped into the gondola of Kejls' airship. But once we were in the air, everything changed.

When Sherm left, as suddenly as if a magician had waved his wand, I stood there for a moment stunned and unable to think. People were everywhere, I had gotten separated from my parents, and for a moment I was totally alone among the thousands.

I picked up the candleholder Sherm had used. The heirloom candle-holder that a husband would use, would receive as a gift from his bride's family

Some friends from university strolled up arm in arm, singing a Borschic song. They asked me where Sherm was, what plans I had for the evening, if I could get away from the official banquet and come with them to Veedirspujl, the university quarter where there would be many get-togethers.

"Sherm had to go," I told them, and they wondered why, and I said I didn't know why, and they strolled on, arm in arm, singing again.

Finally a subdeacon found me and said my parents were waiting in the refectory of the cathedral, the place where there were two seats among hundreds, one for me, and one for my disappeared guest.

The subdeacon ferried me through the crowds, stunned as I was, wondering only where Sherm had gone, and thinking only two things, alternately: *North Americans are horrible people*, and *What have I done*?

We entered a long colonnade that led to the cathedral diaconal residences and seminary, and to the left, in a great grassy quadrangle, an airship was landing and being made fast. The balloon was an oval on its side, ridged horizontally, as long as a locomotive, with a much smaller gondola fastened to it by wooden and metal bars. I looked over and recognized the young man standing by in a peaked naval cap and black overcoat with shoulder bars.

"Kejls," I cried out.

The subdeacon stopped as I did, and clutched at my coat.

"He is a family friend," I told the subdeacon. "I must stop and say hello."

Kejls Muttik turned to me and blinked in recognition, his mouth dropping open. Here was a man, a Borschic man, I thought. Gallant and dashing and one who would risk his life in a flimsy balloon in order to keep our nation safe. I thought to myself, how could I have ever been taken with this Reinhardt fellow, who whacks at a tiny disk of rubber with a childish wooden stick?

"Rachael?" he said, and then mumbled something else that sounded like he had developed a sudden and debilitating speech impediment.

"Kejls, it is so wonderful to see you," I said. "Your airship is perfectly wonderful. Are you the captain?"

He took my hand, reluctantly, I thought, then looked over at it, a two-seater with an open cockpit made of polished wood and ringed with steel, held to the balloon by many heavy wires. It had two propellers, one on the end of the balloon itself, and one attached to an engine on the backside of the cockpit that was a coil of tubes and plates.

"Oh," he said, and mumbled again. He looked over at the

airship, then back at me. "Oh."

"Yes?"

"I'm..." he began. "...not in command."

"Oh, I see."

"I'm in charge of the tethers," he said, and pulled on a rope with a stake in the ground. "And aerial reconnaissance."

"Aerial reconnaissance?"

"I take photographs from the air," he said. "For intelligence purposes."

"Very exciting," I said. "You are a patriot, Kejls."

"Oh," he said.

My spirit deflated like a balloon. Here was the dashing young man of my dreams, in charge of a camera.

"But," he said, raising his chin, "I can pilot it."

"Can you?"

"Oh, yes. I might get her free for a ride sometime."

What I said next was too forward, but there were, in my view, extenuating circumstances: "What about tonight?"

He jumped as if I'd pinched him. "Well, well. Yes. I don't know about tonight. The primary pilot... I mean... must first..."

"Kejls," I said, "if not, it is perfectly all right."

"Tonight," he said as I was finishing. "Tonight. Yes. Tonight. I will bring the air ship tonight and we can go for a ride. It will be cold up there."

"Meet me in my back garden, Kejls," I said. "Midnight. I will make a picnic, with brandy. We can have a midnight snack."

"It will be done," and saluted, his right hand next to his cheek and two fingers next to his temple.

As I rejoined the subdeacon and made my way to the banquet, I knew I had done a thing that would cause shame to my parents. At the same time, it was Kandelmaas, and men and women have been known to do unusual things on this night, things they would not do during ordinary time.

Not that I was thinking Kejls and I were going to...

In my back garden, or in an airship.

Certainly not.

Usually, men and women in Borschland have the excuse of having done unaccustomed things after having compromised their faculties with a dousing of brandy. I had no such excuse.

Unless you could say I was drunk with Sherman Reinhardt, intoxicating, if not poisonous brew that he was.

I made my excuses to Father and Mother, and the other guests of the banquet who were mightily disappointed that Sherm would not be present. This act of Sherm's was highly impolite and disrespectful, but I spent less time on his behavior than on my need to return home and prepare for Kejls' arrival. I said no more than what was true, which was that I felt ill, and not up to the formidable number of courses to be delivered that night. I was really ill at heart, understanding of which registered in the eyes of Father and Mother.

My parents had a quick conversation apart from me, and then Mother took me aside and said, "This North American shows himself to be unsuitable. I know it is a shock for you, but it is best you forget him."

"I know, Mother," I said. "Nothing could be clearer to me."

"Your Papa and I are very concerned. Shall we accompany you home?"

"No," I said firmly. "I want you and Father to enjoy yourselves. Stay as late as you wish. I can take care of myself."

"I know you can, my dear," said Mother. "But please, be careful."

With that, she kissed me and turned away, and I went to Father to be kissed, and I thought to myself, *why is she saying be careful*? Was I being that transparent?

Well, anyway, I thought, Kejls and I are going to have a very short ride in an airship with a bit of brandy and some cheese and bread from the larder. And that will be it.

We do not have live-in servants at our house, though there is a cottage in the back garden for one. The cook and the maid were off-duty, with their own families for their own Kandelmaas celebrations. The house was utterly quiet, except for the ticking of clocks, and dark except for candles left lit in the front windows. It was cold, too, for we had turned down the steam heat, expecting to be gone for many hours.

As is habit in Borschland, I left the electric lights off as I passed through the front hallway, and my sense grew that I was doing something wicked. In the kitchen, I lit a candle, took out the picnic basket and chose a blanket, napkins, china, and silverware. I siphoned into a decanter a half-pint of brandy from our cask, and stopped it tightly.

Food? I felt light-headed, as if my stomach was floating about my body, and the last thing I wanted to think about was eating. Still, Kejls must have his nourishment. I cut slices from a leftover pork roast, wrapped a dozen homemade cheese crackers in a towel, choose two well-preserved apples from our bin, and brewed a pot of hot coffee which I put in our thermos set. The picnic basket was heavy as I lugged it to the back porch and set it there, an hour or so before Kejls was to arrive.

I had some time to consider whether Kejls would actually appear, for he had shaken badly my confidence in him (though, I must confess, I never really possessed much). But as I sat on the window seat in the back library, gazing out at the dark, and the candles in other houses, my thoughts about Sherm gave me fine company-- they spoke much more than I-- and it seemed not long at all before I heard the engine and propellers of Kejls' airship as it circled our garden.

Outside, it was biting cold, but fortunately not windy or snowing, and an experienced pilot, I thought, would have plenty of room to touch down on the snow-covered sward of grass in the middle of our garden.

But Kejls circled. He circled and circled, and finally I called up to him and waved with a hanky. He looked down, and let out a rope ladder, which fell to about ten feet above me.

"That won't do!" I cried up at him, as dogs barked and I thought, *I hope the only neighbor home right now is that* Meestreess *van ter Klaningen who sleeps very soundly.*

"Climb up!" he cried. "I need to do the thetters."

I realized two things then. First, the airship was a two-seater for a reason. You needed one person to pilot, and one person to secure the ship with ropes.

Second, Kejls was drunk.

He was too far away to be looked at in the eyes or to check the color of his nose and cheeks, but the thetters instead of tethers gave him away.

What a horrible, horrible person I am, I screamed to myself. I ran back into the house. I clearly needed to help Kejls back to his post, and this might mean a long journey. I got another overcoat, a couple of blankets, and at the last minute, my passport. There would be much explaining to do to the Borschland Navy, and I might need papers.

Whereas I thought not even once about taking a change of underwear.

When I came out, Kejls was circling lower, just above the treetops. I called to him to throw down a rope, and he did, and I tied the picnic basket to it, thinking of my days as a Loflin Forest Girl. Swinging wildly, the basket tore through a hedge and tipped, and flatware cascaded out where I had not secured a flap. But Kejls managed to pull the thing up.

Then I thought, *this rope ladder climb will be more than a Loflin Forest Girl usually attempts*. But it is in the nature of Borschic women to protect their men, especially when the men have done something stupid in order to impress the woman.

Kejls cut the engine so that the ladder would not move so fast across our greensward, and he managed to lower the air ship far enough that the last rung of the ladder was brushing the ground. I caught at a rung, and held on, and the ladder swung mightily as it drifted to a very large, bare oak tree at the back of our garden.

"Kejls!" I screamed, and he told me to climb. I tried, and got up a couple of rungs, but the tree was looming closer and closer, and we were neither slowing down nor turning aside.

"Reverse it! Reverse it!" I screamed, thinking the only way to avoid the tree would be to push the air ship the other way.

"Reverse what?" Kejls said.

"The engine!"

"The engine is off!" He screamed down.

"Start it! Put it in reverse!"

The engine roared to life, and then gunned. I tangled briefly in oak branches, and a corkscrew of wood nearly parted my hair. But then the oak tree stopped approaching, and instead we started back towards the house, which was almost as tall and quite a bit less endowed with holes.

I got up a few more rungs before the house began to look menacingly large and solid, and I screamed up, "Climb! Avoid our house!"

At which Kejls simply put the engine in forward again. We stopped a few feet from the house, my foot banged against the lower-story stonework, and we started going back to the tree.

"Only a few more!" Kejls said.

It was more than a few more, but now I was confident we could keep going back and forth without pasting me to some large object.

When I clambered, skirts high, into the gondola, Kejls tried to catch me in his arms, but instead he collapsed under my weight and I found myself with my stockings showing above my knees and Kejls on his back trying to avoid what he was doing, which was clutching my thighs and shoulder with either arm.

"Phew!" I cried, and rolled off of him.

"Saints!" he said.

Then I realized I'd been held by two men in inappropriate places, all on the same day.

I knelt in front of him. "You are drunk, Kejls Muttik."

"But you are a woman who makes a man turn cold sober in one military second," said Kejls. "Saints of the fatherland! Women! You are all impossible."

"Kejls! I will ask you to be a gentleman." I tried to smooth my skirts down over my knees.

"I am," he said, and was going to say more, but suddenly the engine made a great chuffing sound, and both propellers went out.

"Saints of the fatherland!" cried Kejls.

"I thought you knew how to pilot this contraption," I said.

"It is bad luck to have a woman in a sailing craft," he said, and went to the pilot's seat to restart the engine. When he had success, he said he would have to have the airship back soon, for his captain had given him only an hour's leave.

"There are still things on the ground," I said. "We need to get them."

"Your luggage, I suppose, for suth a long trip," Kejls said.

I was astonished at how brandy had helped him find and lose his tongue. I shouldn't have been, I know. Poor Kejls.

"We must retrieve the flatware," I said. "That is my great grandmother's."

Kejls was practiced at shinnying out of the craft and "thettering" it, so he cut the engine and went to get everything, finding and bringing up all but a meat knife that I knew was there.

"You shall have some coffee for your efforts," I said, unscrewing the top of the thermos. "And then we shall take you back to your post, for you are most unsafely robbed of your wits."

Kejls allowed me to minister to him. He was near to finished off by the brandy in any case. We drank coffee and he made an attempt at cutting a piece of pork that I had put on a plate. I nibbled an apple, thinking this must be the most unusual place I have ever had a picnic.

Then Kejls leaned over the side and threw up everything he had drunk and more.

It was a good thing it all went into the evergreen bushes on the border of our house and the neighbors.

Kejls lay sprawled on the floor of the gondola. "This has been a lovely time," he said.

"We will summon a cab," I said, "and leave the airship here."

"No," he said, and moaned. "The captain will flay me alive. I may lose my commission."

"You won't lose your commission," I said.

Kejls only groaned again.

I set my eyes on the control stick and the panel with the

little round windows and arrows pointing to numbers. I sighed. Borschic women are nothing if not helpful to their men. And the idea of spending the rest of the night in grief and sorrow over a hockey player was not congenial in the least.

"How does it go?" I said.

CHAPTER 22 - SHERM

The bears almost persuaded me to go to their party.

"Dancing," said Grizzlyfaith. "And you can stay out of sight till the danger passes."

They wouldn't tell me exactly what the danger was, but they noted that Linus Black Jr. was still in town.

I didn't feel much like socializing, and we sat in the car in front of the embassy for a good long time until I got the feeling they were going to push me in there themselves.

So I told them I'd be there but needed to get my evening clothes, and they figured that was reasonable and gave me a ride home and told me they'd wait below.

I smelled her perfume before I saw her. She was wearing a lot, and it was strong, but somehow that was okay. It smelled like incense and a baked ham and some kind of sweet flower like honeysuckle all at the same time, and at first I thought someone was baking some weird clove-studded meat, though there wasn't any oven in the kitchen.

"Anybody here?" I asked, and shut the door.

No one answered. I clicked on the hall light, made my way through the hallway into the living room. She was lying on the couch with her head propped on a pillow, in a pool of light made by several long candles lined up in a circle on an end table. She was reading from a thin, hardback book.

She put down the book on her chest and looked up at me. Her eyes were deep green, and she had on the blackest mascara I'd ever seen, about as much as someone from a Japanese play. Her lips were painted bright red, and her hair, dark red, almost brown but with definite red, was cut short and curled in.

I had no idea how old she was. She was very slim, but in the candlelight, and with the amount of makeup she'd had on, could've been twenty or forty.

We stared at each other, her with her book on her chest, me with my coat in my hand. I thought of a cat. She didn't blink.

"*Waass…ten…*" I tried, and gestured with my hand with the coat in it. "*…hijliche…*"

"My name is Nemeth," she said, in perfect English. "I am from Zimroth. I was engaged by a Mr. Busby."

Like nothing it was totally clear what was going down. "Oh my god," I said. I looked behind me, towards the door, then towards the window. Out in the street the bears were idling their big black sedan.

"How did you get in here?"

She raised her chin. "Do you know Zimroth?"

"Oh, god, Busby."

"He said expressly that I should tell you he engaged me."

"What, is he coming over later?"

Nemeth either ignored my comment or didn't understand. She sniffed, like I didn't understand what a great privilege it was to be with a Zimrothian courtesan.

"Do you know," I said, "what prank means in English?"

"I am afraid I am not up to the minute with the latest English slang," she said, saying *slang* like it was the coolest word in the dictionary. "But if you'd like to teach me…"

"That's fine, that's fine. How long are you, um, engaged for?"

"I always accompany a gentleman until noon of the clock on the day following our evening together. That is my minimum engagement."

"Wow, that must have cost him."

Again, she fluttered her eyelids a little bit, as though she was used to johns acting like jerks. She sat up, delicately swiveling her long legs so that her slippers touched the floor. The silk of her dress rustled, and her long legs made an outline on it.

"Well, I'm..." I was going to say I was tired, but I really wasn't. I was depressed, for sure, but I didn't feel like sleeping. I felt like seeing Rachael again. I felt like I wanted to learn Borschic a lot better, and get smarter, and cooler. Because even though I was the leading scorer in the Borschland Hockey League, I felt like I was behind 15 to nothing to Team Rachael.

And then there were the bears. But they could wait.

"Oh," she said, like she'd just understood something. "Forgive me... but I must ask. You are... inexperienced?"

I sat down in an easy chair across from her, and put my head in my hands.

"You should not be ashamed," she said. "You are very attractive. Someday you will find the right woman."

"Gee, thanks," I said to my hands.

"Mr. Busby is looking out for your welfare," Nemeth continued. "Perhaps you are not confident with women. Perhaps this is why you have not succeeded in finding a woman who is pleased with you."

I looked up at her, and I thought to myself, *she's an absolute nutcase.* And also, *she's absolutely right.*

"I am a very educated woman," said Nemeth. "I have many skills beyond the arts of lovemaking. I think you should be grateful to Mr. Busby."

I looked up and rubbed the back of my neck. "Do you do massages?" I asked.

"I am skilled in that area, yes," she said.

I had gotten used to training massages. Of course, these were done by big hairy guys in wool t-shirts and trousers with suspenders, and Nemeth was probably going to insist on doing it in the nude. I mean, what self-respecting courtesan wouldn't?

Nemeth stood up. Apart from the too much makeup, she

was a very classy woman. "Would you like the massage in your bedroom?" she asked.

"Whoa," I said. "Not so fast."

"Oh," she said, the same way she'd said it the first time. "Then please tell me your desire. I am yours." And she spread her arms and pushed out her small but perky chest.

"How about leaving?"

"That would be harmful for my reputation," she said, and let her arms fall at her sides. "I have never been disengaged before noon of the clock on the following day. That is, em, unacceptable. I apologize."

"Okay."

She sat down again, silk swishing. "I might suggest... conversation and brandy. Many men enjoy this as a prelude to lovemaking."

I did have a bottle of brandy in the house. About the only thing I kept.

"All right," I said. "Hold on tight."

"I'm holding."

I laughed. She was so sincere. Really good English, though I could tell she didn't get much chance to practice, unless she spent her vacations down at the RAF base in Bearland. I got two tumblers, beautiful Borschic glass. They made nice glass in Sichebach. The riverbank sand was the best in the country, Busby told me once.

"Are you hungry?" I asked. "I could go down and raid the restaurant ice box. They gave me a key to the pantry. And the elevator works all night. They don't turn it off."

"This will be fine," she said, taking the tumbler from me so that her hand touched mine. "You are a kind man. This is good."

"Are men not kind to you?"

"Men are not kind by nature. But they can be softened."

"Umm," I said, and thought of Rachael.

"What did you do tonight? How did you celebrate Kandelmaas?"

I thought of the bears in the car below, idling, maybe

freezing. "I'm a hockey player."

She widened her eyes, like she was surprised. "Surely you did not play a game on this holiday?"

"No, what I meant was… I was… I was in public. I was spending a lot of time with people who think I'm a great hockey player. Do you know, I mean, do you know me? Do you know who I am?"

"I do not follow the sport. Many of my sisters do, because men want them to. But my clients are those who do not follow hockey, and do not want to speak of it. Mr. Busby said…"

"It's okay," I said. "That's actually really good. That's actually perfect, in fact."

"Are you weary of being in public?" Nemeth asked.

This girl is good, I thought. She's pretty great. What is going to happen if I decide not to have sex with her? Will I be passing up the greatest night of my life? A Zimrothian courtesan. Thanks so much, Buzz.

"Listen," I said. "There's this woman. Someone."

"Oh," she said, in a different way than before. An enhanced "oh."

"You're not going to… we're not going to…" I tried.

"You mean, you are true to this woman."

"I guess so," I said. It sounded wrong, *true*, but maybe she was right.

"And she is your betrothed?"

"No. No, I don't even want. I don't even know. What to do about her. Does that make any sense?"

"Oh, that makes no innocence at all. I am quite trained in matters of the heart," said Nemeth. "I am a trained counselor in matters of wooing. I think I know what you wish."

"What's that?"

"I will tell your *lana*," she said. "It's a Zimrothian art. I have a deck of cards. You will see. We will find out from the *lanathuia* whether this someone is for you or not."

"The *lana*tha what?"

"The *lanathuia* is the heart of life," said Nemeth. "Of course they know."

"They?"

Instead of answering my question, she leaned over and rummaged in her elegant purse, which must've also had her toothbrush in it. She took out a polished wood box with a fine grain. She took off the lid, and pulled out a set of oversized playing cards with backs that were squiggly lines, or an intricate pattern, or both.

"Bring that over," she said, pointing to a hassock that had the tray with the brandy bottle. I almost jumped. What the lady wants, the lady gets.

She motioned for me to take the tray off the hassock, and she laid the deck face down on it, swirling them around to shuffle them.

"Now you," she said, and put my hand down on the deck. Nice, soft hands with smooth nails. "It is important for your *lana* to marry the *lana* of the cards."

I felt a tingle on my back as I touched the cards and repeated the word *marry* to myself. It was crazy, but Nemeth was fired up to stay till morning, I wasn't sleepy or drunk, the bears were on duty and were going nowhere, and I was worried about Rachael and knowing I didn't want to sleep with a prostitute on the same night we had our first big fight.

"I don't believe in tarot cards," I said. Caroline what's-her-face did. She believed in everything. She believed you could make a wish at 11:11 in the morning and it would come true.

"We are not going to tear the cards. They must remain, em, intact."

She arranged the cards and dealt out three face down.

"The first card," she said, laying a smooth fingernail on the card on my right, "represents your heart. The third card represents her heart." She pointed at the one on my left. "And this card, the middle card, represents the binding card, which tells whether your heart and her heart are *lana*."

"First we will show your heart," she said, and turned the card face up. It was a group of horsemen with long lances galloping into battle.

"Em," she said, and smoothed the card on the cloth of the

hassock. "This is the six of lances. This represents bravery, supremacy, and, em, potency. The *lana* are telling you that you will be a father of many children. You will be a great man."

"That's good, I guess," I said.

"It is good and bad for matters of the heart," said Nemeth. "For a woman, to have a man of this heart means she is also competing for his attention with other things that take him from her."

"Such as hockey," I said, and looked down again at the six men. Just a coincidence, of course, that there were six men on a hockey team. This *lana* thingy knew its stuff.

"And it may also mean you will have many wives," said Nemeth. "Great men in Zimroth often do."

"Whatever," I said.

"Now we look at her heart." She turned over the card. It was of a snow-covered hill, and at the top of the hill a tree with no branches, and a black sky with seven stars arranged like a horseshoe.

That can't be good, I thought.

"Winter," said Nemeth. "Your woman is Borschic, I presume?"

"Totally," I said. "I don't know if there is anyone in the world more Borschic than she is."

"This does not surprise me. These are winter people here. They look for the light, and they find the light of the stars as warming as the summer sun. Zimrothians are different. Winter for us is a time to take a long and very hot bath."

I imagined Nemeth in a bath. It was a nice picture.

"This card represents a woman whose heart is set on purity."

"Purity," I said.

"I do not mean, em, chastity," she said, guessing right where my mind was going. "She is a stubborn woman who must have things all her own way. But she is noble in her desires. She wishes only the best for all, and she will never tell a lie."

I nodded.

"Does this disappoint you?"

"Yeah. No. I don't know. But you're right, she is stubborn."

"Now for the third card." Nemeth turned it over, and gasped.

The card was of a palace hanging in the air, upside down because it was reversed to its normal orientation. It had a golden dome, like one of those palaces in India, and there were people falling from it, one a man in a long robe clutching at a crown that was falling away from him, the other a woman who has just let go of a flowering branch.

"It is the *tor meleth*," said Nemeth. "The phase shift."

"What?"

Nemeth looked around the room. For the first time, she seemed less than composed. "Do you have a wireless?" she asked.

"Yes. Over there." She meant a radio. I had a beautiful wooden one with polished boar's-tusk knobs. The team had given it to me as a house-warming present.

"We must listen."

"What's going on?"

"Your woman is in danger," said Nemeth.

CHAPTER 23 - RACHAEL

The sound that it made when it happened was like that of someone blowing into a bottle. Not a musical blowing, just a kind of *pffft*! loud enough to hear but not loud enough to pay attention to.

I thought it might have been Kejls blowing into the thermos to cool off the coffee.

But it wasn't. It was, as I realized when I looked down over the side of the airship, the phase shift.

In school, of course, we are taught about phase shifts. We are taught the science of it in the fourth form, when we are fourteen years old. We know that the phase comes at irregular intervals. It is like an earthquake in the wide world. For reasons still unknown, the occurrence and time length of a shift can be somewhat predicted, but not with any precision.

We know that the shift affects the entire continent when it happens, and that it affects everyone and everything, birds, insects, and snowflakes, to an elevation of about five hundred meters.

Borschland and the rest of the continent does not seem to be affected, for we still see the same sky and we have the same kind of weather, though not identical.

But once the phase comes into effect, anything that is

above five hundred meters is left behind. That is, if you are a creature such as an eagle that thinks it belongs in Borschland, then you must not climb higher than five hundred meters, for if you do, and the phase shift occurs, you will find yourself at least five hundred meters in the air with nothing but ocean below.

There is no crashing of seas into the hole left behind by Borschland and the other nations. It is simply as if we were never there. Sometimes the shift lasts for an hour, and sometimes it lasts for over a decade. The longest shift, so we were taught, lasted 21 years, three months, seven days, and sixteen hours.

This is why it is somewhat risky for an aeroplane or an airship to be hovering about our continent at a very high altitude, and why it is still very unusual for anyone on our continent to be flying at any altitude, and why our birds are mostly the kind that stay close to the ground.

Now I was taught, at the age of fourteen, in the Deaconess Bujrgujt Kujroos Preparatory School for Young Ladies, that if you did keep your feet on the ground, you would always stay in dear old Borschland. And I remember one of my classmates, Terejsa Scheefl, once asking the mistress what would happen if you were on a ladder hanging a picture at the time.

Terejsa was rapped across the back of the knuckles for that question, and we went on to other topics in meteorology.

So I did not know what would happen if I were not on the ground when the phase shift occurred, but below one thousand meters. It must happen sometime, but the papers never report the whereabouts of the airships of the Borschland navy, and I would expect that the stalwarts of that military organization believe the reconnaissance of some shepherds in the Celtlands is worth the life of a sailor or two to be left behind in a twenty-year phase shift in the middle of the Indian Ocean, hundreds of miles from any stable land.

How did such a thing happen? Saints, it was my fault, but then again, it was also Kejls' fault as well.

I had determined to get my young navy officer back to

base, but Kejls was in no condition to tell me how to work his airship, and I did not know where his base was. However, I did know that there was an airship base on the river in Oststaff, which, even thought it is named "East" (Ost is "East" in Borschic), it is really in the west.

A long story, to be told at another time.

So I decided to head in that direction after I found the compass, and I pulled the lever that said "WAAFT" (lift), and the ship went up and the propellers roared to life, and I felt as if I were free, and Sherman Reinhardt was not a problem any more, nothing was a problem, for I was flying.

Of course there was Kejls, who had begun to smell like rotten apples, and I wasted enough time thinking about what to do with him to not realize how high the "WAAFT" lever had gotten us. In no time, we were so high that the lights of the city were like beadwork on a dress.

The compass would have been of use, of course, but for the fact that I knew not exactly what direction to go in for Oststaff. If it had been during the day I could have managed it, just by staying low to the ground and finding the river. But that would also have meant knowing exactly how to work the "WAAFT" lever.

"Kejls!" I cried, and pulled back on the lever. The propellers abruptly stopped. We were floating, and it was quiet, except for the wind in the metals stays, which made the sound *wing, wing.*

"Are we home yet?" he asked.

I looked over the side. Lights, as far as the eye could see. But in the distance, a long ribbon of darkness.

"The river," I said.

"Forward," he said. "The throttle."

There was a lever that said GAAJ (throttle), and a direction to go that was forward. I pushed gently, and the propellers roared. I felt wind in my face, and the lights below began to move.

"Are you sure this is the right direction?"

"Forward," he said again, but did not get up from the floor

of the gondola. "You are under orders, *demouzeel*."

"Yes, *commandant*," I said, and laughed. Kejls was addressing me at the rank of a typist in the Borschland navy.

"How do we turn?" I asked. "The river is south of us."

"The rudder," he said. "To the right."

I turned the rudder lever to the right, but the ship turned its nose the opposite way, and I realized that to go to the right I would need to turn the rudder left, like a sailboat on the Borschland River.

And I began to have an idea for a poem, *How the air is a sea, and we like leaves are blown about.*

That is all I remember before the *pffft*.

Of a sudden, instead of lights underneath us, there was a very great and impossible nothing, and a very great increase in wind.

The night to that point had been nearly still, which made the cold bearable. But now the gondola creaked and the stays around the balloon sang as a breeze that seemed increasing to a gale took us up into its stream.

"What is it?" Kejls said, blinking, and sitting up.

I could say nothing. I sat down-- almost was forced down-- a chill overtaking me.

"What is it, Rachael?" Kejls scrambled up, staggered, held on, and looked down.

"Is it cloud? Are we above cloud?"

I decided not to shriek. It would have been a womanly thing to do at this point, because there is nothing quite like the feeling of being left behind. Very few dwellers on the Continent have known such a feeling. This is why we try to keep our feet on the ground.

"Are we above cloud, Rachael?" Kejls yelled.

I knew not why he would ask me such a question. He, after all, was the naval flyer. My heart was in my throat, and I was chewing on it.

"It is not cloud," Kejls said. "It was a clear night."

He stared at me, and the glassy drunkenness in his eyes resolved to blind fear. "My god, we are left behind," he whispered. He slid down a side of the gondola and gripped the floorboards.

I sat down and began to cry, silently, tears dropping down and beading on my overcoat. The gondola swayed and shook in the wind.

"My god, my god," Kejls said. "It cannot be. I am drunk. I am dreaming."

That was when my best idea for a poem has ever come to me, and at the same time, my plan for getting back to Borschland.

I saw it clearly: "To be left behind is to lose one's sky." It sounds better in Borschic, though we all must confess it: Borschic is not a terribly poetic language.

Usually, poets who have been left behind, and there are only a few, blessedly, say that the feeling of being left behind is to lose one's earth. Because that is indeed what it is. But to me at that moment, I felt as if Borschland had taken both its earth and its sky, for in the universe I was in, presumably that of the wide world, it was storming, and my own, quiet, windless sky of Borschland was gone.

Then a thought washed over me, and I spoke it. "We cannot be five hundred meters up. We can't have climbed that fast."

"Look at the altimeter," Kejls said, and leapt up, suddenly as sober as a toad. He wiped the face of a dial, though there was nothing on it, and tapped. "589 meters. We are in the wake."

"The wake? What is the wake?"

He clutched the WAAFT lever, but did not move it.

"What is the wake, Kejls?"

"They taught us about it in training. If you are above five hundred meters but below one thousand meters you are still left behind, but you can get swept back to the continent by the wake of the phase. It is like a disturbance of air, a wind, that is sucked back into the shift as the continent goes away."

"Pull down on the lever, then, we must get back," I said, and put my hand on his.

He cast me off, as lightly as if I weighed nothing, and I fell on my skirts, *ker-flump*. It is a good thing we women in Borschland wear thick undergarments. I did not think of Kejls as a strong man, but in the moment he was of giant strength.

"I'm sorry," he said, though he wasn't. "At one thousand meters of altitude the wake comes at two hundred kilometers per hour. It would tear us to shreds, and we would fall to our beloved continent in many pieces."

"But if we descend below five hundred, will the wake be less?"

"We cannot descend below five hundred. The wake will not let us."

"And at five hundred, what is the airspeed of the wake?"

"I don't remember."

"What are you saying?"

"I wasn't listening in class."

"Why not, you miserable wretch of a man?"

"I was writing a poem to you," he said.

"Oh, Kejls." Oh, Rachael. You have terribly forgotten your manners, you miserable wretch of a girl.

"We can climb above one thousand and be safe," Kejls said. "Or we can chance it below and be torn apart."

"If we go above, there is no land for us to get to. We will die in any case."

"We can make for Perth, Australia. About a thousand nautical miles. Or the Kerguelen Islands, to the west. About six hundred."

I stood up, and came back next to Kejls, looking up into his eyes, that would not look into mine. "How far can we get on the fuel that we have?"

"Two hundred nautical miles. Then we drift with the wind." I noticed that he had nudged the WAAFT lever, for the altimeter had begun to creep up past 700 meters.

"And the winds… will take us?"

"Unfortunately," he began, and fixed his eye on me. "Toward Tasmania, two thousand nautical miles."

I shook my head, put my hand on his again, the one on the

WAAFT lever. Kejls had been listening in his geography classes.

"We have food, and drink," he said, almost a whisper. "We can make land. Or hail a ship. There are those."

"We have a picnic," I whispered back through clenched teeth.

"The phase may last only a few..."

His was the voice of reason, I knew. Phases do not always last twenty years. Kejls was right. This one could last a day. Hours. But once you are left behind, you are left behind. And I did not want to be left behind for two decades, or more.

Two decades without my Sherman, blast his stupid American crooked-nose beautiful face.

"Kejls," I said, in as silky a voice as I could muster. I am not a seductress, so this may not have sounded very convincing to him. "Kejls, hold me."

He took his hand off the WAAFT lever, and crushed me to him. He very much almost pinned my arms to me, but I did manage to get one free.

"Rachael, Rachael, we will survive," said Kejls. "And I will..." he paused, and then swallowed. "When we return home, I... I... will ask... your father for your hand."

Such a brave boy. It was a lovely, lovely gesture, and a brave, brave promise, one to which any self-respecting Borschic woman would have held such a man as Kejls, the son of a rich man from Tarlunz. But I was not really thinking on that at the moment. I was thinking that the phase-wake must be much less than two hundred kilometers per hour at the altitude of five hundred meters. It was an intuition, I know, based on nothing except not wanting to be left behind, not for an instant.

But while Kejls held me and buried his face in my neck, waiting for me, perhaps, to allow him to kiss me, and from there to go on to the desperate actions that would drive any doomed couple of lovers, I stopped the WAAFT lever and nudged the LUUREN (fall), and the propellers reversed, and we tipped downward, and Kejls let me go.

"We are not going up anymore," he said, frowning. He looked down at the controls.

"No," I said. "Kejls, don't."

And he didn't, for at that moment, the wind, which had been blustery enough to shake us about quite a bit, suddenly lifted us up in such a terrifying blast that we were both cast off our feet and sent headlong onto the side of the gondola.

"HOLD ON!" he screamed over the shriek of the wind.

I said *side of the gondola*, and that's where we were. The airship had been thrown horizontally, and gravity was no longer holding us to the floor. I found handholds even as I saw the thermos roll down and out into the blackness, followed by the picnic basket and two table settings of my grandmother's silverware.

The wind tamed for a second, and I fell a bit towards the floor again, though my skirts were now completely blousing against my arms and Kejls, if he could see me, would have had a scandalously broad view of my stockings, garters, corset and knickers. As it was, the running lamps fore and aft were still lit for the moment. I felt a rope go about my waist, then pulled tight.

"Emergency!" he screamed. He pulled himself against me and tied the rope. Now in my ear, he said, "Life ropes. Keep us lashed to the ship."

Grand Borschland Navy training had made Kejls cooler under pressure than he would have been otherwise. I gave thanks, silently, to the saints of the waves.

The wind came up again worse than before, and we might have been put upside down, for all I could see after the running lamps were extinguished and two of the stays on the balloon snapped with a stinging *oing* sound that was most dreadful indeed.

I wrapped my legs around Kejls' and my arms around his neck and put myself in the most compromising position I had ever been in, something else, I thought in my madness, I should remember to put in a poem sometime, that when you are about to die the idea of lovemaking is both farthest away and closest to your mind.

But every thought was then blown out of my head by the worst thrust of wake yet, for we were tossed out of the gondola entirely, hands ripped from handholds and flying in blackness around and around, and I had no idea whether the rope still held or whether we were hurtling to the ground.

CHAPTER 24 - SHERM

I turned the knob to on, and the lights lit inside the wireless set-- AKA the radio. It was tuned to Bearland Radio Continental, the only English language station on the continent that I could get.

A low, growly voice rumbled out of the speaker.

"Details not known at this time," the voice said. "No word on how many airships may have been left behind. Bear Air had already suspended flights for the evening. A Bear Air passenger service flight headed to Perth, Australia left Continental airspace at 20:37 hours Brownbakikio time. More information as it comes to hand.

"This is Bearland Radio Continental."

I turned off the radio.

"There's been a phase shift," I said. "You-- the cards-- were right."

Nemeth hesitated, then said, "The *lana* know your beloved may have been left behind in the phase shift."

"What do you mean, know?"

"There is an energy with you and this woman. The *lana* have been influenced by it."

"Well, she didn't take a flight out of Borschland tonight. Anyway, there aren't any airplanes in the country."

"There are airships. Carriages on balloons. Could she have gotten in one of these?"

"I don't know."

"If you value your woman, you must find out."

"But if she were in one of these balloons, wouldn't she be out of reach anyway?"

"No," said Nemeth. "The phase shift card was reversed. Which means that she was left behind, but somehow will get back. Not without danger."

"So what can I do about it?"

Nemeth said, "Turn the wireless back on."

I did.

"Tune to Borschland Radio."

She gave me the frequency, and we listened for a few moments to the rebroadcast of a Kandelmaas sermon.

Nemeth said, "Bearland know about the shift, but Borschland do not. If they were to know, the wireless would be reporting it."

"Would the government know?"

"The Navy might."

I snapped my fingers. "I'll go that one better."

What I needed at the moment was a cell phone. But since there were no public landlines, the next best thing was to get a ride.

"Stay put," I told Nemeth. "You're engaged till noon of the clock tomorrow. And after that… This didn't happen, okay?"

"I never, em, disclothe my clients," said Nemeth.

"Thanks," I said, and pulled on my overcoat.

"But…" she said.

"What?"

"Tell me if you find her?"

I smiled. For the first time ever, anywhere, I felt like a hero.

The bears were still waiting below when I rushed out my front door.

"What took you so long?" one said.

"Only she-bears take so long to be ready," said the other.

"Let's move," I said, and ducked into the backseat. I didn't know exactly what the bears could do for me, but I knew they had a hell of a lot more technology than the Borschers.

The Bearland consulate was lit up with blazing electricity, unlike all the other houses on the street that had hundreds of candles burning in their front windows.

I didn't wait for the bear escort. I ran into the front door into a foyer with vaulted ceilings, flying saucer-sized chandelier, and a marble floor. A guard stopped me.

"Invitation?" he said, and held out his paw, white-gloved, but with holes for the claws.

"What?"

"Ball," said the guard, and looked me up and down. "Evening dress is expected."

I was not in evening dress. My Borschic standard was trousers, shirt, sweater vest, blazer, and cravat, but now it was just trousers, shirt and heavy overcoat.

"I need to see Grizzlyfeather, um, Grizzlyfaith," I said. "It's an emergency."

"Reinhardt?" The guard said.

The driver bears now joined me.

"The phase shift," I said. "I need to know if someone was left behind."

"There's been a phase shift?"

"Bearland Radio's reporting it," I said.

"Wait here," he said.

He went down a corridor, leaving me alone, and I wondered if he had any relatives on the Bear Air flight to Perth.

The guard came back with two bears in tuxedos, one smaller than the other and wearing glasses. I recognized the bigger as Grizzlyfaith.

"This is Churchbear, our communications officer," said Grizzlyfaith, motioning to the smaller bear as he hustled me down another marble-floored corridor. We went into an outer office with desks and typewriters, and then into another one marked PRIVATE.

In here it was the space age. Bearland had definitely come

into the late twentieth century. Refrigerator-sized computers, printers with paper feeding out of it, and terminals with glowing screens.

Churchbear sat next to a terminal while Grizzlyfaith pulled at a scroll of print out.

"Phase shift reported," he said, "to the public in Bearland at 23:22 hours yesterday. About an hour ago."

Grizzlyfaith grunted, continued pulling.

"Phase shift nearly complete," he went on, tapping on keys. "Wake nearly complete."

"Wake?" I said.

"This is a disaster," whispered Grizzlyfaith.

"Forecast is for..." Churchbear tapped some more keys, then hit enter. "A phase lasting six weeks to three years."

"My god," said Grizzlyfaith. "My god. Had they predicted this?"

"Predictions were for..." Churchbear leaned in towards to the screen. "No chance of shift this month."

"Blast it," said Grizzlyfaith. "Scientists."

"What's going on?" I asked, though it didn't matter. They completely ignored me.

Grizzlyfaith said, "Chance they saw it coming and pulled him back?"

"Look at the top secret telex," said Churchbear, and Grizzlyfaith shifted over to a second printer.

"Encrypted message," said Grizzlyfaith.

"Give it me," said Churchbear. "I'll soon have that translated."

He did. "Prime is away," he said. "Prime is away."

"Oh my god," said Grizzlyfaith.

I wondered whether Grizzlyfaith thought God was a bear, maybe a grizzly. Or a polar bear, in a white robe. Holding a bottle of cola.

"We need to act," said Grizzlyfaith. "See if there's been a communiqué from Central. Get all available agents on the job. We need to find Black."

"Yes, colonel," said Churchbear.

"What's going on?"

"We, ah," Grizzlyfaith said, and scratched at an ear with a claw, "to put it mildly, this is not the ideal moment for the Republic of Bearland."

I waited.

"Our prime minister was on a plane to Australia tonight."

"The Bear Air plane going to Perth?"

"No, it was an RAF transport. Because it was a top-secret visit to the PM of Australia, to discuss highly sensitive matters. We don't generally make ourselves visible in the wide world, Mr. Reinhardt. People like teddy bears, but they are scared of real live bears with teeth, especially ones that can fly jets. So almost all our diplomacy is on the quiet."

"So what you're saying is that the president of your country has been left behind?"

"That is admirably concise," said Grizzlyfaith. "Though not entirely accurate. We don't have a president per se."

"But you're okay, per se," I said. "Just let the vice, um, prime minister or whatever take over, and wait until the shift is over."

"Except that this PM was a very important person for our nation. More important than most PMs."

"You mean he was like a dictator."

Grizzlyfaith tried to shake his head, but couldn't. Bears are not good liars-- or maybe I should say, they don't like to lie. Despite their lack of facial expression, you can tell when they're making something up.

"Which means that Linus Black was right," I said. "Bearland is not democratic, and he wants it to be. The way it should be. Probably the way you guys have it set up, with a constitution and everything."

Grizzlyfaith grunted, something like *hummpf*, the Bearish way of saying "Whatever."

"That's why you want to pick up Junior," I said. "You don't want him to know the dictator is out of town, maybe for good."

"Be that as it may," said Grizzlyfaith. "You're with us, Mr.

Reinhardt. For the foreseeable future."

"What do you mean?"

"I'm sorry, but we can't let you leave the embassy," said Grizzlyfaith. "You know too much already."

"I don't know anything."

"Yes, you do," said Grizzlyfaith.

"No, I don't. I really don't. And I do have to leave, because I've got a hockey game to play tomorrow. And I believe they need me."

"We have to keep you until we pick up Linus Black. That way we know you won't have unauthorized communication with him."

"I won't have unauthorized communication. I promise."

"Hopefully we'll have him within 24 hours. We know he's in Borschland because his superiors assigned him to you. It's just a matter of finding him."

"What could I tell him?"

"No one in Borschland knows about the shift-- now. The shift will be reported in the afternoon papers, at the earliest, after everyone has woken up from the Kandelmaas celebration. And no one in Bearland knows about the PM's visit to Australia, except authorized personnel, and you, of course. So no one in the opposition knows. But they will find out soon enough. We have to make sure no one gets the jump on us before we get organized to resist no confidence."

"So what, if I go to Linus Black and tells everyone back home about the PM, they can do something about it?"

"Yes, they can vote no confidence in the government, and the PM would be forced to resign. New elections, and uncertainty about everything."

"But you can just fix the elections and everything will be okay, won't it?"

"It will be a sticky business and everyone's fur will get something on it," said Grizzlyfaith.

"So you just have to hope that this shift only lasts a few days or maybe hours."

"Yes, we do. The PM will come down with the flu. So make

yourself at home, Reinhardt. We will arrange accommodations for you. This shouldn't take long. We'll have you back on the ice in no time."

"I came to you for help."

"How so?"

"I need information on any airships that may have been up when the phase shift happened. My girlfr-- I mean, a friend may have been in the air when it happened, and I need to know."

"How do you know this, er, friend, was aloft?"

I thought for a second, then shrugged my shoulders. "It was the *lana.*"

"What?"

"I can't explain it now. I just need to know."

"We have a record of all Borschland naval activities. Churchbear, get the list for tonight."

Churchbear went to another printer and tore off a printout. "Do you know which ship the friend would have been in?"

"No."

"Any idea what the activity was? It is a she, I presume?"

"Yes."

"Not a naval officer, I presume."

"No."

"On Kandelmaas, in an airship."

"I don't know. Can you just, like, check?"

"There were no Borschic airships scheduled to fly above five hundred meters altitude tonight," Churchbear said. "About a dozen were scheduled for parade and lights around 18 hundred hours."

"Those ones I saw above the city tonight," I said to myself, aloud. "Did any of them take passengers, you know, like, on tours?"

Grizzlyfaith said, "Something like that would've been in the paper."

"Here's something," said Churchbear. "Out of Klaarwatters Base on the river. An officer's airship has been reported missing."

"What's that?"

"Routine communications are intercepted," said Grizzlyfaith. "Not in their top secret stream."

"Who was the officer?"

"A Commandant Kuurtschel."

"Doesn't ring a bell."

"All other ships reported docked for the night," said Churchbear.

"Does your friend know this man?"

Churchbear said, "Kuurtschel didn't take the ship. It's marked code ex jay vee, which means it was taken without the officer's permission."

"Maybe this friend is fond of, erm, riding with junior officers on Kandelmaas. Is she beautiful?"

I cocked my arm back to throw a punch at Grizzlyfaith, but Churchbear stood up and pulled me back. He was pretty strong for being a tech geek.

"If they're left behind," Grizzlyfaith said, "my condolences. But you know my first and only duty is to my country."

"Can't you send out a search plane or something? Come on. It's the least you can do."

"Churchbear, send Clawsharp up here to escort Reinhardt to his accommodations. We'll sort out this phase, and then…"

I still wanted to hit Grizzlyfaith. I settled for growling at him.

"Thank you, Reinhardt, for the alert," he said. "You've helped us. We won't forget that." And he left the room.

I figured I'd have to escape immediately or there would be no escaping forever. Once they put me in the dungeon, I'd probably have to penetrate six layers of security. But right now, it was only Churchbear, the tech officer, and then whoever Clawsharp was. But he was not quite in the room yet.

"I'm going to be sick," I said. "Where's the toilet?"

"Stay right here," said Churchbear, letting go my arm. "Won't be long and we'll get you into a suite."

"I'm going to be sick right on top of your best computer," I said. "I don't think you want that."

Churchbear screwed up his snout and showed his teeth. "Stop it. You're not."

"Where is it? I can't."

"Against the wall. Turn around. Not on the equipment!"

I turned, bent over like I was going to puke, then burst out of the room. It was an ace move, until I ran straight into a uniform, a blindside check with fur and salmon breath. I bounced off, and rolled.

"Stop!" the uniform shouted.

I didn't, though my ears were buzzing. I ran through the room with the typewriters and tried to open the door marked PRIVATE. The door wouldn't go. Click click. Locked. And about a millisecond after I figured that out, I realized there was a bear right behind me.

It was like fishing for a puck on the offensive sideboards with a defenseman gunning for me. I stepped aside from the door at the last minute, and he was going too fast to stop himself. The door was no match for a grizzly going at about a hundred miles an hour.

The guard flew into the hallway, went ass over teakettle, and slid on the marble along with a hundred separate pieces of door. I was out right after him. I ran down the hallway away from the foyer, doors on either side of me.

That corridor led to another one, right turn, which dead-ended in a window, with a stairwell to my left. I heard yelling in the distance, figured on not having time to open the window, and took the stairs up.

Floor 2 was identical to Floor 1: window, corridor, doors. I decided to try offices, see if there was a window open. Maybe I could jump to a roof.

I turned a corner towards the main wing and saw a she-bear in a long dress with an apron stooped over next to a mop and bucket.

Don't they let people take a night off in this place? I asked myself as I flew by her.

Then I was in the air, seriously.

The maid bear had stuck out her leg and tripped me.

"Reinhardt!" she hissed.

"Lavinia?"

"Get in here," Linus Black Jr.'s fiancée said, motioning with the mop to an open door. "I'll hinder them. Open the window, go down the fire escape, and go to the end of the alley. There'll be a cab waiting for you there."

"How'd you?" I began, but she closed the door behind me.

The window was open in that office, and there was a fire escape, as she said. I got out, went down, ran, and met the cab. The driver was a bear.

"Where to, sir?" said the cabbie, leaning over. It was that genteel pirate accent I knew so well.

"Junior!" I said.

"Quiet."

"We have to find Rachael. You have to help. Or I'm not helping you."

"Oh, we know where Rachael is. She's been under surveillance just as you have. How do you think we knew you went to the embassy tonight?"

"You really should give your people a night off."

"It's the republic we're talking about."

"Oh, yes. I forgot."

"Rachael went up in an airship with a certain, er, Kejls Muttik, a *lutnant ter aar* in the Borschland Navy."

"Rachael went up with a what?"

"I'm just telling you what our bear saw."

"But she's-- "

"Yours? Because you kissed her once while skating? Somehow I doubt that."

"With a sailor?"

"He's an officer. And I'm sure he has a bright future. He was so drunk they hardly got underway."

I shook my head. To think I passed up a perfectly good Zimrothian courtesan when she was out doing it in an airship with a navy guy.

"They were headed due south when our bear lost visual. So all we need to do is get you out of town and wait till they come down."

"Come down where? You do know there was a phase shift."

"Yes, we do."

"And you do know that they were left behind by it, but they're going to get back."

"No, I didn't. How do you know as much?"

"Well, the *lana*."

"Excuse me," said Junior, and looked me over. "What were you doing tonight at that flat of yours? Something having to do with the nation of Zimroth?"

"All I know is, we have to find her-- them. They may be in danger. Who knows? They may be lying on a hillside with their legs broken."

"Or they may be off-Continent," said Junior. "If they were too high, they've been left behind."

"But the *lana* said they haven't."

"Well, that's the definitive answer, isn't it?"

I shrugged. If he couldn't believe, then he couldn't believe.

Junior pointed to someplace far away. "We've got to get you across the frontier. You went right into the jaws of the beast. They've been wanting to hold you forever. They were just waiting for the moment when you came to them. Once you go into the embassy that's sovereign ground. The Borschic authorities couldn't get you out. It's against international law."

"But I have information you don't know about. I'm pretty sure you don't."

"What is that?"

"No. You've got to give me your word you're going to find Rachael and this other dude, before I give you the information. I know you have better technology than the Borschic government. You can find an airship, can't you?"

"The Borschers can find their own airships. And they would've found this one if it were under a five hundred meters and not left behind. Unless they were caught in the wake."

"What's the wake?"

"It's a disturbance of air. The phase shift creates a kind of splash when it happens. Waves of air are pushed and pulled. Like when a door slams if a window is open in another part of the house."

"Okay."

"The wake is a high speed disturbance at the level just below a thousand meters and above five hundred. It could push an airship a long way off course. Unless it simply ripped it to shreds."

"Oh."

"But Borschic balloons on airships are aerodynamically designed to fly horizontally in a wake. If the gondola didn't snap off, it may have just taken them on a merry ride."

"And they could have gone a long way."

"Certainly. They were headed south when the shift happened, so they could have flown as far as the frontier of the Twin Kingdoms. From Staff Borsch, that's only about a hundred and fifty miles, as the swan flies. Which is a lucky thing."

"Why?"

"Because that's where you're going. You're taking the next freight train to Alma, the southernmost city in Borschland, and from there a hay cart to the Twin Kingdoms, to wait this one out."

I decided to shut up. There was nothing more I could do about Rachael. Once I was in the Twin Kingdoms I could ask about her. I would have to wait.

"So what was that information you wanted to tell me about?"

"Wait. We're going to find Rachael, aren't we?"

"We?"

"Or you don't get the information. And it's good."

"All right. We. I will personally see to it that we rescue your beloved. So what's the information?"

"If you act fast, you can overthrow your government. Legally."

"Do tell."

And I did.

CHAPTER 25 - RACHAEL

When I woke I believed I was still in snow.

I was in a state of complete warmth and silence. I could feel nothing but the greatest soul-calming warmth ever.

But I was not in snow, I was in a bed. Beams, rough-hewn, extended above me, with straw peeking through the cracks. There was the smell of wood smoke and the snapping of a log in a fire, and the glow of that fire playing about the room.

I tried to stir my hands and was not able to do so, and my eyelashes touched something soft that had been fashioned in a straight line, and I realized it was the end of a quilt, pulled up over my nose.

Then it was that I became aware of my body enough that I knew I was encased in many layers of the warmest quilts anyone could ever imagine. And I was calm, though I seemingly could not move my body.

Some time before I had felt the same type of warmth when I was encased in snow. I had fallen into it, I knew as much, and was meters down in it, and I think it saved my life, for when Kejls and I finally lost the balloon, well and truly, and the emergency rope snapped, and we went headlong out of the gondola that was hurtling through the freezing air, I knew that we were still too high up to survive a fall onto hard ground.

The fact that we fell into snow-- deep, deep snow, which only falls on the faces of very high mountain slopes-- was our salvation.

Once we hit, I wish I could say I lost consciousness, but I did not. I lost sight of Kejls, and said a final prayer to St. Noos for his safety. I hit with a big ploof and it hurt and I thought, *I will soon find out what it is like to be dead*, and *Let's hope being dead takes away this annoying pain.*

But I did not die right away, or at least I did not see my aunt and uncle taking me away to begin my purification before joining the saints. Instead, my leg hurt and I couldn't move. Gradually the pain went away, and I said to myself, *Now I am dying. The pain is going away.*

But I did not die then, either, and I began to think that I must not have been very high up when I hit. After a time I began to see a vague light above me, and though I couldn't move and it was totally warm I thought, *This is the world above me. The world is still there, and I am not that far from it.*

I wish I could say that was when I lost consciousness, but I did not, and I began to fight with my arms against the weight against me, not with much success. And as if I were in a dream, I called out, a weak cry, and I could hear voices.

It is my aunt and uncle, I thought, but it was not. After a time I felt myself being pulled bodily from my prison, and with my last moment of consciousness I smelled clearly the scent of dog and felt the wetness of a dog's tongue against my cheek and the fermented meat smell of his breath.

So then I knew nothing, and did not dream, except for one dream when I saw a woman standing over me, an old woman with the pinkest, most wrinkled cheeks I'd ever seen. And she kept saying something like *poor, poor child*, but it was not in Borschic.

When I woke, therefore, I was not at all sure of where I was, or even whether I was dead or alive. But after checking the ceiling with its beams and straw, listening to the popping of the fire, and letting my eyelash flutter against the quilt, I began to be surer that I was alive, that I was in the world the saints call The Orb of Glass.

And to be frank, I began to feel a bit poetic, and I thought of a line of poesy, *what if the orb of glass were encased in feather down?* which scans rather well in certain Borschic meters. But that was all that came, especially after I turned my head and saw the back of a man's head, his blonde hair cut short from his tiny, pink ear.

Kejls was in bed with me.

He was asleep. I craned up a moment to see his face. His eyes were closed and he seemed at peace. I had never seen him such before. I think his mother would have liked to see such a demeanor upon him. He was handsome, in a young boy sort of way.

Then it all came flooding back, the midnight adventure with the balloon, the loss of grandmother's flatware, not to mention the thermos, and the phase shift and wake.

"We are home, we are here," I said to myself aloud, and it felt as if I had woken from a terrible, terrible dream.

But having Kejls next to me like that reminded me that what I had lived through was real, and that I had been very lucky, and that whoever was the owner of these quilts had been very kind indeed to Kejls and me.

I felt a wrinkled hand on my cheek and looked up. It was the old woman from my dream. She said something again, like *poor, poor child*, but it was not in Borschic. It was in the language of the Twin Kingdoms.

"Grandmother," I said in that language, for I have learned some of it in my holiday winters there, and she started, and took a step back.

"How do you fare, my little granddaughter?" she asked, in a rough whisper that was like a breeze through a bare bush.

"Well enough," I said, which was what I always said when peasants in the Kingdoms greeted me during winter holiday.

"God has let you live," she said. "And your husband."

That was when I had gotten enough feeling back in my body to realize that I had not a stitch of clothing on, and neither had Kejls. My body was laid up against his like two spoons in a drawer. But even more startling than this: as I tried to move my legs away from Kejls', I felt a stab of pain, and the splint against my left leg.

I cried out, and the old woman patted the quilts above the leg. "Rest," she said. "You are hurt."

"Where are my clothes?" I asked.

"Torn, torn," said the old woman. "You are blessed to have your husband's warmth to save you. You live because of him."

Ah, I thought. This is my destiny, to marry Kejls and have many little sensible children, who will never believe we even had an adventure, much less almost died from it. So it has been decreed by the *lana* of Zimroth.

And that is when I first thought of Sherm.

I had never felt so far away from anyone in my life, and yet so near. As if I were the little glass orb of the Continent and Sherm was the wide world. We brush up against one another, and then we are absent from one another, but always, always, somehow, we are one.

Kejls stirred, then startled, and cried out wordlessly.

"He is feverish," said the old woman, putting her hand to his forehead just long enough to confirm her statement.

The good peasants of whatever village in which we had landed had done an admirable job. They had set my broken leg and immobilized me and warmed us as best they could by placing us together to feed on each other's warmth. I owed them my life.

"Thank you," I managed to say, first in Borschic, then in Kingdom speech.

"God's voice to you," she said back to me, which is what the people of Dann and Kaatsch reply to thank you. They are great monotheists and mystics, which comes, no doubt, from living in utter quiet and isolation, and being able to hear the voice of God clearly and unambiguously. In Staff Borsch, the voice of God is quite unable to be heard, except by deacons in very, very quiet chapels. I have gone to such chapels at times to discern God's voice, but ended up only hearing my own. Which is why we in Borschland are so frequently asking the saints to pray for us. And why my poetry is still so feeble, though there are those who are pleased by it.

The old woman brought me a little bowl of broth, the darkest, deepest and most concentrated broth I have ever tasted, and fed it to me by spoonfuls as I lay there. Then she pulled back the covers for a moment and let me stretch, before tucking me tightly in again.

"Rest," she said, and patted the quilts in a quiet rhythm until I fell away again, and knew nothing for a very long time.

When I woke again a sparkle was playing off of all things in the room, and I knew the day was fine out, the sky deep blue. My strength was better for I was able to move my arms and push back the quilts to free them. I turned over, careful of the splint still on my leg, and saw that Kejls was gone. A little shock of fear hurt my heart, and I wondered if his fever had broken.

I sat up, and took in the room, a sturdy, rustic place with the beams I'd seen on the ceiling and walls made of stone, plaster and beams. A window of thick glass let in the light. There was a washstand with a bowl and towel, but no mirror, and a caned chair with a table next to it, and an ashtray on it carefully cleaned. The old women of the Kingdoms enjoy a pipe of tobacco now and then; it is their way.

My leg ached somewhat, but I felt a great desire to stand up, to test it, to see how far along I had come in whatever time I had been here. And I wanted to know where Kejls had been taken.

The old woman came in presently, a little pipe in her mouth, and greeted me gravely.

"Where is my… the gentleman?"

"We must needs move him," she said. "He is not well. My dear, the angel of God is over his bed."

I put my hand to my mouth. "Kejls!"

"The teacher has been in to pray for him," said the old woman. "It is in God's hands."

"I want to see him!" I cried.

The old woman nodded, and brought a heavy, woolen

nightgown for me. She sat me up, carefully making sure my splinted leg remained straight, and let the nightgown over my head. Then she brought me a crutch, and I stood properly upright for the first time since before the phase shift. I felt weak, and dizzy, and I sat back down.

"Perhaps you would wait," said the woman.

"If he is to die," I began, and again the woman nodded.

Saints, I thought. Married to a man for only the briefest of moments, and a widow for life. Many Borschic women never remarry, though I think this is from a surfeit of romantic sensibility-- or from a general intolerance of the baffling ways of Borschic men.

The woman brought me a washcloth, and I stood over the washstand with warm water and cold, and I dipped the cloth in the warm, and pressed it to my face, then the cold, until I felt better.

I used my crutch to walk through the hallway, and emerged in a front room, where the furniture had been pushed back and a large table was set in the middle. Kejls lay under a white sheet, face up, very pale. Several men with long beards stood about him.

I tried to say something in Dannish, but it came out as a little squeak.

"He is not dead, daughter," said one of the men. "It is in God's hands."

We stood there silently, me with my left hand at my mouth, my right leaning on the crutch, and the other men sitting, one of them mumbling prayers.

I was about to say, *he is not really my husband*, for it was, I confess, a moment of weakness for me, thinking that I might have to be a widow the rest of my life.

But in the next instant a young girl of sixteen or so came into the room. She was dressed in a simple, long dress that was gathered just above the waist. She wore stockings, clogs, and a bonnet over dark blonde, combed-back tresses that trailed in ringlets like angel's wings down her back. In her hands she held a saucer of steaming liquid. A tiny spoon rested on the plate that held the saucer.

"It is the death *tisande*," said the old woman. "Leah has made it herself."

"Death?" I squeaked in Borschic.

"Peace," said the woman. "It is begun."

The girl rested the plate on Kejls' chest, and took the tiny spoon. It struck me that she was as fine as the spoon itself, a slender little teenager with long, slender fingers, pale cheeks, a slight, curved nose, and lips that, when pursed, were like a little pearl.

She dipped the spoon in the *tisande*, blew on it, and placed it at Kejls' lips. "Young man," she whispered, the tiniest, sweetest little voice I have ever heard. He stirred, his lips opened, and she inserted the spoon.

"Oh," he breathed out, and I remembered all his oh's from the other night, when I used him-- used him!-- to console myself for Sherm Reinhardt's cloddish behavior. It was my fault that he was in this predicament, wholly and completely my sin that put him on this hard table under this unforgiving white sheet.

If you live, you will have my total devotion, I silently vowed to my darling Kejls. *And if you die...*

I stopped myself there, shameless thing that I was.

Leah, the girl, again fed him the *tisande*, the same as before, and I noticed that there was a spot of water on the sheet, just off of Kejls' covered shoulders. What a clumsy girl, I thought at first, she's spilling the medicine, and then I saw a drop of liquid fall from her cheek.

Saints above, I could only think to myself. Those are tears.

We stood there for an eternal moment while Leah, the weeping maiden, fed Kejls nearly all the *tisande*, and when she sighed and the spoon clinked at the bottom of the saucer, Kejls turned his face towards mine and his blue eyes appeared. They did not focus on me, but rolled back, and caught sight of Leah's angelic mien.

"Oh," he said, and startled a bit, and the man who had been mumbling prayers stopped.

We all gasped.

Leah hurried from the room, wiping her cheek, leaving the plate and saucer on Kejls' chest.

"It is good," said one of the men.

"Will he live?" I managed to ask.

"No, child," said the prayer mumbler. "But if he does, he will have ruined his own good death."

CHAPTER 26 - SHERM

I had never hopped on a freight car before, but I didn't think it would be that difficult. You just run as fast as you can and hold on to the handholds and pull yourself up.

Junior was smarter than me. We got on when the train wasn't moving.

We sat in the boxcar wedged in between bales of hay. Junior told me he couldn't accompany me very long, and didn't, only about a mile or so, and then he hopped off, because any bear traveling with any human is going to be noticed.

"We will get in touch with you when you are over the frontier," said Junior. "You will have no other contact with bears until then. In the meantime, this hay will keep you from freezing to death tonight."

The journey to Alma would take a long time, said Junior--over eight hours to go about a hundred and thirty miles. I needed to check in to a hotel on the outskirts of Alma that catered to guest workers from the Twin Kingdoms, and wait there until a guy in a hay cart came to get me. Then I would need to ride the last thirty miles to the frontier in a farm wagon, mixing with the guest workers and using the fake passport given to me by Junior.

"Good luck," he said, picking out his place to jump off.

"Same to you," I said. "By the way, I forgive you."

"For what?" he almost growled.

"For saying that guys were throwing games for me."

Junior continued to stick his snout out of the mouth of the freight car door. His eyes twinkled in the moonlight.

"How do you know it's not true?"

"Because I know you'd lie to save your country if you had to," I said. "And also because you're a bad liar."

Junior turned to me, and gave me a smile.

Then he jumped.

I never spent a colder night than the one in the boxcar. I spent the first hour unbaling enough to make a cocoon of hay for myself, and the last seven I spent rubbing my hands together and trying not to fall asleep.

The rail yard was deserted except for a few stray dogs. Snow was piled up along the sidings. The sun came up in a crack between the mountains, and half the sky was black with mountain.

I walked in the rail yard for what seemed like miles, until I found a hole in the fence and walked into an area of warehouses. A limp-eared dog passed in front of me, shivering.

On a street corner some men were warming their hands over an oil drum fire. They were mostly under five six, with skin like cracked leather, and scruffy beards. Definitely not Borschic folk.

I nodded at them as I joined them and put my hands out in front of the fire.

"Vaan Osten Guest House?" I tried.

"*Anfvorische*?" said one of them. They knew I wasn't a native speaker.

"Dannkaatsch," I said. "I go to Dannkaatsch."

They all looked at one another, their eyes wide.

"I take you to Vaan Osten," said one of them. "You take this."

And he took out an envelope from his inside jacket pocket. It was a letter. "To my family," he said.

"And to my family," said another, and took out a letter.

"And to mine," said a third.

They all had letters.

"You have no money for stamps?" I said.

They shook their heads.

It must have been about 8 AM when we got to the hotel, and it was not all that much warmer inside than it was out, but I was glad to get out of the cold.

The front desk man said, "You look for Levi. He come tomorrow."

So I waited most of that day in the kitchen of the hotel, where the stove kept things warm and I got fed about eight times, along with the men who would come now and then to the back door for a mug of coffee, steaming hot soup and a roll.

I slept in a cold room under a thick quilt, and the glass of water next to my bed almost froze. The next morning Levi came by in a hay cart, and fifteen or so of us, all Dannkaatschians who had stayed in the hotel, got up in it and sat in hay while he drove the twin donkey team.

Levi was brown and battered, and he spoke Borschic so slowly and simply I understood all of it. He and I had something in common. Borschic was a foreign language to us. We had to speak slowly and simply.

"When you come to border, don't say nothing, except Borschic maybe. Act you don't understand."

The other men were all tinkers or cobblers and had kits. I had nothing, but Levi said it didn't matter.

"You are son of tinker," he said. "You learn."

I showed him the letters the guest workers had given me.

"You don't have this on you," he said. "Contraband. Crime to hand carry letters to Twin Kingdoms."

He was about to throw them on the ground, but I caught his hand in mine. "This is their families," I said. "This is news for them. I buy stamps for them."

"No," said Levi. "No. Hold them. We will see."

I was feeling sore assed and hungry as we rolled into the

border station that evening, just as the sun was going down. The station was a two-story building along a stone-paved road that had been cleared of snow. Many carts were lined up to get across, and the Borschic guards, dressed in black with peaked caps with a black and white feather on the front that looked exactly like a striped border crossing gate.

"Hard man go home to dinner," said Levi as we waited. "Easy man now."

I saw what he meant when we met our guard, a very tall and skinny young man with blue-green eyes who knew Levi.

"Going home?" he asked, and motioned to the group of us.

"You see," said Levi. "As always."

Being six feet tall and pale-skinned, I stuck out to the guard, and he gave me a long look. If he'd been from anywhere but the sticks, he would've recognized me. Levi produced papers for me as the son of one of them, a five foot eight redhead

"This one is from an Anvorian *schpuns*," said the young man. I won't translate *schpuns*. "You must stop holidaying down there. Too many brats to feed, eh?"

Levi bristled. He was proud, even if I wasn't really that guy's son.

The guard was about to wave us through. But it couldn't be just that easy.

From down below we heard a hey-oh, which is the Borschic way of saying "hold up." Levi flashed me a look.

It was the "hard man." A guy appeared in the light of the street lamp below us, dude about the size of Norbert Grimm, huffing and puffing up the mountain and waving a scrap of paper I'm sure that said be on the lookout for the kidnappers of Sherm Reinhardt. But it wasn't.

"Telegram from TK," said the heavy-set guy as he came up to us. "TK" mean Twin Kingdoms. "Foxes."

"What?" said the tall one, and the heavy-set guy let him read the note.

Banditry across the border, said the telegram. Armed foxes abundant.

"We have to shut the crossing," said the tall man. "You

have to go back."

Levi hunched forward. "No place to stay, *lutnant.* Too cold outside. Guest house in Dann country. Just over frontier, see?" And he stuck out a knobby arm.

"Go back," said the tall man, pointing the opposite way.

Right then there was a bang and a crack and a shingle on the guardhouse fly up in the air, sliced in half.

"Take cover!" shouted the heavy-set guy.

Shots continued, and bullets drove into the ground around us. Both the guards drew pistols, but they lay behind the cart and didn't try to return fire.

Then the cart started moving. Maybe it was the donkeys that were spooked, but they walked forward, and the cart went with it.

Our group crouched behind the cart and crawled as moved towards the crossing. The gate moved up, like it was automatic.

Shots continued to fly over our heads.

"No," said the heavyset guy. "No crossing! Not authorized!"

Levi said, "Cart go, we stay behind. All safe that way, and you."

The cart rolled across the line and sank into the muddy, unpaved Dannkaatschian road. The border gate went down. The guards were now on Dannkaatschian soil.

"You go back, Kommandant," said Levi to the heavyset one.

"And the foxes kill us? No fear," he answered.

"Foxes gone," said Levi.

He was right. The shooting had stopped.

We raised our heads. It was dark on the Dannkaatschian side, no streetlamps. Their customs house was down the road, a distant twinkle of light.

The heavy-set guy trained his gun on Levi. "Do you have contraband?"

Levi held up his hands. "You in Twin Kingdoms, Kommandant. You know?"

"Not for long," he said. "Take the cart back, and all the

men. We're searching you up and down."

But then there was an *o-ho* from the road coming up from the Twin Kingdoms side. Border guards.

"Solomon?" said the heavy-set one.

"Wilvred?" came an answer.

"We heard shooting."

Two men appeared, panting. They had rifles slung over their shoulders on straps.

"Foxes," said Wilvred, holstering his weapon. "You have the telegram?"

"Always foxes," said Solomon, who was short and wiry and had a squared off beard.

"This cart has contraband," said Wilvred.

"Shalom, Levi," said Solomon. "*Evre tov.*"

Levi shook both guards' hand.

"We need this cart to come back." Wilvred insisted.

"What, have you found some unstamped letters?" Solomon said.

Levi poked me in the ribs with an elbow, and unzipped my jacket. The letters fell out.

Levi said something in Dannkaatschian to the guards, and they laughed. "So, Levi, pay the fine."

Levi said, "Fine? Cart stood in front of bullets for these men. Saved life."

All the men laughed.

The Borschic guards grumbled, but they went back. Three letters, two pistols, two rifles and a donkey cart added up to a story both sides would tell their friends-- in different ways.

"How far to a town?" I asked after we left the border guards.

"Schleeboz," said Levi. "Over mountain pass."

"Those were foxes?" I said.

Levi only smiled.

The path narrowed as we climbed, and we couldn't ride in the cart anymore-- too steep a grade. A mist began to form and lower as we walked, and the shreds and puffs of cold vapor lit up by the moon that had just risen, I felt like I was walking in a crowd of ghosts.

"Not far now," said Levi. "Less than ten kilometers."

Just then one of the men cried out something, and we all stopped. We were in a place of boulders, and even without the mist you wouldn't be able to see far. The path wound between the rocks. Every twist you'd think you were out of the maze, or above it, and every twist there'd be another rock.

The man in the front threw a rock up at a boulder and it skipped off and clattered away. Then he threw another one, and we all heard, as clear as anything, a growly voice saying "Ow!"

No one said anything. All of the men opened their coats and revealed guns of every description. Sawed-off shotguns, pistols, guns that had little brass attachments. They began firing in every direction. Contraband, all right. Now I knew what had happened up top at the Borschic crossing.

I crouched behind a wheel of the cart and tried to see something, anything. Then a figure ducked out from behind a boulder and aimed, almost point blank. It had a snout and a tail and was bundled in a heavy coat and cap.

Foxes I thought. Then, *I'm about to get shot.*

One of the men with the brass attachment gun fired, and out came a little ball that exploded against a rock and put up a cloud of purple smoke right in front of the fox in front of us.

"Run!" said Levi.

The foxes continued to return fire, and bullets whizzed and whined all around us, and bounced off boulders.

I looked back, and the smoke was all I could see. With the smoke and the mist they couldn't hit us in a million years, I thought. What a great idea.

And at that moment I felt a sting in the back of my thigh, and I went down like I'd forgotten how to run.

My leg flopped by itself and my pants leg turned dark. It felt like a puck had gotten through my pads and nailed me and it also felt like somebody had punched a metal bar through my knee. It also felt wet, kind of par for the course when you get shot.

I screamed ow and cursed several times and stupidly tried to turn over and sit up and look at the wound, but then the pain sort of took over and I lay on my side and just cursed a blue streak.

Two guys on either side of me pulled me up by my arms and dragged me through the snow. A line of blood trailed behind me as I bled into my boot.

They didn't drag me far, because I screamed holy hell at them that my leg was shot and they were making it hurt worse. They put me down inside a line of trees, on a bed of pine straw.

The shooting continued, but I couldn't hear it as well. I was screaming inside and outside with pain. One of the guys pulled out a big knife, cut my pants with it, and tore off the leg at mid thigh. My leg was gushing with blood. He took a bundle of gauze out of his pocket, wrapped the knee tight, and tied it with surgical tape.

Then somebody put me on his back and carried me, all the while with the leg feeling like it was going to fall off.

Finally somebody hit me with a shot of morphine, and that was it.

I woke up in a room somewhere, I don't know where, with my leg elevated and heavily bandaged. I think I must have been coming down off morphine, because as I woke up my leg started to throb, and the rest of me began to shiver.

Then I thought to myself, I wonder if I will ever play hockey again.

A nurse came in, a woman with a bonnet on and a white, stiff dress, and fed me some broth. There was a fireplace, and a big window, and she opened the screen and threw a chunk of wood in.

After a while a doctor came in, bald, with a little goatee, and undid the bandage on my leg. It hurt, but I was glad of it, because at least that meant it wasn't so bad that I had to have it taken off.

The doctor said, in this little high voice, with his lips bowed in and working his tongue, "You are lucky."

"You speak English," I said.

"We are paid by the bears," he said. "This is their facility."

"Where am I?"

"In the Twin Kingdoms. In Dann, about ten kilometers over the frontier from Borschland. It is a small town called Schleeboz. Very charming place. There is a lake that feeds an ice hockey pond. Many Borschers come here to ski."

"How's my leg?"

"You are lucky," he said again. "The bullet passed straight through the top of the patella and touched none of the cartilage. It was either a lower caliber bullet, or more likely, it was a piece of a bullet that had fractured in two, one of the pieces going one way, and another through your leg."

"Will I skate again?"

"I would not do so for several weeks. You must heal."

"But I can. I can continue to play hockey, can't I?"

"We will see," said the doctor.

"Is Junior here?"

"If you mean Mr. Black, I should rather say he has gone back to Bearland. They are having a governmental crisis there. The Prime Minister has been left behind-- so they are reporting."

"And what about Rachael? Did they find her?"

"I know nothing about a Rachael. A Borschic lass, I presume?"

"Junior promised he'd help find her."

"Nothing has been said to me," said the doctor.

A wireless set was brought in that got Bearland Radio Continental, and for the next two weeks I listened to all the political news, about the parliamentary procedure and how long the phase shift was going to last, and whether they should dissolve the government and call new elections. They had experts on from everywhere, and they interviewed all the RAF personnel and asked them how they felt about being away from their own world, and one of them said, *It's a bit like being in Antarctica, isn't it. You can't get in or out of there half the year, can you?* And everyone was very optimistic that the phase shift would be over soon, and the Prime Minister would come back from exile in Australia. The ruling party was hoping the phase would be over and they could retake power, and the opposition was hoping the phase would take a long time and the PM would not come back to organize his crowd.

I listened to the hockey scores, and to the speculation about where I was. No one knew. No one even in the town of Schleeboz knew. As I began to stand up and walk around on crutches and look out the window at this incredible blue lake that was ringed around with mountains, and snow on all the slopes and plenty of pine trees, I never got to go outside or even talk to anybody except my doctor and the stray Bearland opposition intelligence officer who came by and said I was a hero.

"When we take power again, we'll see you are decorated," said one of the officers.

"What happened to those foxes who ambushed us?"

"We took care of them," said the officer.

Te Staff lost all three of its games in those two weeks. It didn't matter who they played. They lost. In the meantime, Matexipar won two and tied one, and they took over first place in the league.

Bearland Radio reported that all Borschland was constantly talking about our Sherm and when he might come back. The doctor even said that some Borschland international investigators came to Schleeboz to see if perhaps I had come over the frontier at some point. They left with no knowledge, for no one except the doctor, his nurse, and the bears knew where I was. But they did watch some pretty good Dannish hockey, apparently. The local team had a great reputation.

One day, at the end of the third week, they allowed me out of the hospital to watch some hockey. The team was playing another team that had come over the mountain, kind of a local rivalry.

I'm not usually into watching a lot of hockey. I get antsy and I need to play. But since I was sick and tired of staring at white walls without a TV or a laptop or even a book, Sherm

Reinhardt became a big fan of Schleeboz hockey.

Turned out I wasn't the only one in the stands with a busted leg.

CHAPTER 27 - RACHAEL

I must confess that I shed not a few tears for my dearest, darling Kejls in the hours following the death *tisande* ceremony with the young girl, Leah.

And never had I been so moved to ask the prayers of all the saints. I remembered most of them from my school days, and asked them all in turn to preserve Kejls' life so that we could be married.

For many hours I prayed, or seemed to, as prayer can be very tedious, and my mind wandered for saints know how long. Tears streamed down, and eventually I came to pray to the Great God of us all, about whom Borschic people are very shy, wondering how great a being would ever concern himself or herself or itself with such small creatures as ourselves.

But being in the Twin Kingdoms made me feel closer to that Great Spirit, as the people there very easily converse with God and make their needs known and even are freely angry with God, so my father's friend, the Great Teacher, once told me.

So just before my exhaustion took me into a deep slumber, I asked the God of the Twin Kingdoms to heal my Kejls and forgive me my sin of self-pity.

It was the most religious I have ever been.

The next morning I rose, quite late it turned out, and there was a snowstorm outside. I immediately took this to mean that Kejls had gone, for I am a great believer in omens.

But nothing could have been further from the truth.

I lifted myself from the bed. A fine fire was going in the hearth. I found my crutch and rose, feeling stronger even than the day before. My body, it seemed, was determined to be better even if my heart were broken.

I hobbled out to the room where I had seen Kejls on the table the day before. I expected to see the sheet over him. I expected to be a widow the rest of my days.

Instead, the table was gone, and there were chairs set up in a half-circle.

In the chair in the center of the bow was my Kejls, looking very hale indeed, dressed in the trousers and sweater and boots of the men of the land. He had a mug of tea in one hand, steaming away, and on a little table next to him, a plate of rolls and a pot of jam.

On his right and left were two of the men I'd seen the day before, leaning back and smoking pipes. The old woman who cared for me was sitting at the edge of the assembly, next to Leah, who, as soon as she saw me, blushed scarlet.

"Rachael, you've awoke at last!" said Kejls. "Thank the saints you survived. They tell me you have just a small broken leg."

I could say nothing. The man who was on death's door the night before was thanking heaven for my safety?

The old woman stood up and went to get another chair, as I continued to stare at Kejls, who took a sip of tea from the mug and grinned stupidly at me, and then at all the rest of the group. Leah continued to look down at her hands in her lap.

When I was seated, Kejls said, "It's fantastic. Do you know what kind of adventure we've been through? They thought we were married, can you imagine?"

"Kejls" was all I could say.

"But I've made it clear we are not. It took much effort, but in the end I kept pointing to my finger and showing them there was no ring. Then they went and looked at your finger, too. I think they've finally gotten it into their heads we are not even betrothed."

Kejls, your promise I was about to say, but he went on babbling. "I tell you it's fantastic. I asked them how long I was asleep, and they put their fingers around the edge of that face right up there-- " he pointed at an ancient wooden clock over the mantle-- "thrice, which means about 36 hours I expect. But then I asked what day it was, and they showed me a calendar. We've been in this place for two weeks, dear Rachael!"

"That's not possible, unless…"

"Yes, unless we were lying in snow all that time. They've told me about that part as well. We've had a fine conversation this morning, Rachael. They told me how we were found face down in a snowdrift as tall as a house, and the balloon of the airship was punctured and tangled in a tree above. They still haven't found the gondola, just some wire and braces. It may have smashed to bits on a rock face." He gulped at his tea, coughed, and everyone leaned forward. He shook his head as if to say, *No, no, I'm all right.*

"My dear Rachael," he said after he'd composed himself from the cough, "we have survived a great adventure." Then he nodded at all the others in the room, who nodded back.

I said to the old woman, "He has told you he is not my husband?"

"Yes, child," said the old woman.

"He is not in his right mind. His wits have been taken by the fever."

The old woman clucked. "Tut tut, daughter. He is perfectly in his right mind. God has healed him."

"But we are marr… betrothed. He gave me his promise."

"Ah. But you are not betrothed unless he has chosen you and your father has given consent. Has he?"

I had to shake my head, for I am not given to dishonesty.

"So then," said the old woman. "It is quite clear. You are not betrothed, for he has not chosen you and your father has not given consent."

"But up in the air," I protested, jabbing my finger at the ceiling. "Up there, he promised me."

"We must not hold men to promises made in the very face of death," said the old woman. "Men are excitable and prone to say anything at these times."

"Rachael," said Kejls, "what are you speaking of? You seem vexed." He put down his mug on the little table.

"Kejls, how could you?" I said, and slapped my knee.

It was at that moment that the beautiful and darkly blushing Leah burst out of the room, sobbing.

Kejls bolted up as she left, upsetting his tea and rolls. Suddenly everyone seemed to be standing except me, and then everyone was on his or her knees, mopping up spilled tea, righting the basket, hunting down stray rolls.

All during this time, I simply stared at Kejls and he stared at me, with this very frightened rabbit look.

"When we return to Borschland, you are going to go straight to my father's house and ask for my hand in marriage," I said.

"Oh."

"Don't you remember what you promised? Don't you remember saying if we made it through this you would marry me?"

"Oh. No. I hardly remember-- "

"Remember what?"

"Even going up in the airship. I think I must have been very drunk."

"Well, you were. Shamefully."

"And so."

"And so what?"

"And so I do not remember promising you anything." He rubbed his hands on his thighs. "Truthfully, Rachael. If it were any day but today, I think I would have been glad of it."

"It?"

"Yes. Your wanting me to marry you. But now it's different."

The others had stopped their cleaning to listen to the conversation. They were still on their knees.

"What do you mean, different?"

"Well, you see. Now there's someone else."

"What? What are you saying, Kejls Muttik? I prayed for you. I prayed for you to be healed."

"I know," said Kejls. "Or at least, I'm sure you did. But you see, the girl that was just in here. Her name is Leah."

"Yes, that little skinny thing?"

"Yes. Well, when I woke up this morning she was there, I mean, here, next to the table where they'd put me. She was waiting up. She hadn't slept. And when I saw her, I-- "

I rolled my eyes. Unbelievable. *Unglaaberlickt*, as we say in Borschland.

"Just wait, Rachael. Listen. Then they all came in here and told me she had saved my life with a special tea."

"She is much too young for you."

"She is only three years younger than you, Rachael. I asked, and they counted out on their fingers. And her father here"-- he motioned to one of the bearded men-- "has already given me permission to marry her, after I have worked in his sawmill for a year's time, and I have proven myself a worthy groom."

"What? You have already worked out a deal to marry this child?"

"She is not a child. She is marriageable. They have said so." We stared at each other for a time, and then he said, "Be honest, Rachael. You are not even very much older than she is."

"You cannot even SPEAK Dannish," I burst out, shaking my fists.

"Quiet, quiet," he said, as if someone were ill in the next room. "Calm down. It is not so difficult to speak when you are speaking of matters of *Te Hart*."

He looked all about him. The others were on their knees, nodding.

"Girl," said the old woman, finally getting up, "Be gracious. A man who has survived the death *tisande* deserves the woman who gave it to him."

The others grunted in approval, and I put my hand to my temple. "So you are resigning your commission in the Borschland Navy, I presume?"

"I must. I have greatly shamed my country by destroying its property. But the saints and angels have seen fit to put me in a place where I will be happy. I will go back after the proper amount of time, and face charges, make restitution, and then return here."

"And be a woodchopper the rest of your life?"

"As long as it is with Leah, it will be a good life."

Well, I thought. Let's see how well he likes it after a year breaking his back with an axe and coughing up sawdust while waiting for a girl who doesn't even speak his language.

Doesn't even speak his language. The words rang like a bell in my head, and I realized: that describes a certain other foreigner I'd lately been interested in, Sherman Reinhardt.

What a fool's errand I've been on, thought I. The only blessing I can see now is that possibly it will be grist for my poetry. Though terribly embarrassing it will all be if I do happen to write about it. I thought I must stick very definitely to nature poems.

Poems about the purity and chastity of snow.

There was nothing for it now, but to find a way back to Borschland. I asked how far it was back to the frontier, and the old woman said not far, perhaps thirty kilometers down the mountain. Was there a telegraph in the town? I asked. No, she said. But there was one in the town of Schleeboz just over the ridge, and I could send a messenger if I liked with the next bag of mail.

I wrote out a message to my parents saying Kejls and I were both safe, but nothing about Kejls' marriage plans. I expected he would want to break the good news to his family on his own.

The snowstorm delayed the mailbag a day, and in that time

I talked with Kejls again about the phase shift, and he said it was quite likely we had lost time during the shift and that was why we came out two weeks later.

The next day the weather was fine, and the entire town was setting out to Schleeboz for a hockey game with the local eighteen of their town.

"You must come," said Kejls. "A bit of hockey to warm up your Borschic heart?"

Kejls was unrepentantly cheerful and pink-cheeked. I hated him for it. But I had to admit, as we were loading sledges with provisions and blankets, this land and this people agreed with him. Sometimes it just takes a change of scenery, and a people to believe in you, for your natural talents to blossom.

The horses' harnesses went a-jingle as we cut our way through the deep snow on a path that was hardly big enough for us. There may have been a hundred of us in the procession. That is how small that town was. When we topped the last ridge, a long, sparkling lake came into view, with a collection of stone houses trailing up a hill nearby. For the first time since I'd been in the Twin Kingdoms, my heart thrilled. I was safe. Soon I'd be home. And I would see my beloved Papaa and Muuttuj again.

We piled into the public room of a guesthouse, where the teams had a meal and there was music and speeches and storytelling and much Dannish beer and wild berry wine. As a woman I was allowed no beer, but by the end of the meal I had lined up quite a few tiny glasses of the wine, which was very sweet and potent.

Then we all repaired to a pond where there was an ice rink, and the people lit up the area with torches. Everyone stood on the banks of the pond, or, in the case of the old women and me, in a rough-hewn hut, out of the elements on chairs under many blankets.

The young men played a rough and ready game, with the puck flying about like an electron, and the boys flying after it in masses. At times they would pass it about expertly as if imitating Te Staff, and then it would all break down into chaos, usually ending with someone whacking the puck past one or the other confused goal minder.

After two periods the score sat at 7 goals to 6 in favor of Schleeboz, and our side was ecstatic with the team's efforts. "We have not won or drawn versus the city in many years," said the old woman. The sun was setting behind clouds and the shadows lengthening, and as I had had perhaps one wild berry wine too many, I began feeling very romantic about this lovely place and setting, as our little contingent from the small town in the mountains was holding its own against the taller and heavier Schleebozians.

Then it was that I saw two things I never thought I would see.

At the start of the third period, a slight young man strapped on a helmet and skated out with the boys.

Everyone in our group began screaming "Kejls! Kejls! Kejls!"

A man below me said to the other, "These Borschlanders are great skaters."

I was astonished. But then even more so when I saw, limping up the hillside toward me, the last face I ever dreamed of seeing.

He took me in as if I were the first woman he had ever seen. "Rachael?" he said, as if it were the first woman's name he had ever said.

I tried to nod but could only stare. Part of me was still angry at him for leaving me during Kandelmaas, but the wild berry wine made his face look ever so much more beautiful than I remembered it.

"*Unglaaberlickt*," we said at the same time.

The old woman cocked her head and took her pipe out of her mouth.

"You're hurt," I said, and he pointed at my leg, that stood out from the blanket at a right angle.

"I look for you," he said. "Every day I think, where is Rachael?"

"You've found me," I said.

"I thought..."

"You thought I was dead?"

There was a great roar. The Schleebozians had scored a goal, and were celebrating. At the other end of the ice, Kejls was rallying the troops.

"Your officer?" said Sherm, motioning down to the ice.

"Not mine," I said. "He is betrothed to another."

Sherm stuck his hands in his pockets. "Good," was all he said.

"Good? In what fashion, if I may ask?"

"I want to marry you," he said. "Please."

The old woman said, "You see how God knows best, child. Here is your husband."

I stood up. "Sherm Reinhardt," I said, "You are *unglaaberlickt*."

He limped towards me, and though he seemed very weak, he took me in his arms in such a decisive way that it was impossible not to kiss him when he brought my lips up to his.

We took a long time on that very first kiss. Time seemed to stop. Maybe there was another phase shift. I had a sense that we were losing weeks out of our lives. I must have tasted shamefully of wild berry wine to him, but he had been, I think, eating mints and violet blossoms all day, and his rough beard against my cheek felt like finest silk.

Then there was another roar from the crowd, and the Schleebozians had scored another, and we both disengaged our faces from the other, and Kejls was being helped from the ice with his arm crooked next to his chest.

"He is a hero," I said in Sherm's ear.

He looked at me, maybe for the first time, with understanding of who he was and who I was. At least that is what the depths of his eyes told me. "I love you," he whispered.

I gasped. It is almost never in the life of a Borschic woman that she will ever hear these words from a man, even her own husband, though it is greatly rumored there are some from Vinasola who will say it for the sake of receiving even one kiss.

Borschic men are very reserved (Kejls, poor broken-winged Kejls, having now proved an exception) and most of the time their women must be content with the knowledge that their man has provided for them and speaks well of them outside the home.

"I love you, darling," I managed to say. I thought it very stupid and inappropriate. But he seemed not to mind, as we began another weeks-long kiss.

All crowded around, and the game was quite forgotten, except for those who were playing it, and for Leah, of course.

Sherm's physician joined us finally, and as he spoke fluent Borschic, Dannish, and English, was able both to be informed and to inform on all the goings-on.

"The bears of the opposition party in Bearland expect he will be able to return to Borschland very soon," the physician explained. "They are hopeful that after parliamentary elections there will be recalls and prosecutions and everyone who was an enemy to Sherm will no longer be in Borschland."

"I wonder if you will marry us this evening, doctor," said Sherm.

"I cannot. But there is a teacher in town who I'm sure will be willing. We are very big on weddings here."

I whispered to Sherm, "In Borschland we are married after we have spent a night together."

"Wow."

"But if you wish it."

He smiled. All of the confidence of the ice was in him now. He told the doctor we would want a party and a short ceremony. "And then we go home and your father-- we are in a big church-- and I can invite my sister Cathy."

But I had another idea, for I was still feeling the effects of the wine. "Let's not go home yet. The phase shift is still on and your sister cannot visit. Why don't we honeymoon in our cottage near Dejndeech, south of here? It is so beautiful and cozy. We can ski every day."

"Or not," said Sherm, and I giggled like a girl.

"There is no direct train to Dejndeech," said the physician.

"Most people walk a day's journey over the mountain and then another two days down the mountain to the valley. There are guest houses along the way, and a train in the town of Khaan Koob."

"Do we really have to walk?" I said.

"You might get the Bears to take you in their airplane. There is a strip not far from here."

"No, thank you!" I said.

"What about a wagon?" Sherm said.

"We will think of something," said the doctor.

So it was that Sherm Reinhardt and I were married that very night, and I came into the knowledge of him and he of me. It is not appropriate to speak of what happened exactly that night, for there were some complications with legs, but we both contented ourselves with ourselves and managed to love each other with deep passion and with the soaring of angels above us. We laughed about it for many days afterwards, especially along the way to our cottage, a journey fraught with snowstorms and meetings with folk who thought we were well and truly insane to be traveling by donkey and guide at that time of year, but who opened their homes to us one and all when they found we were newlyweds.

That is a story for another book, I think.

We took a darling little train down the mountain, and a spur line took us directly to the town of our cottage, where the telegraph operator had a lovely message of congratulations from my parents. We spent a good long eight days in our cottage, using our injuries as an excuse not to ski. I wrote much bad poetry during this time, and while I wrote Sherm read from our library and improved his Borschic mightily. Then we took the train to Dejndeech and there a physician took an x-ray picture, removed my splint and proclaimed that I was very much on the mend and a lucky young lady indeed.

Then, with the knowledge that in Bearland the emergency elections had gone splendidly for the opposition, which was now the ruling party, we took the train home for Borschland, where we were greeted by the thousands as returning royalty, and my mother and father had both the stern words of devoted parents (though they had found, at least, the meat knife that Kejls could not) and the practical sentence that I knew someday would be on their lips.

"When do you wish your father to perform the ceremony?"

CHAPTER 28 - KADMUS

The return of Sherm Reinhardt and Rachael Martujns to Borschland was almost as momentous as the return of Sherm Reinhardt to the ice of Te Rijngk.

In the four weeks Sherm was gone, three weeks not knowing a thing, and a fourth for the honeymoon with his best beloved, and a phase shift thrown in for good measure, Te Staff had played a total of 5 games, and had won 1, lost 3, and tied 1. Fortunately, they had won thirteen of their first half games and drew only with Matexipar and Atterische, so now were sitting at 14 wins, 3 losses, and 3 ties, with ten games left to go. Matexipar, who had gone 2-1-2 in the same stretch, had 14 wins, 2 losses, and 4 ties; by the calculus of the league, therefore, Matexipar stood with 46 points at the top of the table, and Te Staff with 45, right behind them. The decisive battle with the Iron Sticks would be happening in one week's time. If, as all believed, Te Staff could rally and gather itself and win that game on home ice, they would be inspired to win the rest of their games and win the League's Championship at 24-3-3 even if Matexipar won all theirs and finished 23-3-4.

Borschland was overjoyed to welcome back its newest married couple, *Meester* and *Madaam* Reinhardt, who repaired to the home of Archdeacon Martujns amidst much pomp. The next day, Sherm reported to practice with the team, a scant four days before the Matexipar game. He was first fined by the team for going absent without permission, and docked his five games' pay, but then the team paid him the customary wedding gift, which was five games' pay, and so he came out even.

Of his adventures in the Twin Kingdoms Sherm would say little, except that he went to find Rachael, whom he knew somehow had been blown south by the wake of the phase shift. Rachael said only that she had accepted the invitation of a young naval officer for a ride in his airship, and that they had unwittingly been caught up in the phase and the wake, and were very fortunate to have landed in a deep snowdrift when the wake finally squirted them out of itself next to a mountainside in Dann.

The young naval officer, Kejls Muttik, would stay behind in the hamlet of Lamedh, some thirty kilometers from the frontier of Borschland, to work at the business of his father-in-law-to-be. It is said that Dannkaatschian lasses are among the shyest in all the Continent, but our intrepid journalists managed to get a shot of the couple sitting in her father's house amid tea and rolls.

So this might have seemed the end of the story for those readers who are concerned with romance. But it is not quite the end of the story for the rest of us, for there is another and quite a dark chapter still to be told, which I greatly wish did not have to be.

But that is the way of *Te Hart.*

CHAPTER 29 - SHERM

I think the thing that was most surprising was that I didn't need Busby anymore.

Back in Staff Borsch he was one of the first ones at my side, but when the questions started coming I understood them and answered on my own, and he stood behind me and after I was done he turned away.

Before practice he sat in a corner in the locker room, arms over his chest, looking miffed. He didn't ask me about Nemeth, and I didn't say more than "hi" to him.

But the guys had plenty to say.

Unlike Rachael they talked mostly hockey, with a bunch of dirty jokes mixed in, like any hockey locker room. I wasn't surprised, really, based on how they'd been before I understood.

"So you are back," said one guy. "Do you have any legs after that honeymoon?"

"Give him a break," said Chrujstoff. "He has been learning another game. He is only used to one kind of stick."

"But he has been scoring many goals with the other one," said the first guy. "He is tired out."

To which I said, "So sorry, boys, but it looks like you yourselves have been using your dicks for sticks the last few weeks."

They all woo-wooed and whistled. Chrujstoff said, "This poetess is clearly teaching you all the wrong words."

Then someone was quick to say, "But all the right moves."

This broke them up, and they held their sides from laughing, and it would have gone on a long time, probably forever, except that *Meester* Chrojstenkaamps entered the locker room along with his two assistants, and stopped right in front of me.

"Reinhardt. Good to have you back. The doctor tells me you were shot in the leg. Well, get out there and skate the best you can."

Suddenly it was quiet as a funeral. It was the longest speech he'd ever given, the entire season. And it was the first anyone heard that I'd been shot in the leg. That shut everyone up quick.

I was examined by the doc when I got back, and he saw the entry hole scar and the exit hole scar, and said I was really lucky, and did I feel okay to skate? I told him I wouldn't know until I got out there.

And so I did. I put on all my gear, feeling rusty and creaky, and stretched out best I could, noticing that the bad leg would not really stretch quite right.

Out on the ice, I took a few laps and bent into a couple of shots. I nodded at Chrojstenkaamps, who nodded back. We were playing Mat X in a few days and needed to win. It was personal with Cramps, I could tell. He wanted it bad.

We went over offensive strategy a bit, standing out there and leaning on our sticks, and then we did a bit of light scrimmaging, everyone quiet and tense, because they were worried about me.

At the end of the practice, I said I felt okay, though my leg was aching, and the guys bopped me on the shoulder or tousled my hair. Gone, the jokes about scoring goals in a new game with a different stick.

"You really got shot in the leg?" said Norbert.

It was going to be a tough week.

When I got home to my apartment, Rachael was there with the windows wide open and the place freezing.

I had told her about Nemeth, the *lana*, and the cards during our honeymoon, but she said that when she got to my place it still smelled like her perfume.

"So you would not lie in love with this temptress?" Rachael said, in her very dramatic and poetic way.

"She was disappointed. Wasn't used to being, um, not taken."

Rachael laughed. "And did you engage her yourself? As a salve against losing me?"

"No," I said. "She said it was Busby. He was always interested in me, um, having one."

"I don't like that man," she said. "There is something… *eenickt* about him."

"*Enicht*?"

"False. Hidden."

"He's been good to me. He is a bit…" I wanted to say that Busby had issues, but was basically good. I couldn't express it exactly in Borschic. "…He has a few problems."

"*Enicht*," she said again, and we spent a long time talking over all that he had ever said or done. We had that kind of time to hash things out.

I mostly took Busby's side, but when I got back that whole conversation colored the way I looked at him.

In the old days, he and I would've gone out to dinner after practice and we could've fought it out about Nemeth. But he disappeared, and I was eager to get home to Rachael anyway.

We took a cab over to the parents' house and had a nice dinner with wine and then went out to see a show with a bunch of photographers trailing after us, and I forgot about Busby till practice the next day.

It was funny. Everyone else was nursing little injuries, and their legs were heavy from skating all season. I'd taken a few weeks off, and I felt pretty good stamina-wise. But my hurt leg stopped me from skating all out.

"Matexipar will be testing you, Sherm," said one of the

assistants one day. "Do not be surprised if they stick hack you on the back of your leg."

The papers had gotten wind of my injury, and though no one knew the details, that didn't stop people from speculating. In Matexipar, it was all over the front page. "Reinhardt nursing gunshot wound" was the nicest. There was also "Reinhardt injury proves North Americans bring violence to Borschland." And then, the most ridiculous, "Is it safe to be at a hockey game with Reinhardt playing?"

Telegrams and letters started coming in from all over, mostly people wanting me not to play if I was not okay. But several came from Matexipar, or at least Their supporters, who told me I should get out of Borschland as soon as the shift was over.

A couple even said I shouldn't play.

Then there was the anonymous letter that said YOU WILL NOT LEAVE THIS GAME ALIVE.

I didn't show Rachael that one. I wonder how many the team intercepted and didn't show to me.

Busby was scarce. Someone said he was translating documents for a goaltender out of Bearland who was going to join the junior team in Oststaff, and maybe he'd be that bear's translator.

Two days before the game the team told us we couldn't go out after dark, none of us on the team, but I knew the rule was aimed at me.

Rachael and I spent the last two nights in my apartment looking in the papers for new digs.

The next day, the phase shift tossed us back into the real world.

And it was like the full moon times a thousand.

CHAPTER 30 - KADMUS

It does not often happen that a phase shift occurs during an actual hockey game.

Shifts can occur any time of the day or night. And most of the time, they are not noticed. But if it is an awkward shift, the phase has some of the properties of an earthquake. There is a shudder, a movement of the earth under one's feet, even a sense that one's vision is blurred or the whole world goes out of focus for a moment.

I have never seen the city at a greater fever pitch. Our Sherm seemed to have arrived in the nick of time, and even to have given himself a week to patch himself up and steel himself for the most difficult game of the year. Of course, we did not know at first that there had been some kind of gunplay involved in Sherm's disappearance. Guns are not frequently seen in Borschland. Wars are something we try to prevent. Violence, in general, is confined to the checking of an opponent on the ice, or perhaps, a tiff between two swains for one girl.

So everyone was quite astonished, and many theories were tried out in the papers, until the team gave an official version mid-week, saying that a Dannish hunter's weapon had gone off accidentally while he was guiding Sherm and Rachael through the mountains of the Twin Kingdoms. This gave the nation something to talk about for another 36 hours, until some columnist or other (certainly not me) found a way to prove that that account could not be true, by the basic laws of physics.

On the ice, Sherm was skating and moving and stickhandling, and the team let the press attend a number of workouts, not of course with any sensitive strategies being discussed or tested. We asked him how he felt, and he showed off his Borschic language prowess, which, so his wife had told the women's section of the paper, he had been gaining all along, except that the team wished him to be perfectly understood until he could express himself properly.

"I am ready," he said many times. "I am confident that as soon as the game begins, I will be my old self again."

That "as soon as" was pounced on by the myriads of writers whom the papers assigned to Sherm himself, as an indication that he was not quite his old self yet. And that was true, because he was not his old self when the game began. He was not Sherm Reinhardt at all.

The Rijngk had never been so full. The grandstands were bursting, and the standing room on the other side of the bank was stuffed with humanity. In the press box, we could hardly sit down. I could not believe the number of men who had gotten credentials.

Matexipar skated out as shiny as you please, with their red uniforms with black piping and silver skates, big and imposing and confident and very cognizant of the fact that Te Staff had tied them on their home ice in the first half. If they could win the game, they would even be able to lose one of their remaining games or draw two, and still win the championship. Even a draw in this game would mean a crown if they won the rest of their games. The only thing between them and glory was Te Staff and its lamed first-line center.

The roars for Te Staff began as soon as our boys took the ice, white sweaters with black and gold trim. Sherm skated out, number 6, the usual number for the first-line center, and the teams whirled about in their own end while the electric lights bounced off the ice and the flash bulbs of the photographers blazed.

Then it was time for the game to begin, and Te Staff lost the first faceoff, and from there it was pure disaster.

It was as if Te Staff was a collection of little boys standing on the beach with little pails of sand, watching wave after wave come in and obliterate their little sand houses. Nothing the team did on offense came to fruition, and one or more of the forwards would be knocked on their teakettles and spinning about while Matexipar began a rush to the other side of the ice.

The Iron Sticks rocketed puck after puck at Norbert, who stood fast for about a quarter hour. Then, like the city of Bevinlunz when the Vinasolan Navy attacked in the year 165, he was breached. By the end of the first period, the score was two to nil, and the whole city sat in stunned silence.

On the wireless, venerable announcer Smick Silbersglaad could hardly raise his voice above a whisper, while analyst Jaan Blink, who had been a great first-line center himself, kept saying that Reinhardt must not be himself.

Sherm hardly played. He would take a shift and skate aimlessly about, chase a puck that was too far away, let a puck go that was close enough to take. He missed passes, was knocked down, and could never set himself to shoot. Gradually, *Meester* Chrojstenkaamps began limiting his shifts until he missed two at the end of the period.

In the second period, Chrujstoff took over as first line center, as he had been in the five games of Sherm's disappearance. Without Sherm, the team seemed to find itself, for it had grown somewhat used to no Sherm, and scored a surprising goal at 5 minutes gone in the second period. The team had been able to besiege the Matexipar goal, and the officials had called a penalty, and Hauke Sybranduj tapped in a puck on the weak side with the Iron Sticks one skater the less.

Then Matexipar's ebb tide reversed, and they were pounding on the castle walls again. Fortunately for our boys, Norbert stopped everything, and the period ended with Te

Staff on the short end of a 2-1 score.

Talk on the wireless and in the press box had shifted from Sherm-- for we all believed he had been injured in the first period, and that was why he did not come out for period two-- to the possibility that the team could win even without the superstar North American.

The team sent up a message between periods just to this effect, that Sherm had re-injured his leg and would not return.

Which was all the more confusing when, at the beginning of the period, number 6 took the first faceoff, won it, and smartly guided the puck to defenseman Gerd Droobink, who sent a headman pass to right winger Alois Kveck, who sprinted into the corner as if he'd been strapped onto a cannonball. He then passed back to number 6 behind the goal, who shrugged off a defender like a light spring jacket, and stuffed the puck into the goal on a wraparound, a move Sherm Reinhardt himself had popularized.

You never saw such an overturning of coffee mugs and dropping of brandy flasks in a press box.

Nor did you ever see a group of men scribbling on scraps if paper or pounding on keys faster and more feverishly.

Nor telegraph machines tapping nonstop to telegraph offices from Vinasola to Bearland.

The crowd was perhaps not delirious, but more than that, ready to be institutionalized. I had never heard such a noise before. It struck the very heavens and bounced down, amplified all the more because the little glass orb that is our world had its glass ceiling while phase-shifted. The bank on the other side was a solid wall of black and white scarves, moving, flaring, a blur.

Then it was on. Two teams of men, equally matched, equally motivated. This number 6, whom we had not seen before, had transformed Te Staff from a team that was desperately hanging on to the edge of a cliff to a band of marauders fanatically dedicated to plunder, pillage and rapine.

Matexipar, for its part, seemed to hesitate for a moment, shudder, and stall, but then threw the throttle into full forward.

The result was mayhem, bodies flying, the puck screaming from end to end, the officials bewildered and as much become onlookers as any one of us.

We all looked through our field glasses at this new number 6, fully expecting to see some alien face, perhaps one we had never seen before. Instead, we saw Sherm Reinhardt, clean-shaven, the way we'd seen him early in the season before he grew the beard. Had he simply shaven between periods, and like some reverse Samson, gained strength from the loss of locks?

After that first goal, Sherm came back for more, won the faceoff, and Te Staff steamed into Matexipar's end. Left wing Uwe Sipken stung a shot at the goalie, who let it come free right in front of the goal. Sherm was there and directed the puck to the goalie's left shoulder. Only a miracle-- and the top of the pipe-- stopped that scone from going in.

If it had gone in, I have no doubt we would have won the game 20-2. But the actual final score was just as astonishing.

CHAPTER 31 - SHERM

When I got to 14 Waatersdram that afternoon I was called immediately into the office.

Cramps was there, along with the assistants, the owner of the club Mr. Vujlsbarron, his assistant, and Busby.

"Sit down, Reinhardt," said Cramps. The overhead bulbs swung as the door slammed behind us.

"Here is the situation," said one of the assistants. "You know you've been getting a certain number of… er… letters."

The other said, "And Mr. Busby has had an idea. We think it's a good one."

Busby said, in Borschic, "You know I've been… ah… absent for a couple of days. I've been looking for someone who could help us."

I shook my head.

"The death threats you've been getting. We think-- the police think-- they are credible."

"We don't want you in the game, Reinhardt," said the first assistant. "Just in case someone wants to harm you, publicly, for some political gain."

"So…"

"So we've engaged a double," said Busby. He looks like you. We will give him a helmet on the pretense that you are just being cautious after your ordeal. Under a helmet no one will notice. This man can skate. He's played hockey. He understands the danger. But we've fitted him with a bulletproof vest. He'll go out there for the first period, and the police will comb the crowd. If we can see there's no danger, you can go out for the second period."

"That's…" I tried. "That's…"

"It's for your own good, Reinhardt, and the good of the nation," said Vujlsbarron. "If there's one thing we don't want, it's an assassination. There hasn't been one for some time, and we don't want there to be. We realize we are being cautious, but some things, er, are more important than hockey games."

"Let me go out there," I said. "Let me put on the helmet and the vest."

"We want you in one piece, Reinhardt," said Vujlsbarron. "It's one period. After that, you can go out and play."

"We've got to beat this team."

"Anyway," said Busby in English, "it'll be more dramatic when you do win."

"What are you talking about? Did you fix this game?"

"In Borschic," said Crampsy, and Busby immediately went into translator mode.

"He's concerned. I'm trying to encourage him, but he's concerned."

"Well you might be," said the assistant.

The other said, "We need you, Reinhardt. We'll win. We're on home ice, and you're going to give the boys a big charge when you come in."

"Listen," I said. "I need to know one thing before I agree to this. You need to swear on your mothers that when that puck drops, no one on either side will just give me the game. Just because someone…" I didn't know the word for fixer. "…Wants me to win. You're not telling the players to go soft or the other goalie to let one in. They're not being paid to let me score goals."

The room went as silent as a graveyard. First of all, it was the longest speech I'd ever made. They all stared at me like I'd accused them of sleeping with their grandmothers. Only Busby had an expression that was anything less than total shock.

Cramps said, "Busby, one period."

And that was it. We went to the pre-game press conference, where it was established I was okay but not completely one hundred percent. It was a great smokescreen that I was answering all my own questions. They all wanted to know what it was like being me now that I was a real person-- you know, a Borschic speaking person.

I skated a warm-up, and went back in the locker room with everyone else, and the other number 6 laced up his skates and went out with the team.

Once everybody was gone, Busby motioned me to get up. "What's going on?"

"Let's go," Busby said. "We can't have anyone in here thinking you're not out there."

We took a back hallway to an equipment room and sat down on packing crates, me in my gear, socks, t-shirt and suspenders, and Busby with his sweater vest and tie, looking like a kid with graying red hair.

"You're really looking out for me," I said.

"It's my job," he said. "Always been my job."

"Like for example that prostitute."

"Yeah, I didn't get a chance to ask you about her. How'd you like her?"

"Well, I have to thank you. She helped me out a lot more than I thought she would."

"How so?"

"Buzz," I said, "I've always wondered. How did you come to be in Borschland? You're the only guy I ever met from North America in this place."

"You mean the only poor god-forsaken bastard from North America besides you," he said.

"Whatever."

He took out a flask from his pants pocket, offered it to me. I shook my head.

"You want the story. Okay." He tipped the flask. "In the

old days, I was you."

"What? What are you talking about?"

"I was going to be you, Reinhardt. I was the skater in the strange land, going on twenty years now. No one remembers me, because they never told anyone about me."

Busby's eyes went glassy, and from time to time he would shake his head as he spoke.

"I was a pretty good left winger for a team out of Charlottetown, Prince Edward Island, and I was being scouted by some major teams. They knew I wasn't big enough to really play in the NHL, but I could mix it up and in the meantime I skated pretty well. So one night after a game in Rivière-du-Loup we all got drunk and I got into a fight and I hit this guy and he fell weird and whacked his nose on the bar and his bone backed up into his brain and he died on the floor of the bar.

"I didn't kill him, see? I could never hit that hard. But you bang your nog on the edge of a tabletop and anything can happen.

"I was scared. I didn't want to go to jail. And the guy was a Quebecois. He had relatives. I got a court date, paid bail, and the police told me to watch out for big Frenchers with clubs. I remembered there was this flyer up on the bulletin board in the locker room. Play hockey for money overseas. It was a place no one had ever heard of. That's a great place, I thought. I'll lay low there for a while, people will forget about me, I'll do penance or whatnot, and when I come back all will be forgiven. Kind of like prison, but playing hockey while you do it.

"So I take a little pleasure trip to the States, just over the border, and hole up for a while and write away to them. When they say yes, I say can I come early, as in right now. It's the offseason for them, but I'm a wanted man, I need to make myself scarce. They send me the money for the plane ticket, and I get as far as Perth, and there's the threat of a phase shift, so there's no airplanes out for a few days. And in that time I'm outside playing some beach volleyball with some guys and I tear my ACL."

"You tore up your knee playing volleyball?"

"I just caught my foot in the sand and the next thing you know I'm on the ground holding my leg."

"God, that sucks."

"And I got the worst sunburn of my life, too. So there I am with my torn ACL and a plane ticket to Bearland and nowhere else to go except back to Quebec and the dead guy's family and the law."

"So what did you do?"

"I took the plane to Bearland two days later, and they had a team official meet me there. They saw I had a limp and asked what it was. I tried to play it off-- I didn't know what I was doing, I was just a kid-- but he was smart, he set up an appointment with a British doctor at the RAF base, and the doctor diagnosed my tear. He said I should have surgery right there, or I'd never skate again.

"I spent six weeks at the base rehabbing my knee, and by then the season had started and everyone forgot about Busby the Canadian if they even knew in the first place. The press never even wrote one story about me."

"And I never did play hockey again. I tried to train, but I tore the ligament again and that was it."

"The Borschers are sympathetic old souls. They gave me a job washing jocks, and I learned Borschic and rose up in the hierarchy. And now I am special assistant to the club manager and I do whatever the hell they ask me and I am getting old in this effing place."

"Why didn't you ever go back to Canada?"

Busby looked me over, then at his watch. "You want to listen to the game on the radio?"

"Buzz, tell me, why didn't you ever go back?"

"Reinhardt. I don't want to do this, but sometimes you have to look out for number one." And he took out a pistol from his waistband from behind his suit jacket.

"What the-- "

"You're not going back, Sherm," he said. "You're not going

back to play that game. I put a lot of money, my own money, on that game, and I've got someone down in Bearland who'll give it to me in British pounds. And I'm going to get out of here and not look back, as soon as this phase shift is over."

He pointed the gun at me as he spoke, standing at the door to the equipment room. "See, I'm not going back to Canada. I'm going to Australia, and I'm going to live well."

"A lot of people are going to make money from this game, and they will all be happy for me. See, Their is a full goal underdog with you playing, and officially, you are playing. So a bunch of fools in Borschland started betting that Te Staff would win with you out there, and they drove the odds down. Right now, if Their wins by one goal, it's 8 to 1. And if they win by 2, it's 36 to 1. I put down about a quarter million shillings for Their to win by 2. That comes out to almost 9 million shillings won on that long shot, which would come out to a little over one and a half million Australian dollars. I figure that'll be a fine stake to go to Oz with."

"What is that, your life savings?"

"Yeah, pretty much. It's what I managed to put away lo these many years. A lot of funny money that didn't really amount to anything. But my connection in Bearland gave me this little proposition."

"Uh huh."

"To guarantee that Their wins by 2 at least, and probably more, I agreed to keep you out of the game. And a number of other people, a small group of investors if you will, are going to benefit from this as well."

"Yeah, but what if we win? Hey, what about that?"

"You kidding me? They lost to Domaatische during this streak, three zero. They beat Sichebach one oh, the worst team in the league. As soon as they find out you can't go in the second period, they're going to wet their pants and Their is going to bury them. I know this team. It's pretty much the same team we had last year, minus you."

"So how are they going to find out I can't play?"

"They don't know we're in here. We're supposed to be in

the locker room, waiting for the all clear."

"So they're going to come in at the break and we won't be there, and they're going to freak?"

"That's about it."

"And what if I yell for help?"

"I should just shoot you now. Then you really couldn't play. Shoot you in the knee or something."

"But you wouldn't get your money. They'd find out I didn't play and all bets would be off."

Buzz stood there with the gun pointing at me. I knew shooting me wasn't his first choice.

I said, "You need me to lay quiet until after the game and you get your payoff."

He waved his arm; I followed the pistol with my eyes. "Well, what would it hurt? God, you're the greatest thing to happen to Borschland hockey since the invention of the rubber puck. You've got a long and happy career ahead of you. You married your true love. You're going to have plenty of money. It's fine and dandy, Shermy. All good. Why don't you spread a little of that good luck my way?"

He was right, in a way. I was in a fairy tale, and he was in hell. A knee is a hell of a thing. And he'd paid so many dues, never to be able to step a skate out onto the ice, to always be looking at other guys getting the glory.

"Listen, put away the gun," I said. "Okay, don't worry. I'll do it."

He didn't put away the gun, but he did lower the barrel.

"We don't have to win tonight. What are the chances we win the championship if we lose tonight?"

"Like I care."

"Come on, tell me. You're the stat man."

He glared at me, but I was right. He knew the game, knew the league. "Not terrific," he said finally, setting his mouth. "Their might lose one more game, but if they do, you will too. It doesn't matter. If you don't win this year, you'll win next. Or whatever. It's not like the Stanley Cup. This is minor league hockey at best."

"Still, it means something to the guys, doesn't it?"

"So what?"

"You don't care about the team, any of the guys?"

"I've done my caring. Now I want to do some not caring."

"Okay," I said. "Okay. Fair enough. Can you answer me one more question?"

"Sure, Gretzky, sure."

"All this success I've had. I mean, were people throwing games? Were people letting me win, letting me score goals?"

"Yeah, that's weird, that speech you made. You must have that on your mind."

"I'm just wondering. I don't want anyone to let up on me."

"You want to know my theory?"

"Yes, Buzz. Yes, I do."

"All right, here it is. Remember that first game, that first play, when you rushed the Tarlunz d-man and you got a stick on his pass, and then you shot and scored?"

I smiled and shook my head. "Unreal."

"Yeah, unreal," said Buzz. "When you did that, it was like you were some superman. You could do no wrong. Suddenly you believed in yourself. And so did your teammates. And the crowd. Even Tarlunz believed in you."

"So what are you saying, I--"

"You became a superstar because you believed you were a superstar and so did everyone else."

"Because of that one play?"

"That's all it takes. The mental part. See, you've got all the physical tools to compete in this league. But you didn't know you could until you did."

"So it was luck."

"That, and you believed your own luck. So."

"So."

"Yep."

"God, you'd make a great coach, Busby. You'd make an effin' great coach."

He stared at me, saying nothing, with the gun in his hand, and turned the dial on the radio.

It was nearing the end of the first period. Matexipar was up 2-0 and the announcers sounded like it was a funeral.

"I can never understand these guys," said Busby. "After twenty years, I still can't hear what they're saying when they get heated up."

We listened for a while. Norbert Grimm was getting lit up like a pinball machine, but he wouldn't hand out a third goal.

"Wouldn't it be great if you could pay off Norby," I said. "Then you'd be guaranteed your win."

"I'm guaranteed it now," was all Busby said, but he leaned over the set and bit a fingernail. He was listening, and understanding, I knew. You don't spend twenty years with a team and fail to figure out what someone is saying about it.

"They're hanging tough," I said.

"Only a matter of time," he said. There were only about 2 minutes left in the period, and the announcers kept saying, "*Unglaaberlickt mujnen*," unbelievable save.

Busby must have had some fierce divided loyalties.

"We get that third goal," he said, "and it's over right now. They won't come back."

But "we," meaning Mat X, didn't get that third goal, and I shut up when Busby cursed, because he still had the gun in his hand, and I wasn't stupid enough to make him angrier than he was.

"Okay," he said, turning off the radio. "No one is coming back here, so all you have to do is button your lip. And if they do come back here, just follow my lead."

The clomping sound of men on skates filtered in to us. I sat there, and Busby kept the gun on me. Buzz was right; no one would have a reason to come back into the storeroom. The trainers had what they needed right there.

We heard a commotion then, assistant coaches yelling my name and Busby's. Busby motioned for me to get up and stand against the wall next to the door.

There was a lot of yelling, and then quiet, and then more talking, low. You couldn't hear anything they were saying, except when one of the coaches was saying, *quiet, quiet.* There was about ten minutes of silence or near silence, and then more clomping as the guys went out to skate warm-ups for the second period.

"They've called the police, you know," I said.

We turned on the radio again. It didn't surprise me that the team played better. You get the news that your star player is missing again, your coaches give you the talk, and you go out there loaded with adrenaline. Plus, Mat X was bound to lose a little pace after working so hard. When we got a penalty for a hook, I could hardly keep quiet. In Borschland penalties go for five minutes, and a power play goal is pretty much a fifty-fifty proposition, whereas in the NHL a good team only makes twenty percent of their chances.

Buzz got red in the face when Te Staff scored, and we stared at each other for a second.

"Second period boost," Busby said. "They're going to lose it in the third."

"Probably," I said.

"Here," Busby said, producing an electric shaver from his coat pocket. "Shave off that beard."

"What for?"

"Just do it. We'll be on our way in a sec."

"I thought I was just going to stay here."

"Plan B."

I did what he wanted. He turned up the radio so he could hear while I was running the shaver over my beard. I had a pretty thick one by that time, and Rachael had gotten used to it and liked it, so I hadn't shaved it when we got back to Staff Borsch. The shaver was loud, and old.

"This yours?" I asked.

"Yeah, brought it from Canada," he said, glancing up from the radio.

"Needs new heads," I said.

"Your yap," he said. "Can't hear."

"What are we going to do?"

"Shut up, I said," he yelled, and trained the gun on me.

I put my hands up and took the shaver away from my face.

I was about half done. The thing continued to buzz.

"Hurry up," he said.

The radio announcers gurgled on, and Busby waited for Mat X to score again and put him in the clear. I took my time on the shaving. I did a really good job. Near the end of the period, Buzz turned up the radio even more. And that's what gave him away.

There was no warning when the door to the equipment room opened. Someone had put the key in fast and just swung it open. We couldn't hear a thing with the radio going so loud and the shaver scouring my face.

It was Jorduj, one of the trainers. He was fat and squat and had a vacant look in his eyes most of the time, but he turned out to be sharp and quick on his feet where guns were concerned. Buzz was standing with his back to the door, bent over the radio, and I was the first one who saw the door open.

Jorduj looked in and his eyes bugged out. He was wearing one of those old style long-sleeve wool t-shirts with the Te Staff castle logo on it. I shook my head to tell him to leave, but he went "Oh!" really loud, and Buzz turned to him and brought up the gun.

There was the bang of the gun that made my ears ring, and the sound of glass shattering out of the door, and the door slamming, and then the radio again.

"Holy Christ," I said.

Busby kicked his way through the glass, opened the door, turned to the right, aimed, and fired. Busby said, "Shit. Come on, let's go."

We went out of the storeroom and turned left, away from the locker room. Jorduj was lying in the hallway, bellowing. The corridor dead-ended in a locked door. Busby got out a set of keys and opened it, and sent me ahead of him with the gun at my back.

We went upstairs. It was sleeting, and cold. I only had my gear on and socks. When we got to the top of the stairs, there was an alleyway, and at the end of the alleyway, a cop.

Policemen in Borschland do not carry firearms. They carry

tronschonnen, a long, polished wooden stick. The stick is no match for a gun in a fight, and if a crook does have a gun, which they don't often have because you can be hanged for committing a crime with one, they let them go and live to fight another day.

Busby showed his gun to the cop, and the cop stepped aside. But then we got out into the street, and there must have been four dozen cops and soldiers besides. And the soldiers had rifles, some of them with scopes.

The soldiers aimed their rifles at Busby, and the cop who stepped aside said "Hands up!" and I dropped the shaver and Busby dropped the gun and that was it.

The newspapers the next day said, "Kidnapper betrayed by sound of radio."

CHAPTER 32 - SHERM

Jorduj was not dead, thanks be to all the Borschic saints. He was definitely shot through the ribs and the bullet grazed a lung, and they were hustling him out of the building when I came back down to the locker room accompanied by three policemen.

The guys were hunched over the lockers looking sweaty and beaten, and all the coaches' ties were undone. I have never seen such wide eyes and such a big roar when I came in with the police.

"Saints, Reinhardt," screamed Norby after the first yelling died down. "You bastard magician! You really know how to make yourself disappear and reappear!"

The rest of the guys crowded around and slapped me on the back of the shoulders.

"Hell of a game," I said. "I've been listening."

"You lazy *schtupper*," said Chrujstoff. I will not translate *schtupper*. "Are you ready to finally play twenty minutes of hockey?"

"You don't need me," I said. "You guys fight like hell."

"But we're playing the devil," said Norby, and everyone laughed.

The coaches got us calmed down and said a few things,

none of which I remember. I pulled on my number 6 sweater, and laced my skates, pulled on my gloves, and I didn't feel shaky at all.

Then I tried to grip my stick, and it fell out of my hands.

"I can't feel my fingers," I said.

Chrujstoff put the stick in my hand and slapped me hard on the face. "Better?" he said.

As a matter of fact, it was.

I don't remember going out on the ice or warming up or much about the goal I scored in the first ten seconds of the period. I know that the other guy on the draw, Karlin Kreesters, just stared at me when he saw who was taking it, and it was an easy win. Then adrenaline took over, I rushed to the back of the net, the puck came to me, and I just decided to stuff it. Someone was on my back but I was so juiced it didn't matter.

There was a big pileup on the ice, and I almost didn't get out of there alive. I skated around and roses were falling from the stands. Usually you don't get roses until the hat trick or at the end of the game, but these came raining down.

I skated up to the bench to knock gloves with the boys, and there was Rachael on the bench, bawling. I picked her up and twirled her around a couple of times while the girls skated out to pick up the roses, and Mat X stood there waiting at center ice because there were 19 minutes and 50 seconds left to play in the hockey game, and it was 2 to 2 and no one wanted to go home playing to a tie.

I looked up at the sky, and it was all ice fairies, sleet trickling down, and my breath going up in clouds, and I thought, it can't get any better than this, but then Sybranduj came over to me and slapped me hard on the shoulder and said something like *come on let's win this* and I realized there was plenty more work to do.

Matexipar were on their heels, and we took it to them. It would've been the easiest thing to get that third goal and bury them, but I hit the crossbar on that first shift after goal number 2, and Mat X must have thought the saints had decided to smile on them.

We lost a little bit of jump, too, because the adrenaline wore off and the guys had already played two draining periods. People say that it's a tough thing to come back from a deficit in sports. If you come back from 2 goals down in hockey, and the other team didn't give it to you, but are fighting hard as they can, well, the odds are bad that you're going to win that game. You're going to be too tired to push through that last goal, and they're going to capitalize on your fatigue and someone's going to make a mistake, and then the floodgates are going to open into your goalmouth.

Mat X made a rush down after the crossbar dinger, and Norby made a ninja save on them, and we rushed down and Chrujstoff nearly scored, and their goalie coughed up the rebound and we roped it in to him again, and he caught it in his glove.

I came back on the ice and won the draw and we ended up in a big scrum in the center and someone whacked me in the jaw and didn't get penalized for it. I had a bloody lip and a tooth was bent, but the referees let us play. In fact, they pretty much let us play until one of the goalies melted down a puck or it went flying into the stands.

Usually Mat X would have taken the opportunity to get in a few free shots, but the game turned into a track meet, with each team racing down the ice, putting a hard, clean shot on goal, and then the other team picking it up and doing the same thing at the other end. Neither goalie was giving an inch of empty space. There might as well have been a brick wall built over each goal.

I couldn't feel anything except now and then I'd taste a little sweat that had dropped from my upper lip. I felt like I was in a flying saucer, gliding out there. My stickhandling was fine, too, even though I couldn't feel my hands. I'd throw the puck on net thinking *I will try the three hole this time*, and it would go exactly there. The only hitch was the blocker of Heiko Moordfvors, the Mat X goalie: it'd always be there before the puck got through.

It was looking more and more like there would be a 2-2 game, which would've been bad for us, because in a tiebreaker for the championship, you look for the head-to-head record, and the team that has the most away goals wins if you tie twice. So Mat X gradually started to turtle up, and when there were 3 minutes left, they were keeping their center between their circles most of the time and the rushes had ended and we were just blasting away.

Then there were 2 minutes left and they were able to break out and noodle around in our area for a half a shift.

Then there was 1 minute left and we slammed one into Moordfvors, and he melted it down, and we called a timeout to regroup and put a clever one on net.

Cramps called for the Borschland River Twig, which is a variation on the Borschland River.

The Borschland River play is one where you win the puck, pass to the left wing, who sends it around the boards to the right wing, who fakes a pass to the center and then sends it back, and then everyone's attention is on the area behind the boards, and the left wing fakes sending it back again, but turns and passes it across the goal mouth and the center or the other wing taps it in on the weak side.

The Twig is something Cramps put in for me. In the Twig, instead of letting the puck go through the first time, I intercept it behind the goal and either fake a wraparound or pass it front for someone to tap in. I assisted on a lot of goals off of that play because everyone hates to be scored on a wraparound, and they all rush to knock you down before you can sweep around to the other side of the goalie. So instead of keeping the puck I flip it to the front of the net, and whoever's there has a clear shot on goal.

So everybody comes out of the huddle saying "Twig" to one another, and we line up, and everything works to perfection. I win the draw, send it to the LW, he fakes, and I drive to the back of the net. He sends the puck behind, I take it, and decided to stuff it in. But Mat X isn't interested in being whipped that way. So one of their guys clocks me in the temple.

I go down on the ice, my ears ringing. I don't hear the referee's whistle. Everyone is standing over me, and then I start hearing, "Penalty shot, penalty shot."

The penalty shot is given when the officials determine that a player who has a clear one-on-one shot on goal with the goalie is illegally impeded from that shot by a defender. Usually that type of thing is awarded when you're on a breakaway in free ice. But this time, I guess they thought I was about to score on that wraparound, and the only thing the defender could do was punch me.

"*Alles ergut*?" The assistant coaches asked when I skated up to the bench while the referee skated over to center ice to place the puck.

"*Alles ergut*," I said, although not everything was *ergut*.

"How many fingers?" someone said.

I looked over and saw three up, and mistakenly said "two" because the word two and three in Borschic are very similar (*dej* and *twej*) and I always mix them up.

"Don't you mean three?" the same someone said.

"Yeah, *twej*, *twej*," I said.

It didn't matter if I had a concussion. I was going to take that shot.

CHAPTER 33 - RACHAEL

It is one thing to watch a hockey game and be interested in the outcome. It is quite another to watch a hockey game where your husband is playing.

Or even not playing.

I was in the Church of Borschland box with my father and mother when the game began, and there were a dozen archdeacons there and a number of others that had managed to prevail upon the sacred powers that be to set up a chair under the eaves of Te Rijngk.

When the number six-sweatered man skated out for the first period I knew in a second it wasn't Sherm, even though the man on the wireless kept saying Sherm is a bit rusty, it must be the effect of the gunshot wound.

I told my mother what I thought, and she brought her field glasses to bear, but she couldn't see exactly. "Why ever would they put a lookalike out there for our Sherm?" she asked me.

"Saints and spirits," I said, which is the same as saying I have no idea.

In the second period, when he did not come out at all, we got a message from the team that he had disappeared, the authorities were seeing to it, and we were not to say anything to anyone. We spent that period in an office next to the rink with a team executive, and I wept and begged to be let go to try to find him.

Then, near the beginning of the third period, another message came up that Sherm had been found, that it was Busby who had kidnapped him, and that he was coming out to play the last third of the game.

I made my way down the stands amidst the crowds, everyone staring at me, and I reached rink level as Sherm was taking the first faceoff. Then only a few seconds later he had scored, was skating about the ice like a champion, and we had a joyous and tearful reunion.

"You complete fool," I remember saying.

"I love you," he said. I would have to get used to a man saying that to me.

Then someone made room for me on the bench and I sat with the boys for the rest of the game, letting them play and not saying anything, for I knew they would need all their concentration to win the game.

I had almost decided that it was a fair outcome for the game to end tied when they took their timeout and made up their play, and I sent up a tiny little prayer to St. Noos for a good outcome.

Then a Matexipar player brutally punched Sherm in the head, and I was outraged and wanted to punch that player myself. But Sherm got up, skated over, said he was fine, and lined up for the penalty shot.

The hush that came over that crowd was like the silence of purgatory when you have spent your life telling lies. You can say nothing more, nothing more is said to you. There is simply a total silence of silences.

It had been sleeting, and continued to do so, and as Sherm skated up, took the puck, and flew down towards the Matexipar goal, the only sound may have been his skates and the prayers of the saints.

Which made it all the more remarkable when the phase shift occurred.

Coming out of the wide world is not much noticed, but

going back in is sometimes wrenching, and this one was wrenching. There was a sigh, as of wind, which everyone could hear because it was so quiet. And then there was a blurring of everything. For a moment you could not look at anything straight on. And then you felt this wrench, as if someone picked up your chair and moved it two feet.

And after that, there was a blizzard.

We were back in the weather of the wide world, and in this weather, a great snowstorm was raging.

Snow was falling so hard that you could not see but a few paces in front of you.

And everyone cried out and wondered where Sherm Reinhardt had disappeared to, for there was nothing but lights bouncing off of snow, and it was several minutes before someone found the puck in the back of the net and my Sherm lying on the ice with his fists in the air, celebrating.

It is in the rulebook of the Borschland Hockey League that if a phase shift occurs during a regular and sanctioned game, it shall not interfere with the progress of the game unless it is determined that the shift has made the game unplayable.

A snowstorm such as this one might be said to be such a case, but as there was something less than a minute left in the game, the officials dropped the puck in the storm and the whistles went off several seconds later and the game was over and Matexipar had lost and Te Staff had won.

Matexipar lodged a formal complaint with the league, but the masters of the Borschland Hockey League, considering the sport a religion, are not prone to question acts of God, and they denied it.

We will never know whether the goal that Sherman Reinhardt scored was as a result of his own skill, or because the snowstorm disoriented the Matexipar net minder, or because it happened to bounce in a way that no one could anticipate. Sherm himself has told me that he remembers nothing of making the shot and never saw it go in. He says the only thing he really remembers is kissing me afterwards. Which is another way of telling me he loves me.

CHAPTER 34 - KADMUS

The extraordinary hockey game of 28 Fefvruar, Sankt Noos's Day, will be remembered forever, even in Matexipar.

And it will be remembered here in Staff Borsch, though there were many twists and turns before Te Staff was crowned champion of the Borschland Hockey League for the 75th campaign, in the year 329 of our reckoning. Matexipar, you see, lost no more games that year, and most of the time dismantled their opponents. We won almost all our games, tying one, a game when the goalkeeper Norbert Grimm was taken out for an injury and the good men of Meechen scored three goals in the last period to tie Te Staff 3-3. And the teams finished identically, with records of 24-3-3, but Te Staff won the title because of their superior head-to-head record with Matexipar of 1 win and 1 tie.

There were no more phase shifts that year, and I was glad of it. It is always a bit alarming, and besides that, foreigners are much discomfited by it, especially in this case Sherm's sister, Catherine, who joined him as soon as she was able after the phase shift, and decided to make her abode here with him and Rachael.

As for the strange case of Mr. Kevin Busby, he has been extradited to Canada to face charges of manslaughter and flight, and will stand trial here for conspiracy, kidnapping, and fraud.

In Bearland, the Free Democracy Party headed by Linus Black Jr. continue in power, with Linus' cousin Ethelredge "Smokey" Black having been elected the Prime Minister.

I have heard that both Rachael and Sherm are writing their own books concerning the events of this year, and I expect they shall have their own insights and perspectives. My own humble efforts are those of a journalist, seeing the story from the outside, but being, as it were, an objective observer. So that regardless of what one says one did or saw, the journalist's role is to give an account of what can be verified. And that is what I have done.

At the same time, there must be a note of mystery to this year's happenings, and a humble acknowledgment that we do not now nor can we ever understand the import of them. That is the nature of *Te Hart*, may the saints bless us.

May the saints and the spirits always bless us.

EPILOGUE - SHERM

Borschlanders say the world is ruled by something called *Te Hart*, which is about the same thing that the Zimrothians call *lana*. As for Bearlanders, they probably would say everything's just about dumb luck. They never go in much for magic or destiny.

I'm not a religious guy either. Even though I married the daughter of a deacon, most theology doesn't make much sense to me.

Cathy's the opposite. She is thinking about going to seminary down here and becoming a deacon. She always had a knack for finding God where there seems to be empty space.

Me? I'm always looking for empty space-- at least at the goalmouth. That's about all the theology I'm good for. See, all I know is, if a phase shift comes when you're putting the puck on net, try for the five hole. You want to keep that hunk of rubber as close to the ground as possible.

ACKNOWLEDGMENTS

I should like to thank a number of people for their help in bringing this book, these voices, and this story to the wide world. First and foremost, my undying gratitude goes to Dr. Heeledine Thruusbeck and the Benefactors Trust of the University of Borschland Daamensveltinstitut for generous travel, insurance and research grants. Hearty thanks also go to President Dean Koharski at the Vestphalia University of Pennsylvania, which houses the only freestanding Department of Continent Studies in North America, and to Department Chair Marujke Oosens, and for the assistance of graduate student interns Lisel Gutchard and Francis ("Hobs") Hobbelin. In Borschland as well I encountered many who helped me, but none more than Meester Erki Turkommen and his wife Naykki. Lastly, I would like to thank my wife and family for permitting me the great and grand pleasure of travel to the Continent with full knowledge of the risks involved.

ABOUT THE AUTHOR

D.W. Frauenfelder grew up in Borschland: that is, he first devised the world of the Continent as a boy and has been working on and deepening its geography, culture, language, and characters ever since. While not in Borschland, he is an instructor of Latin and Greek with an academic specialty in Greek mythology, and is the author of *Growing Up Heroic: Adventures in Greek Mythology* (Duke Talent Identification Program, 2009). Much more about the author, Borschland and the Continent may be found at breakfastwithpandora.com, the official website for all things Borschic.

Made in the USA
Charleston, SC
15 June 2013